MATIAS YL

Hell Pulp

Published by Matias Ylikangas
Helsinki, FI

ISBN (Paperback) 978-952-88-0003-3
ISBN (eBook) 978-952-88-0004-0

Cover design by Matias Ylikangas

Cover artwork: *A human head dissected: "In Memoriam"* by R. Ellis, modified and licensed under Creative Commons Attribution 4.0 International License

matiasylikangas.com

HELL PULP

Essille

CHAPTER ONE

A hand pushed out of the ground and fumbled for something to cling to. A sluggish whirlpool of dirt formed around the hand as its fingers tangled in grass that jutted like the fur of a hissing cat. The hand clenched into a fist and pulled, inching the man buried in the dirt closer to the surface.

Four of his fingernails were missing, two had split in half, and another dangled from the cuticle. Yet, he felt no pain—or rather, he was in too much shock to register it. What he did feel, however, was air brushing his skin for the first time in who knew how long, and this gave him more strength to fight than any pain ever could. He kicked against the heavy soil holding him down and pulled at the weeds with a firmer grip.

Finally, his face broke through the surface. Black dirt filled his eyes, nose, and mouth and clung to his scruffy hair in stiff clumps. He tried to gasp, but dirt clogged his windpipe and coated the inside of his mouth, like burnt stew stuck to the bottom of a kettle.

He fought the earth sinking around him until he was halfway out of the hole. He beat and clawed at his chest, gagging and coughing. At last, a ball of dirt dislodged from his throat, and air rushed in. The sensation was so overwhelming that he passed out on the spot.

And so, Oscar was born.

Some moments later, Oscar awoke to a sharp pain in his lungs. Inhaling felt like swallowing embers, and exhaling ignited a series of violent coughs, making him curl into a spasming ball. When the coughing fit finally passed, he rolled onto his back and wiped the dirt from his eyes.

Above, resin-colored clouds covered the sky, hanging low and bloated like overripe fruit. The light that filtered through the clouds cloaked the world in a hazy, bronzed dusk. A black moor stretched out in every direction, its grassy hills lined with dilapidated tombstones. Here and there, mausoleums lay in half-collapsed heaps. The ground shook and rumbled in a steady, numbing tremor, and mist slithered between the headstones, carrying a faint yet noticeable stench of decay wherever it drifted.

But none of this really registered with Oscar. None of it carried any meaning. Everything was an amalgam of blurry shapes, vague colors, and distant sensations. He knew nothing else but his name and that he shouldn't be here—wherever *here* was. And even these fragments of knowledge were so distant and muffled that they might as well have originated from someone else's mind.

What sounded like drunken singing sharpened his senses—a little, at least. The raspy voice belonged to an old man. Oscar couldn't make out the words from the toothless, garbled drawl, but he recognized the rhythm and melodic pattern of a sea shanty.

A person. He can help.

It took great effort to get his stiff body to bend to his will, but finally he managed to sit up. Before him, a dark hole yawned in the ground—the one he'd just climbed out of. Above it perched a granite headstone, tilted to the side as if curiously observing him. The stone's face was unmarked, void of names, dates, or an epitaph.

Strange poppy-like flowers grew in lush clusters around the grave. Bent stems cradled their silvery-gray heads, and a withered wreath of leaves covered their necks like medieval millstone collars. The flowers wouldn't have caught Oscar's attention if not for one detail: this grave—*his* grave—was the only one adorned with flowers.

His attention shifted to a ball of light hovering in the distance, its faint glow receding in the shroud of mist. The light bobbed and weaved between the tombstones, now a dozen rows away. The drunken singing seemed to originate from the same source.

Oscar tried to call out to the singer but only managed to produce a pathetic wheeze which was followed by a series of coughs. He crawled away from the edge of the pit, staggered to his feet, and immediately collapsed back down. Gritting his teeth, he tried again, slower this time. His legs wobbled as if molded from wet clay, and the world spun in disorienting somersaults. He grabbed support from a nearby tombstone and managed to stay on his feet.

"Hey! Wait!" he croaked, the words scraping the back of his throat raw.

He tottered down the corridor of graves, leaning on the tombstones, spitting and sneezing loogies of dirt. The black grass crackled and crumbled beneath his stride as the mist parted before him and stitched back together behind him.

Gradually, his legs began to grow stronger. His pace

quickened. With every step, he had to rely less and less on the tombstones as crutches. His gait remained clumsy and uneven, but at least the distance between him and the drunken singer was no longer growing. Oscar was gaining ground.

But then his foot caught on something, and he slammed facedown on the ground.

He looked back at what he'd tripped on and first mistook the thing sticking out of the ground for a tree root. Then he felt the thing tighten its grip around his ankle. He blinked and refocused: the "root" was covered in skin. And it had five fingers.

Oscar's face twisted in disgust. He kicked at the hand with his free foot, but its grip remained firm. Panic took over, and he kicked again and again, his entire body joining the frantic motion. After half a dozen kicks, the wrist made a sickening crunch, and the fingers uncoiled.

Oscar scrambled to his feet and wobbled forth, hugging himself, shaking his head from side to side.

Oscar was some ten graves away from his target when the singing stopped. Whoever he was following had apparently heard him approach. And here Oscar realized that the singer wasn't alone. Four figures stood on a beaten path that cut through the grave-riddled moor. One held up a lantern, casting a dome of warm light around them, shrouding their figures with heavy shadows.

Beside them loomed a sorry-looking Victorian mausoleum, buckling under its own decay. With the mist enveloping the group and obscuring the lantern light, the scene resembled an ominous vision emerging from a crystal ball.

One figure towered above the others with the demeanor of an iron statue. A trench coat hung from his broad shoulders like a stage curtain, and a brimmed hat and a bushy beard hid his features. Upon noticing Oscar, he shuffled to the side, shielding a ragged wheelbarrow with a possessive stance.

Oscar staggered closer to the group and collapsed at their feet.

"Water," he wheezed.

The one with the lantern shone his light on Oscar. A shovel rested on his shoulder, and his cagey movements resembled those of a mangy rodent. His twitchy body arched forward like a fishhook, and he was about as stringy as one, too. From the waistband of his tattered jeans jutted a folded cutthroat razor. A few strands of hair clung to the sides of his head, and his sickly pale face was twisted into a lizard-like leer.

Leaning closer, he ogled Oscar as though he were a product on sale. The proper response might have been to run away, but Oscar, numbed by the shock, could only shrink further into himself.

The remaining two members of the group hunched on the sidelines: a young woman with a bob cut and a teenage boy wearing broken glasses, both smeared with dirt from head to toe. Both of them also bore a teardrop-shaped gash below their left eye with fresh blood trailing down their cheeks. The teenage boy shivered violently, his mouth agape with fear, while the woman's expression remained ghoulishly blank—burned out, detached, her stare fixed on a horizon a thousand yards away. The last detail that should have sent Oscar running was the nooses hanging around their necks, the loose ends of the ropes tied to the cagey man's shovel. But Oscar didn't. He remained kneeling and begging for water.

"Another child for the forest, Ernie?" asked the trench coat man. His voice rumbled with an almost inhuman baritone.

"Maybe," Ernie replied, his reptilian features widening. He reached out to slick back Oscar's hair. Oscar flinched at the touch but retaliated no further.

Ernie turned to the trench coat man, his hand still

lingering in Oscar's hair. "Pass me the water, Heinrich."

"Water," Oscar echoed.

Heinrich reached into the wheelbarrow and tossed Ernie a sloshing leather pouch. Ernie caught it midair and unscrewed the cork with the few teeth he had left. He poured water over Oscar's face to wash away the grime.

"Let's see what the good Lord has blessed us with today," he muttered.

Oscar tilted his head, gulped down the water, and rinsed out his mouth. The water was murky and rank like sewer sludge, but it also felt more refreshing than anything he'd ever tasted.

"It's a pretty one alright!" Ernie hooted at Heinrich.

Oscar wasn't listening. Most of the dirt had now washed off his face. He no longer had to squint against the grit scratching his eyes nor did his mouth feel like a maggot-infested hole in the ground. But beneath the earthy taste of muck, he noticed something else: the sour, rancid tang of decay. His breath reeked of rot, as though some animal had crawled down his throat and died there. He gagged and spat.

"We already got you a pretty one," Heinrich said.

"But the pretties are so rare." Ernie squeezed his voice into a high-pitched whine. "Why can't I have nice things?"

"Taking more than we can handle is redundant," Heinrich said, cold and quiet. "Not to mention risky."

"But family's supposed to stick together," Ernie said, still whining. "And we are a family. A big happy family. You don't have to worry about the kiddies. You know I can keep 'em in line."

Ernie and Heinrich stared at each other a beat, locked in a wordless conversation.

"Fine," Heinrich said, breaking the silence. "But all of his rations come out of your end. I'm not sharing anything with him."

"We have a deal, my friend," Ernie smiled. He turned back to Oscar and introduced the rest of their group: "That pretty lady over there is Daughter. The boy is Son Number One. That makes you... Son Number Two."

"More water," Oscar wheezed. "Please."

"You're a needy little fucker, ain't you?" Ernie grinned and gave Oscar the water pouch. "Here."

Oscar drank voraciously. The murky sludge was a sweet nectar compared to the foul rot clinging to the back of his throat.

"Let's start with a test." Ernie crouched down to meet Oscar's eyes. "What's your name, boy?"

"Oscar," he managed between labored breaths. "I'm Oscar."

Ernie's fist sprang like a mousetrap, jabbing Oscar on the cheek. Oscar's head snapped to the side, his face throbbing. Despite Ernie's wiry frame, the punch packed unexpected strength.

As Oscar reeled from the impact, Son Number One whimpered and cowered as if the blow had landed on him. Daughter flinched but quickly sank back into her dissociated haze.

Oscar's eyes watered, but the pain barely registered—it was like a whisper in a crowd, unable to reach him, drowned out by the mush of his mind. He stared blankly at the patch of dirt where Ernie's punch had steered him, doing nothing, feeling nothing.

"No, you dummy," Ernie laughed carelessly. "What is your name, *Son Number Two?*"

"Wha—"

Ernie punched him again. This time, the pain came through, igniting hot pressure on Oscar's cheek.

"Your name!" Ernie barked.

But Oscar couldn't answer. His brain felt like a useless slab of meat. He wept in confusion and shielded his head, not knowing what else to do.

"Don't cry. This is supposed to be a joyous occasion." Ernie smiled, his expression a strange blend of warmth and insult. "After all, you're part of the family now."

He helped Oscar to his feet with surprising gentleness and walked him over to Heinrich. "You'll feel a lot better once we make it official. Heinrich?"

Without warning, Heinrich wrapped Oscar in a crushing bear hug. His massive arms locked around him, squeezing all the air from his lungs. Oscar's mouth moved involuntarily, unable to produce a word or a sound. His heart raced. His pulse throbbed against his eardrums. It felt as though his body was trying to shake him out of this stupor, demanding him to take action, to resist—to do *anything*—but the sensation left him feeling only more helpless, lost, and empty.

"Family is forever." Ernie grabbed Oscar by the hair and flicked open his cutthroat razor with practiced ease. He brought the blade to Oscar's face, just below the left eye. "As are scars."

CHAPTER TWO

Night settled over the cemetery as the amber clouds dimmed to a bluish black. Dusk became darkness, and somewhere from the distance rose the echoes of howls, screams, chants, and fits of laughter. Together, they blended into a cacophony of madness, pounding against Oscar's temples with the pressure of a bass drum.

Heinrich, leading the way, pushed the ragged wheelbarrow down the cemetery road. The wheelbarrow carried two duffel bags, a shovel, some leather pouches, and a small stack of bricks, pacing the chaotic soundscape with a steady rhythm of clatters and squeaks. A lantern perched at the front of the wheelbarrow, casting light over the ravaged road, the graves lined on both sides, and the mist that hung limp and still like a carcass in an abattoir.

To Oscar, these sights and sounds filtered through a cocoon, leaving him stuck in a liminal state between a feverish dream and reality. This haze dulled not only his senses but also his grasp of the danger he was in. A teardrop-shaped piece of skin had now been cut from his cheek, but the cocoon shielded him from this pain, as well.

A noose hung from his neck, forcing his head into a bow. The rope, along with the ones tied around Son Number One and Daughter, coiled around Ernie's shovel. Daughter slouched beside Oscar while Son Number One shuffled ahead of the two.

The prisoners trudged in silence, compliant as sheep. Their hands were unbound, and the ropes hung loose, but the oppressive dynamic was clear: it would take Ernie one firm pull of the shovel to tighten the ropes and smother any attempt at retaliation. But there was none of that. Except for Son Number One's quiet sobs, the prisoners remained submissive.

A jolt ripped Oscar from his funk as Ernie broke into song at a full volume. He recognized the melody from before. It was the same tune that had first drawn his attention and lured him to this group. This time, he could make out the words, though they made no sense to him:

From the morgue I was towed to the old moor road,
But this old moor road leads nowhere at all.
They killed me once, so I can't die twice—
Lord, has my grave been here long before I?

"Ready to do some digging?" Heinrich hollered from the front, cutting Ernie's performance short.

"How's about we settle for stragglers this time?" Ernie called back. "We've wasted too much time. That newborn shock's going to wear off sooner or later."

"The client wants them fresh out of the ground."

"They won't know the difference," Ernie countered. "You go find us a couple of stragglers while I keep the kiddies in check. You really want to bust your ass all night? If the client gives me shit, I'll sell 'em one of my pretties. I'll sell a whole bunch of 'em. There's a few I'm this close to getting sick of."

"What happened to 'family is forever?'" Heinrich muttered.

"They'll always be my children, even if I sell 'em."

"Where are you taking us?" Son Number One asked, interrupting the two. "Are these ropes really necessary?"

"They're for your own good," Ernie spat. "Now shut up."

"But where are you taking us?"

Without warning, Ernie pulled Son Number One's rope with full force, sweeping the boy's feet from under him. He hit the ground hard, gasping for air. Ernie seized him by the neck and pressed his razor on the bridge of his nose.

Oscar froze, holding his breath. A diluted wave of pity reached him, but the stupor remained stronger. All he could do was watch.

"When I tell you to shut up, you shut up," Ernie said. "One more word out of you, and I'll cut your pretty little sniffer. Understand?"

Daughter took a step toward them.

"Get the fuck back or you're next!" Ernie slashed the air with the razor, the blade flicking only inches from her throat. She flinched and did as told. Ernie turned the blade back to the boy. "Say you understand!"

"I want to go home," Son Number One wailed, tears streaming down his dirt-streaked face.

"Well, ain't that convenient," Ernie crowed. "Home's exactly where we're going."

"Enough," Heinrich snapped. "All this drama is giving me a headache."

Ernie lifted his hands in mock-terror and grinned at the prisoners. He pulled the boy to his feet, barking, "Come on, get!"

The convoy continued its grim procession down the

cemetery road, the prisoners dazed and aloof, the captors sulky and on edge.

A moment after the altercation, Oscar realized that Daughter had taken hold of his hand. He looked at their intertwined fingers, their palms pressed together. Her hand was cold, but the gesture warmed him. When he lifted his gaze, her eyes met his with a frightened yet strangely reassuring expression. She seemed to tell him it was okay to be afraid, that he could depend on her.

Oscar would later look back on this moment and wish he would have returned the sentiment. But at the time, all he could give her was a blank stare.

Daughter tilted her head, her attention shifting somewhere over Oscar's shoulder. Following her gaze, Oscar saw a shadowy figure hunched in the clutter of graves. The figure, a lean man based on his posture, seemed to move in tandem with their group, skulking in the shade of the tombstones, staying close but not too close. His darkened outline flickered between the headstones, his movements sly and fluid.

Oscar watched the man trail the group for a while before his figure melted into the deeper shadows. Once he was out of Oscar's sight, he also slipped from his mind.

The road stretched on. Ernie and Heinrich wrapped up their discussion regarding stragglers. They concluded that Heinrich would scout the area while Ernie escorted the prisoners to an intersection further down the path. They would rendezvous there once Heinrich had captured two new stragglers.

Heinrich reached into his trench coat and pulled out a horn crafted from bone. Its ancient-looking body was etched with strange, arcane symbols and decorated with pagan trinkets made from what looked like wads of hair and human teeth.

"Blow the horn if there's trouble," he said, handing the grotesque instrument to Ernie. "*Auf Wiedersehen.*"

"We can handle a little trouble, can't we, kiddies?"

The group watched as Heinrich's hulking figure ventured into the mist, his silhouette fading with the light of his lantern. Ernie lit a torch, secured the prisoners' ropes to the wheelbarrow, and tossed his shovel in the cart. He pushed the wheelbarrow forward, and the prisoners trailed behind like marionettes.

Some five minutes after Heinrich's departure, their convoy came to an abrupt halt with a voice calling from the dark: "Good evening." The voice was low, gruff, measured, and it punched Oscar's heart up his throat.

It seemed to have a similar effect on Ernie, because suddenly his fishhook posture straightened, and he stopped still.

"Who's there?" Ernie asked, his voice wavering. His fingers curled around the razor tucked in his waistband.

"Just a prospective buyer," the voice responded calmly. "I'm going to light my lantern so you can see me. Is that okay?"

"No funny business," Ernie said. "I've got a friend nearby. You don't want to cross him. He'll fuck you up good."

"No funny business, no fucking anybody up, no nothing."

A light flickered behind a nearby tombstone, and a stranger emerged, his hands raised in surrender. An oil lantern dangled from his satchel, shimmering like a talisman. The man, likely in his forties, had intelligent features marred by scars that streaked across his face and neck, glistening in the lantern's glow. His skin was sallow, and dark, ghoulish bags hung under his eyes. Despite his ragged appearance, there was an air of sophistication about him. His clothes, though worn and torn, suggested a certain refinement: his shirt, trousers, and vest all matched, forming a carefully coordinated ensemble. Rust-colored stains spotted the shirt, yet even these marks seemed to fit the outfit's color scheme.

"What do you want, fancy pants?" Ernie asked.

"A newborn," the stranger said. "Can I buy one?"

"The ground's full of 'em. Go get one yourself. It's free."

"I don't like getting my hands dirty."

"Shit, stranger," Ernie guffawed. "You really are a fancy pants, ain't you?"

"Look," the stranger said, lowering his hands. "I need an able-bodied person who can speak English. I'll make it worth your while."

"Don't look like you have much to give in return," Ernie said.

"I've got all kinds of much stashed nearby." The stranger's gaze veered to the rest of the group, settling on Oscar. "How about the kid in the back? Hello. You speak English?"

Oscar stared back blankly, unable to respond.

"Please, you have to help us!" Son Number One cut in, crying. "They'll kill us!"

Ernie slammed a fist against the wheelbarrow, his face twisted with rage. He yanked Son Number One's noose, forcing him to the ground. "If only I *could* kill you," he hissed.

"Just wait a minute." The stranger stepped forward. "None of that now."

"None of what?" Ernie snapped. "Don't tell me how to raise my kids. And get back!"

Son Number One lay trembling on the ground, Ernie slumped over him. "Please! They're—"

Ernie's razor flashed like a sharp, unexpected breeze, and a crimson stroke trailed the motion over the boy's face. He cupped his hands over the wound, screaming as blood spilled from between his trembling fingers.

What little color there was on Oscar's face drained,

rendering him so pale he became almost translucent. The violence—the sudden, terrible explosion of it—and the sight of so much blood made his knees buckle. But there was something else, too. What? Thrill? Fascination?

"There! How do you like that?" Ernie crowed, jumping in place like one of the early humans discovering fire.

Son Number One curled into a ball as blood pulped freely from his face, pooling on the dirt road.

While Ernie was focused on the boy, the stranger made his move. He snatched the shovel from the wheelbarrow and raised it over his shoulder. He took a readied stance and caught Ernie's attention with a whistle.

He swung the shovel just as Ernie spun around. The shovel connected with the side of his face. A hollow, metallic crunch rang out, and Ernie's remaining teeth shot out of his mouth like shotgun pellets. The impact hurled him to the ground, leaving him whimpering in a semiconscious daze.

The stranger tossed the shovel somewhere between the rows of tombstones and rushed to Oscar. He removed the noose, grabbed Oscar's arm, and pulled him away from the group. "Come on, kid. You're with me."

Oscar shook his head in near-hysterics and slipped free from the stranger's grip. He ran back to Daughter, who stood hugging herself and gasping in panicked staccatos. He tried to loosen her rope, but his hands trembled uncontrollably, fumbling the knot without avail. He felt helpless, useless, and pathetic.

Before Oscar could get the noose off, Ernie yanked Daughter's rope, sending her tumbling. With both of them now sprawled on the ground, Ernie positioned himself next to her and placed the razor on her throat.

Next, Ernie reached into the wheelbarrow, grabbed the bone horn, and blew into it. The horn let out a rusted groan, like some ancient machinery creaking back to life after a hundred years of neglect.

"Heinrich! Heinrich!" Ernie screeched into the night, blood spraying from his mouth.

"Ernie! I'm coming!" Heinrich's voice boomed from somewhere close by.

The stranger stirred from the baritone voice. "We gotta go!" he yelled.

The stranger grabbed Oscar by the arm, tighter this time, and broke into a run. Oscar stumbled and dragged behind, but the stranger wouldn't let go, forcing him to match his pace.

As they fled, Oscar glanced back. Daughter lay on the ground, Ernie's blade still pressed on her throat. Their eyes locked, and he felt her despair and disbelief, her stare like a judging beam of light.

Then her figure disappeared into the mist and was swallowed by the darkness. Her cries melted into the night and became indistinguishable from everyone else's suffering.

The stranger lit their path with his lantern, dragging Oscar through the fields of tombstones and mausoleums. Oscar had no more fight left in him. He staggered wherever the stranger led him and, dazed and exhausted, focused on the hiss of the black grass under their stride. The sound was almost trance-inducing, and Oscar welcomed any sensation that'd distract him from the realities of this nightmare.

They pressed on, and soon the tombstones grew sparse and the grass thinned. The terrain shifted to rugged hills where black moss peeled from the bedrock like charred skin. Up ahead, the terrain rose to a jagged stone ridge, its sharp edges dividing the view in two. Somewhere beyond the ridge, fires burned, casting hues of tangerine and garnet against the dark sky.

The stranger slowed their pace to navigate the challenging

terrain with more caution. They climbed up the slope and stopped at a secluded spot just below the ridge, surrounded by boulders and slabs of stone.

"I think we lost them," the stranger said.

He sank to the stony ground and pulled a leather canteen from his satchel. Oscar remained standing, arms wrapped around himself, rocking with jittery moves.

"Have a seat. It's okay. We're safe for now."

Oscar sat down, slow and awkward, still hugging himself.

The stranger took a sip from the canteen, swallowed, took another sip, gurgled, and spat. He held out the canteen. "Have some water, kid. Wash off that rot."

Oscar hesitated, but the word "rot" seemed to amplify the rancid taste in his mouth. He accepted the canteen and drank. The liquid was more refreshing than what Ernie had given him, but it was still far from clean. It also carried a strange tang he couldn't quite place.

"What's your name?" the stranger asked.

"Son Number Two," Oscar mumbled.

"What?"

Oscar cleared his throat. "Son Number Two."

"I don't mean the name those grave looters gave you. What's your real name?"

"Oscar."

"Oscar," the stranger said. "I'm Nathaniel."

Oscar said nothing. His shaky hands fumbled with the canteen's cork. Nathaniel studied him for a moment, then gently took back the canteen and handed him a pencil instead. Oscar accepted it without hesitation and rolled it around and around between his fingers like an unlit cigarette.

"You take good care of that," Nathaniel said.

"We left them," Oscar whispered, guilt burning in his throat.

"You mean the woman and the other kid?" Nathaniel

asked. "Didn't you see them? They ran off together. They got away."

The image of Daughter flashed in Oscar's mind. She was lying on the ground with Ernie's razor pressed to her throat, her eyes both pleading for help and accusing him of abandoning her.

"I don't... I'm so confused."

"It's okay," Nathaniel said, nodding empathetically. "I'll explain everything once you're in a more stable state of mind. But first, we gotta get out of the cemetery. I have a safe place nearby. We'll head there and figure things out. Sound good?"

Oscar didn't respond.

Nathaniel stood up but suddenly doubled over, clutching his stomach, his teeth clenched. He sank to his knees. "Give me a minute," he said, his voice strained. He turned away from Oscar, unbuttoned his vest, lifted his shirt, and began breathing heavily, his body trembling. "Just... just give me a minute," he stammered, his back still turned to Oscar.

Oscar's focus drifted to the garnet glow beyond the ridge. He got up, legs wobbling, and climbed the rocky embankment to get a better look at the source of light on the other side.

Below, a sprawling ghetto of dilapidated shacks and labyrinthine streets stretched into the darkness. Firelight flared from its claustrophobic corridors, creating a shimmering dome of red and orange above the slum. The chaotic architecture of flat-roofed shacks and illuminated alleyways looked like the earth had cracked open to reveal its molten core.

It seemed Oscar had found the origin of the cacophony. It rose from the ghetto like a unified entity, spreading its gospel of torment all around. The stench of rot, blood, infection, and waste surged from its depths, fouling the air. Oscar stared at this decaying spectacle, the horror and dread it evoked muffled by his overloaded senses.

Nathaniel soon joined him at the ridge, his back

slightly bent, his hand pressed against his stomach. "That's Shantytown. That's where we're heading. Unfortunately."

CHAPTER THREE

A path zigzagged down the sloping embankment, guiding Oscar and Nathaniel to a desolate street on the town's outskirts. Ramshackle huts built with sticks, boulders, coffin boards, tombstones, and mausoleum cinder blocks slumped on the soggy, iron-and-manure-reeking dirt. The dwellings, all unfinished and barely intact, huddled tightly together and lined Oscar and Nathaniel from both sides in a disorganized fashion, like a crowd parting for convicts heading to the gallows.

Faint lights emitted from some of the shacks, filtering through the branch-woven walls, and the street's damp surfaces basked in their glow. The chaotic noises still echoed from deeper in the town, but the acoustics here muffled it all into a distant hum. It was a welcome relief.

But what little comfort the quiet brought the oppressive air smothered. It hung thick and suspended, a humid, sweaty, sticky, unbreathable vapor, staining the walls with a slimy film that sweated death in olive-green streaks. An itchy tissue of the same stuff clung to Oscar's skin and clothes like glue. He shivered through a wave of nausea and fought back a gag reflex.

Oscar and Nathaniel set off down the street. Ankle-deep puddles and thin streams of sludge spotted the ground with yellowish foam swaying in the grime in marble-like formations. The gooey dirt sloshed beneath Oscar's feet and seeped through his shoes.

The glow of Nathaniel's lantern bled into the lightless shacks on their sides, revealing huddled figures inside. Some shrank away from the passing light; others were drawn to it, their fingers probing through the cracks in the walls, their milky eyes glistening with curiosity.

Above, the reddish haze of the town spread across the dark like a veil, blurring all sense of direction. They might as well have been trapped in an air bubble in the Mariana Trench or drifting through outer space.

Oscar's head swam, partly from the foul air, mostly from fear. He fumbled for Nathaniel's hand and clasped it tightly. Nathaniel gave an affirming squeeze in return.

The corridor opened to a wider street, revealing a harrowing spectacle. Some two hundred people crowded the street. Some of them sat huddled in the muck, clutching their knees, pulling at their hair, shivering like orphaned cubs; others staggered aimlessly up and down the street, their backs hunched, heads bowed, their movements hiccupy from spasms and convulsions.

The people's sickly faces gleamed waxy in the glow of bonfires and torches, their pallor dotted by wounds and bruises like patches of mold in a bowl of fruit. A low, collective rasp of labored breathing rose from the mass. A few wailed openly, but most were too drained to join the chorus, their pain weathered and as old as time. It was as if a plague of suffering and squalor had swept through the street in one great wave, infecting everyone in its path.

Oscar froze, his feet rooted in the sludge. He couldn't bring himself to take another step.

"It's okay. You're safe with me." Nathaniel wrapped his arm around Oscar and coaxed him into motion.

"People come here and build raggedy-ass shelters or find abandoned ones to squat in," Nathaniel said, gesturing vaguely at their surroundings. "There's plenty of space out in the desert, but many choose to stay here and wallow in communal suffering. I guess misery is best shared with others?"

Oscar noticed a change in Nathaniel's posture. He seemed half a head taller, his shoulders wider, and his chest more puffed, keeping the townsfolk at bay with a nasty demeanor and a determined stride.

Up ahead, a man in a tattered military tunic paced the street, moving from side to side like a caged animal. He clenched a metal pipe with white-knuckled devotion and muttered to himself through gritted teeth, his whole body trembling with suppressed rage, ripe to burst.

Nathaniel released his arm from around Oscar's shoulder and rested his hand over a knife holstered on his hip. Oscar instinctively slid closer behind him. Although he didn't fully understand the situation, fear throbbed against his temples in a slow, relentless rhythm. They veered to the other side of the street and timed their steps to avoid crossing paths with the man.

Thankfully, the patrolman didn't give them any attention, and the two slipped by without hassle.

Nathaniel led Oscar toward another corridor, away from the main street's misery. The corridor's black mouth yawned before them, looking about as uninviting as everything else in this town. The people near the entrance took one look at Nathaniel and quietly parted from his path.

Then something hollow swept through the air, followed by a blunt smack. Oscar flinched and turned around.

Little ways back, the patrolman stood in the middle of the street, gripping his metal pipe. A man lay crumpled at his feet, clutching his head and struggling to get up. The patrolman screamed something unintelligible and swung the pipe again, bringing it down on the man's skull.

A loud crack whipped through the street, and the victim went limp. Nearby onlookers sank their heads into their laps, curling into shivering balls. Others disconnected altogether, their eyes locked in a vacant trance.

Oscar's jaw dropped. The sensation he had first felt back at the cemetery, back when Ernie had slit Son Number One's face, returned. It buzzed beneath his skin like a faint electric current—a tickle akin to thrill, a mixture of disgust and fascination. The sensation felt bizarre but not entirely off-putting.

"Stop staring," Nathaniel said. "It's rude."

He tugged Oscar into the shadowed corridor. Oscar tried to resist but soon forgot what he was resisting and fell back in line behind Nathaniel.

The dwellings closed in tighter and tighter, and a chaotic cobweb of alleyways and dead ends snaked between their crooked structures. The shacks leaned over the streets in wobbling arcs, teetering on the brink of destruction. In one corridor, a two-story hut had keeled over and was now propped by the shack across the street. Oscar and Nathaniel quickened their pace as they passed beneath it.

Half a dozen blocks later, Nathaniel stopped in front of a small yet sturdy-looking hut. Twined sticks crisscrossed its walls with red mud slathered between them, and a bed of black grass spread over the rooftop, sagging over the ridge.

"Here we are," Nathaniel said. "The safe place."

He pulled back a tattered cloth hanging from the doorframe, revealing a sliding door. He untied a thread suspended at the top of the frame, and something inside clicked in response. Then, he retrieved a rusty key from his pocket, unlocked an equally rusty padlock, and slid the door aside.

"Watch your head," Nathaniel said as he stepped inside.

Perched above the doorframe was a wooden board impaled with nails, their pointy tips staring back at Oscar. The board was attached to a lever that connected to the thread—a lethal snare for anyone unfamiliar with the mechanism.

"Can't be too careful," Nathaniel said.

Oscar ducked under the trap and followed Nathaniel into the hut. The one-room shelter was as shabby inside as it was outside. A coffin stuffed with pelts and blankets sat in one corner, its lid propped against the wall. Above it hung a handheld mirror, its dirty surface fractured by a long, jagged crack. The floor was strewn with worn-out clothes, rags, paper scrolls, and notebooks.

Nathaniel slid the door shut behind them, and the town's noises softened. The walls, thick with solid mud, insulated the humid climate of the streets, and the air inside was musty but also dry. Oscar considered it a welcome change. Some tension melted from his body, and a long exhale escaped his lips.

Nathaniel placed his lantern and satchel on the floor. He adjusted his trousers to avoid creases and sat on the edge of the coffin bed, hand pressed against his stomach.

"This fucking town." He shook head, took a swig from his canteen, then handed it to Oscar. "Creeps under your skin, doesn't it?"

Oscar sank to the floor and gulped down the water. The taste of rot in his throat faded, replaced by that strange, foreign tang. He drank some more. Only then did he realize he'd lost the pencil Nathaniel had given him somewhere along the way.

"I dropped the pencil," he said. Dread pooled in his

stomach at the thought of going back to find it. Hadn't Nathaniel told him to take good care of it?

But Nathaniel only responded with a listless, "Don't worry about it."

Oscar let out a shaky breath of relief and began rocking back and forth. The motion soothed him, and his mind cleared just enough to question the situation he'd ended up in. He glanced at Nathaniel. In the faint, flickering light, the scars on his face looked like squirming maggots.

"How did I get here?" he asked. "I can't remember anything."

"All in good time," Nathaniel said. "I know all this is confusing, but as long as you're with me, you don't have to worry. Just focus on clearing your head. You're not stable enough to hear the answer yet."

"How am I not… stable?"

Nathaniel measured him for a beat. "Look at your hands."

Oscar did as told. His hands were slathered in dirt, shaking. They felt stiff and unresponsive, almost as if they weren't his own. And only now did he notice the state his fingers were in. Four fingernails completely gone, three more badly damaged. One nail stuck out at a weird angle, barely clinging to the cuticle. His heart shrank.

"Oh," he whispered.

"You're in shock, Oscar," Nathaniel said. "Explaining anything to you would help fuck all at this point."

Oscar noticed that most of Nathaniel's fingernails were missing, too. But while Oscar's fingers were bloody and swollen blue, Nathaniel's were smooth and calloused, covered in grayish skin where his nails should have been.

"We'll gather our bearings and go visit a friend of mine," Nathaniel continued. "He has a couple of things I need. Then we'll get out of this town for good. We'll reassess the situation after that. But first, we're going to have to treat those hands."

"Treat them?"

Nathaniel nodded, scooted closer, and inspected the hands. He pinched the crooked fingernail between his thumb and forefinger. "Look away," he said. "Does that hurt?"

Oscar shook his head, humming to himself. Nathaniel slowly pulled at the nail, and Oscar felt a tug somewhere far away. A hideous rustling sound followed as the nail separated from its place. But that was all. There was no pain, only numbness.

"I got it off," Nathaniel said.

He washed Oscar's hands, whipped out a roll of gauze from his satchel, and patched the fingers. "Don't play the piano for a few weeks," he added.

Oscar tried to smile but felt too nauseated to do so.

"You'll also need some new clothes," Nathaniel said. "That suit's done for."

Oscar looked down, studying his attire. He hadn't even realized he was wearing a suit. It was smeared with mud, the pockets were heavy with dirt, and the jacket had torn in various places, its seams split.

"I think I fell into a ditch," he said.

"That's one way of putting it."

Nathaniel rummaged through a pile of clothes stuffed into a corner. He handed Oscar a pair of trousers and a short-sleeved collared shirt two sizes too large for him. The shirt was torn and missing buttons, while the trousers were riddled with holes, gnawed by corrosion and time. The clothes reeked of putrid sweat and were speckled with dark stains of varying stickiness.

Oscar stared at the damp pile of rags in his arms like it was roadkill.

"I'll step outside," Nathaniel said.

"Don't... I... don't leave," Oscar stammered. The thought of being alone in this place frightened him.

"Fine. But I'm not dressing you up." Nathaniel turned away, giving him privacy.

Oscar faced the corner. He shed the mud-smeared suit onto the floor and immediately felt ten pounds lighter. The parts of his skin that weren't coated in grime were wrinkled and frail, tacky to the touch like cork oak leaves. His boxer shorts were stained with dried piss and shit. He made sure Nathaniel wasn't looking and stripped naked. He kicked the rags into the corner and quickly shimmied into his new attire.

The change of clothes did nothing to improve his state. He felt just as miserable and dirty as he had in the old ones. He wondered: was it the clothes that made him feel uncomfortable, or was it his ill-fitting skin?

CHAPTER FOUR

Oscar and Nathaniel traversed Shantytown's labyrinthine streets like rats in a science experiment. The corridors spread forth with the intricacy of an ever-expanding mycelium, but Nathaniel navigated expertly through it all. He led the way with a determined demeanor, vigilant and suspicious of every doorway and person they passed. Oscar followed, a roll of blankets tucked under his arm and a stack of branches on his shoulder—items Nathaniel had taken from the hideout and assigned him to carry.

As they headed deeper into the bowels of the town, the decay that'd settled on Oscar's skin grew thicker, slimier. Now even his eyes felt waxy and itchy, blurring his vision. He kept clearing his throat with rattly snorts and spitting pus-colored phlegm.

The townsfolk seemed to suffer similar symptoms. Their oily skin, grease-matted hair, damp garments, and damaged bodies gave the impression of creatures crawling out of some cursed swamp. Some of their behavior matched the sludgy madness of their appearance: the town's chatter seemed to originate more from people talking to themselves than from social interactions; a few of the passersby pulled out wads of their own hair and chewed them like cows in a pasture; one denizen stood in an odd pose, his arms bent over his head, one leg suspended in the air, petrified by catatonia; a woman cradled a baby, bloated and pale, staring wide-eyed into an oblivion no child should come in contact with; and on one corner of a street, a man held a schizophrenic sermon, flailing a Bible around to emphasize his nonsensical monologue. He had torn some of the pages and sewn them all over his naked body, the patchwork prophet.

A few streets away, panicked screams broke out, followed by pained cries, then more panicked screams.

"What's happening?" Oscar asked, his throat tight.

"Sounds like someone's throwing a tantrum. Might get ugly in a cramped alleyway." Nathaniel glanced over his shoulder at Oscar, saw his distress, and added, "We're moving away from the ruckus. We're safe."

Oscar realized that if he lost Nathaniel, he wouldn't know where to go, what to do, or whom to talk to. He didn't know how far this labyrinth expanded, what lay beyond it, or whether there even was a way out of it. He was completely dependent on a stranger—a stranger who had said, in so many words, that he was Oscar's only chance at staying safe. He sank deeper into the cocoon of shock and detachment to hide from these facts, but some of the dread still dripped through.

The two men arrived at a bustling street of slogging townsfolk. They stopped in front of a shack, its porch sealed off with a fence. The fence was a mishmash of sticks, barbed wire, and rusty nails, looking like some medieval torture device. One could peek through the sparsely wound fencing, although doing so would subject their eyes to the rusty nails.

"This is Kareem's shop," Nathaniel said. "The friend I mentioned earlier."

He yanked at a rope hanging next to the door; on the other side of the fence, a bell rang.

"What?" a voice barked from inside the shack.

"It's Nathaniel."

"Never heard of him."

"Funny. Let me in." Nathaniel turned to Oscar. "Don't worry. Kareem's alright, mostly."

A faint sense of self-preservation stirred awake in Oscar, making him hesitant to enter the premises of yet another stranger. But he also knew it would be a bad move to displease the only person who could help him, so he kept his doubts to himself and said nothing.

"Is there someone with you?" Kareem asked.

"Picked up a newborn from the cemetery. Don't mind him. The kid's basically catatonic."

The wooden porch creaked as a dark figure appeared on the other side of the fence. Various locks and chains clattered and rattled, and the porch door cracked ajar. A man with a shaggy head of hair and a straggly beard peeked out, his suspicious eyes measuring Oscar and Nathaniel from head to toe. Then his face eased into a smile.

"Oh, *that* Nathaniel." Kareem swung the door open. "Get in."

They entered the porch. Oscar set his eyes on the floor and crossed his arms, unable to decide which one should rest over the other.

Kareem bore the same wan sickliness as the rest of the people here although the smile peeking from under his beard and his warm aura made him seem more... *alive* than his fellow townsfolk. He had no visible wounds, either, although they simply might have been hidden under his clothing.

He locked the porch door and gestured at the shack's entrance. "Go on in. Make yourselves comfortable."

"'Comfortable' is a strong word in a town like this," Nathaniel said.

"Make yourselves slightly less uncomfortable, then."

The inside of the shack was padded with rags and blankets to insulate the noise and stench from outside. A rug covered the floor except in one corner where a trapdoor lay locked and bolted shut. In the middle of the snug room stood a knee-high table with a lit oil lamp.

Oscar and Nathaniel sat by the table. Kareem followed them in and covered the entrance with a heavy tarp. The voices outside muffled, and an intimate atmosphere descended upon the room. He took a seat on the other side of the table and rested an elbow on a hooked knee.

"So, you're digging up newborns now?" he asked.

"Me? Come on," Nathaniel frowned dismissively. "Rescued the kid from a couple of grave looters, if you can believe it. Had to fuck one of them up."

"Better not be any of my associates," Kareem said.

"How can you call them your associates?" Nathaniel muttered.

"Hey, they bring in good merchandise from the cemetery. That's all I need to know. That's all I *want* to know."

"See no evil, hear no evil, huh?"

"I see and hear just plenty, my friend," Kareem said with a tired look. "And you're telling me you just decided to save someone out of the goodness of your heart?"

"Something like that," Nathaniel shrugged. "The kid's going to help me with something. But don't mind him. He's still a little shaken up. Hasn't realized that he's—" Nathaniel swept his thumb across his throat.

Oscar saw this, but his mind refused to interpret the

gesture.

"Let me guess: help you with Dean Theodore?" Kareem asked, holding on to his tired look.

Up until now, Oscar had barely registered the conversation, but now something stirred inside him. *Dean Theodore.* The name carried an essence, something that seemed to demand his focus. His ears pricked up.

"That's right," Nathaniel said. He leaned halfway over the table and spoke as if he were on the brink of some grand discovery. "I found him, Kareem."

"Good for you." Kareem shared none of Nathaniel's enthusiasm. "Is that why you asked me for the map?"

"The route through the mountain range." Nathaniel settled back into his seat. "It's just too good a shortcut to skip."

"What's the rush? All we have is time, no?"

"I have to get to him before the trail goes cold." Nathaniel paused, impatiently drumming his fingers on the table. "So, did you get it? The map?"

"Indeed I did," Kareem said, smirking. His faux-tiredness was gone, replaced by smug pride. He flipped through a pile of scriptures behind him and slammed a folded piece of paper on the table. "I present to you the map of the mountain range. Guaranteed safe passage included."

Nathaniel leaned in to inspect the map, as did Oscar. The map portrayed clusters of mountains and forests circling a valley, with a red path traipsing through the region. In the lower left corner was an arrow pointing left with the inscription *Cometerium (occidens).*

"Cemetery. West," Nathaniel translated, his finger below the text. "I don't think compass directions apply here, Kareem."

"It's more of a figurative thing," Kareem said. "According to the map, we're currently west of the mountains, so you'll be heading east to get there. You'll enter the mountain range from this side of the map. See that X at the start of the red trail?

When you get to the edge of the forest, look for a tree with an X carved on it. That's where the safe route begins."

Nathaniel nodded, his eyes fixed on the map, scratching his chin.

"I got this map from—" Kareem waved his hand, searching for the right word, "an anthropologist. She's studied different areas, documented them, drawn maps, and so forth."

"And she's good at what she does?" Nathaniel asked. "I have a low tolerance for errors."

"The word you're looking for is *nitpicker*."

"You say it like an insult, but all I hear is a compliment."

"The anthropologist is a nitpicker, too. No errors."

"I hope so." Nathaniel tucked the map into his breast pocket. "My compliments to the anthropologist. And to you, as well. This saves me a world of trouble."

Kareem nodded. After a beat, he slapped his hands together with the enthusiasm of a perky salesman. "So, what else can I get you boys? I've got a ton of military equipment. Guns might blow up in your face, but they'll still give you authority in a tight spot. I have Kevlar, helmets, explosives… although that stuff I don't keep here with me. Too unstable."

"I don't want to look like I'm heading out to war," Nathaniel said. "I want to give the impression that I'm just passing through, minding my business. I want to be someone not worth bothering."

"How about some drugs, then?" Kareem suggested. "When you haven't slept for a week and get ambushed, amphetamines will do just the trick to—"

"I'm all set prescription-wise," Nathaniel interrupted. "And aren't you forgetting something? The map's not the only thing I came here for. I believe you still owe me some travel supplies."

Kareem's enthusiasm deflated. "Well… I have good news and bad news."

Nathaniel said nothing, but Oscar felt a coldness rise from him, his relaxed demeanor dwindling.

"I got robbed," Kareem sighed. "I was bringing the supplies here, but some sons of bitches jumped me."

Nathaniel remained silent. He rested an elbow on the table and rubbed his temples as if to subdue a budding headache.

"They had knives pointed at me," Kareem added defensively.

"And the good news?" Nathaniel asked.

"The map was the good news."

Gloom descended over Nathaniel. "I need compensation for this, Kareem. The travel supplies are *essential*, understand?"

"Listen, I'm—" Kareem stopped. "Your friend okay?"

Oscar had tried to hide his growing dread but could no longer. He doubled over and clasped his chest, feeling like his lungs were shrinking.

It was the same thought that'd already occurred to him, but now returned heavier than before: Nathaniel was Oscar's only chance at staying safe. The weight of his dependence on the man hadn't truly hit him earlier, not while Nathaniel had shown him nothing but kindness. But now the sudden shift in Nathaniel's behavior triggered something in Oscar—an instinct that screamed danger. The man he'd been counting on had just revealed that maybe he shouldn't be counted on after all.

"Oscar?" Nathaniel asked. "Maybe you should step outside?"

Oscar lifted his head and stared at Nathaniel, eyes wide with horror. *That's all it took?* he thought. *That's all it took for him to get sick of me? To abandon me?*

"Please, no," he stammered.

"Not *out* out," Nathaniel said, correcting himself. "Just wait on the porch. It's safe there. Shit, it's probably the safest place in town on account of all the locks and such."

"I don't mean to brag, but it is," Kareem nodded.

Oscar tried to laugh but couldn't squeeze out a sound.

"These newborns," Nathaniel said, turning back to Kareem. "So dramatic."

A moment or two had passed since Nathaniel had ushered Oscar out of Kareem's shop. Oscar sat cross-legged on the porch, hugging the roll of blankets Nathaniel had assigned him to carry. The worst of his anxiety had now been replaced by numbness although an uneasy aftertaste remained. Nathaniel and Kareem's argument inside the shop had continued this whole time. The hissing, pickering, and overlapping accusations now formed a dull monotone in Oscar's ears. He couldn't keep track of the sour exchange between the two men. Instead, he focused his attention on the street beyond the fence, on the sludge and its people pulsating in the firelight like ghosts flickering on the brink of invisibility.

Oscar's gaze drifted to a shack across the street. The front door was modified from a coffin lid, illuminated by torches perched on either side. Something hung from the door. It moved like a spider turned on its back, helplessly flailing its legs. But this spider-like thing had only five legs. Oscar squinted and realized what he was looking at: there was a severed hand nailed to the door. A dry rivulet of blood ran down from the hand's stump, and its fingers twitched as if playing an invisible harp. A coldness oozed through him.

How in the fuck...?

His concentration broke as Nathaniel stormed out of Kareem's shop, a morose look on his face. An age-old military-grade messenger bag hung from his shoulder with two pairs of leather shoes tied by their laces to the strap.

"I got you more shit to carry." Nathaniel dropped the messenger bag in front of Oscar's crossed legs.

Oscar picked up the bag and hung it over his shoulder. He tried to adjust the strap, but his hands were still shaking. The damaged fingernails made intricate tasks, such as buckling a strap, nearly impossible. Nathaniel knelt down and helped.

As he tightened the strap, Oscar's eyes veered back to the severed hand. It wasn't there anymore. The door had opened, and inside loomed only darkness. Oscar shivered and looked away. Somehow the dark with all its ominous possibilities frightened him more than the severed hand.

CHAPTER FIVE

At the town's eastern outskirts, the crammed architecture dispersed into a desolate neighborhood. Ramshackle huts stood scattered, and save for a few small groups gathered around bonfires in silent congregation, the population was sparse. Unlike back in town, the stench of decay was less invasive here, the rotted humidity less palpable. Oscar took a deep breath, and both his physical and mental state improved, like a foggy mirror that clears with the swipe of a hand.

Above, the first signs of a new day presented themselves with apocalyptic dread. Slits of light appeared on the black clouds, revealing their amber-glowing innards like the punctured skin of some mythical fire lizard, its flesh embers. Bronzed beams of light pushed through the clouds and dissipated mid-air, not quite reaching the ground. Oscar watched the strange sky unfold as Nathaniel led him through the outskirts.

"What's with the sky?" Oscar asked. Despite his improved state, he realized he still sounded—and felt—drunk.

"Dawn's breaking. Good timing. We'll get some distance from the town before it gets dark again." Nathaniel extinguished the lantern hanging from his satchel. "Thanks to Kareem's contribution, we're doing okay equipment-wise. But it's the lantern fuel that worries me. We have only two pouches of the stuff. If we regulate and make camp every night, maybe—*maybe*—we'll be alright. Making camp every night really fucks up our timetable, though. But we can't go fumbling in the dark, can we? And we can't stay in town any longer to collect more fuel, either. I promised to keep you safe, but I can't do it in this fucking town."

By this point, Nathaniel's ramblings had become too much for Oscar to process, so he blocked most of it out.

Nathaniel went on: "And then there's the forest up ahead to consider. I hear the safe route is so overgrown no daylight gets through. No idea how we're going to pull that off without more fuel."

Oscar said nothing and resumed staring at the sky.

"Good talk," Nathaniel muttered.

The dawn progressed, and the sky's glowing slits widened. The black clouds around them paled until they were glowing, too. The darkness below receded, and from that darkness emerged a rock-ridden desert, barren and discolored like the corpse of a petrified colossus. Its stony terrain consisted of mounds, craters, and canyons. Patches of vegetation scattered across the scenery, all of it withered and dead. Everything was either gray or black and tinted with dusty sepia tones wherever the light reached. Far off in the distance, mountains pushed through the horizon like an uneven row of blackened fangs. Not even a gust of wind stirred the heavy air, and the atmosphere hung still as if locked in time.

The landscape unraveled itself before Oscar like some

creature spreading its leathery wings. A visceral fear crept through the numbness and hissed in his ear: *Where are you going, Oscar?*

He stopped. "Wait. Where are you taking me?"

Nathaniel measured him. "Are you in a lucid enough state to palaver?"

"I just want to know where we're going."

"Okay. Let's sit down for a moment."

They found a heap of boulders nearby. In their shade lay a blanket of withered grass, dotted with bone-dry tree stumps. Nathaniel dusted off a rock with a handkerchief before taking a seat. Oscar stood by, hugging the roll of blankets.

"Have a seat, Oscar. Never waste a chance to get some rest. There's a water canteen in your bag if you're thirsty."

Oscar sat down on the grass, opened the bag, and found two canteens.

"One is water, the other one's lantern fuel," Nathaniel said. He patted his satchel. "I have the second fuel pouch. Figured we shouldn't keep all our eggs in the same basket."

Oscar uncorked a canteen, smelled it, and took a swig.

"You wanted to ask me something?"

"Yeah. Where are you taking me?" Oscar found himself nervous; asking questions might result in unwanted answers. He tinkered with the bandages on his fingers.

"I'm looking for a man named Dean Theodore," Nathaniel said.

Oscar stopped the tinkering. There it was again, that demanding pull. The name fascinated him although he couldn't tell why. It felt instinctual—the way a full moon incites insomnia.

"Who?" he asked.

"Look, Dean Theodore has studied this place for a long time. He's gathered information very few have been able to obtain. I'm something of a researcher myself, but I'm a novice at best compared to him. However"—he lifted a finger—"a little while back, I got lucky and discovered something quite… *significant.* I need to get this discovery to Dean Theodore. With his know-how, we can change things. So, to answer your question: I'm taking you—*asking* you—to seek Dean Theodore with me."

Much of Nathaniel's explanation was beyond Oscar's current state of comprehension, but the conviction in his voice did not escape him. Oscar found it hard not to feel enthralled by it. His mouth moved, trying to form a hundred questions at once, but no words came out.

"I know this is all very vague," Nathaniel said, "but I can't reveal my discovery until Dean Theodore is there to hear it. I can't risk the information getting to the wrong hands. It's too precious."

"So… what do you need me for?"

"I need an extra pair of hands to help with the practicalities. Carry the gear, share guard duty while we camp, keep me out of trouble, keep me company—shit like that. In exchange, I can offer you protection and guidance. You're still a bit out of it, but I bet you've noticed that it's not safe here. Well, I can keep you safe, Oscar. I know my way around this place."

Oscar was quiet, eyes set on his lap. He was back to tinkering with the bandages. "You keep saying 'this place.'"

"Yes. That's something you'll have to figure out on your own."

"Why?"

"If I told you, you'd never believe me," Nathaniel said. "Once you figure it out, I can stop being vague about everything. I promise."

A lump formed at the back of Oscar's throat, flaring a burning sensation. The situation felt unfair and raised more suspicion than trust. Nathaniel was essentially a stranger who expected Oscar to follow him into a desert. Yes, he had kept him safe so far, but how long would that continue once they were alone, far from others? The more Oscar tried to figure it out, the more his head ached and the more his thoughts scattered. He frowned and shook his head, sick of feeling so helpless and lost.

"You don't trust me," Nathaniel said, summarizing Oscar's thoughts.

"It's just... I don't know you. And I'm so confused, and my head hurts. Everything hurts. And I can't... Why can't I remember anything?"

"That would be the amnesia. You've just been through a major traumatic experience. Give it time. It'll pass. As for the trust part, I get it. Shit, I'd be worried if you *did* trust me by now." Nathaniel paused, contemplating something. "Check your bag. Side pocket."

Oscar reached into his bag and found a knife there. He took it out, unsheathed it from its leather holster, and studied it warily. The wooden handle had chipped, but the blade itself was well-maintained, sharp. The knife turned slippery in his sweaty palm. Once again, behind the confusion and queasiness, he felt a thrill, like hot breath against the nape of his neck.

"Now you have the means to defend yourself in case I betray you."

Oscar said nothing.

"I get that you're confused by all this, so let me break it down for you. Either we part ways, and you try to make it on your own—head back to Shantytown, see how long you'll last—or you take your chances with me. Tag along, and I'll guarantee you safety and, when you're more lucid, an explanation to all this. Those are your options. It's far from ideal, but that's the crossroads you've come to."

Oscar wasn't sure if this ultimatum strengthened or weakened his trust in Nathaniel. Either way, the man was right: turning back to town definitely meant trouble, and going along with Nathaniel's plan *might* mean trouble. Even in his current state, Oscar understood the difference between the two. He fiddled with the knife and felt the lump in his throat expand.

"Time to decide," Nathaniel said abruptly. He got up and left the spot without so much as a farewell.

Oscar watched Nathaniel's slouching figure recede into the desert dawn. His chest tightened—not because he was afraid of losing his guardian, but because he was beginning to realize just how much power this man held over him. He rubbed his face as if it would ease his frustration, gathered his gear, and caught up with Nathaniel.

"Nice bluff," Oscar muttered.

Nathaniel said nothing. Oscar studied him from the corner of his eye and, to his surprise, detected something akin to guilt on the man's face.

Oscar clenched the knife, and somewhere ahead, Dean Theodore waited.

The murky dawn faded. A thick raft of resin-colored clouds spread across the sky, hiding whatever infernal lights blossomed above, while a steady glow of amber filtered through. The clouds sagged low and oppressive, like a ceiling bloated with moisture.

"There's no consistent day-and-night cycle here," Nathaniel said as they trudged deeper into the desert. "The day might last an hour, five hours, fifteen. The same applies to nighttime. We'll just keep moving until it gets dark or until one of us keels over."

Oscar felt too sick to focus on Nathaniel's words. The mist that had numbed his mind was now clearing, and he realized that the numbness hadn't affected him only mentally but also physically. His body felt... *foreign*. It was as if something familiar had shifted in a deeply intrusive and unsettling way—like returning to an empty home after a long trip only to find all the furniture rearranged. This sense of unfamiliarity manifested with nausea and various aches that danced through him like malignant spirits. His muscles convulsed randomly; one moment his heart beat with the force of a jackhammer, the next it seemed to stop altogether. A hardened lump had taken residence in his stomach, sending feverish signals that made him shiver. He felt unnatural and broken. Paradoxically, the more his mind cleared and the more he reconnected with reality, the more estranged he felt from it.

An explosive boom derailed Oscar's thoughts.

The dusty ground shook, sending tremors up through his feet. He hunkered down, covering his head. Nathaniel jolted as well.

From behind a nearby rock ledge, a geyser of water shot high into the air, its immense pressure slinging gravel all around. It ended as abruptly as it had begun, leaving behind the clattering of falling stones and a fine mist that suspended in the air like an echo, sparkling golden in the amber light.

"Holy shit!" Nathaniel laughed.

"What's happening? What was that?" Oscar didn't know if he was more surprised by the explosion or Nathaniel's reaction.

"I'll show you. It's nothing to be afraid of."

Nathaniel offered his hand to help Oscar up, but he waved him away. "Was it a bomb?"

"A bomb? No. Just come on already."

Oscar and Nathaniel headed for the rock ledge which stood ten feet high and descended into a lowered desert plain. In its shade hunkered a waist-deep pit filled with murky water. Its surface bubbled and fizzed as the water level rose, descended, then rose again. Next to the pit stood a few crooked, lifeless trees. The few branches they had left held leaves at their bony fingers—black, shriveled, and leathery like the wings of a dead bat.

"The theory is that there are subterranean tunnels flowing with water. It's a sort of natural sewer system," Nathaniel explained. "Sometimes the tunnels overflow—probably because of the earth's movements and the pressure points it creates. Whatever the case, the excess water gets released through small cracks in the ground. Sometimes they cause flooding, and sometimes they develop"—he snapped his fingers and pointed at the pit—"springs."

They descended the ledge and reached the bubbling waterhole.

"Let's stock up on water and wash off all this Shantytown gunk," Nathaniel said.

"It's safe to drink that?" Oscar asked.

"Supposedly. Truth be told, I don't know if it has the same chemical composition as water. But it's similar enough. Your body hasn't adapted to the bacteria here, so you might get the runs, though. Just something you have to endure."

It doesn't have the same chemical composition as water, Oscar recited. He didn't ask for clarification. He was already deep enough in the rabbit hole of Nathaniel's enigmatic remarks. He had no desire to sink any deeper.

Nathaniel drank his canteen dry. He placed a rag over the canteen's mouth as a filter and sank it into the spring, filling it to the top. He passed the rag to Oscar, who followed Nathaniel's steps.

"Now what?" Oscar asked.

"Now we clean up." Nathaniel hung his satchel on one of the trees and unbuttoned his vest. "Every time I visit Shantytown, I feel like I've been dipped in slime. It's disgusting. You keep a lookout. Once I'm done, we'll switch."

Unease bubbled in Oscar's gut. The location was secluded, they were alone, and this man was essentially asking Oscar to get undressed. Was this where Nathaniel would make his move—whatever that move might be? He fiddled with the knife holstered in his belt, thinking, *What am I supposed to do? Fight my way out of this? Kill him? This is absurd.*

Nathaniel removed his shirt, revealing an array of cuts and scars riddled across his pale, lean body. One gash in particular nearly made Oscar's eyes pop out. It ran halfway across Nathaniel's belly, curving like a tight smile, cutting all the way through the skin. A shoelace threaded through the wound. This makeshift suture was presumably holding Nathaniel's stomach together. But it also looked like one firm yank could unravel it and eviscerate the man. Oscar turned away, feeling dizzy.

"I see you noticed the cut. This is what happens when you're not careful around here." Nathaniel shed the rest of his garments and descended into the pool. He shivered at the cold water but soon settled in like it was nothing. "And before you get all bent out of shape: this happened probably months ago. I've been dealing with it just fine. I can see from your face that you're about to start fuzzing over it. Don't. I don't want to talk about it. I'll manage."

Knees buckling, Oscar sat on the ground and pressed his head between his knees.

"Sure, take a breather." Nathaniel splashed water on his arms and shoulders. "But you better get up that ledge soon and keep watch. Someone might have seen that geyser. Water draws in predator and prey alike, you know."

Which one are you? Oscar wondered.

CHAPTER SIX

The darkness spread across the dangling clouds like mold, and dusk settled over the desert. The temperature dropped from bland to brisk, and the distant screams and bursts of laughter rose in volume. Their echoes raced across the desolate landscape, aimless and mad, like spirits freed from their shackles. In the midst of all this, Oscar and Nathaniel headed on at a sluggish pace.

"This is what I meant by an inconsistent day-and-night cycle," Nathaniel said, gesturing at the sky. "How long has it been—a few hours?—and it's already getting dark."

Oscar's clothes glued to his damp skin, and the drop in temperature cast shivers through his body. He'd dried himself with one of the blankets after bathing in the spring but apparently hadn't been thorough enough. Having taken the risk to bathe in the spring while Nathaniel had kept watch had improved Oscar's mental state, but he still felt very much disoriented. He tried to piece together everything that had happened since the cemetery, but most of the memories simply weren't there, and the few he had left were hazy and unreliable, as if he'd been blackout drunk up until entering the desert.

"I don't know how much longer I can keep up," he said, teeth clattering.

"Well, we should make camp before it gets too dark anyway. Let's get out of the open first, though."

They found a spot nearby where a moss-covered boulder and a few dead trees sheltered a patch of grass. They reached the spot and set up camp. Nathaniel passed a collapsible spade to Oscar and told him to dig a knee-deep hole for a bonfire. Oscar did as instructed, sucking in air through gritted teeth as flares of pain pulsed from the tips of his damaged fingers. Nathaniel set up wires around the camp by tying them to sticks he planted in the ground. He yanked the suspended threads, and the metal shrapnel dangling from them clattered like wind chimes.

"Tripwires," he explained.

For what? Oscar thought but didn't dare to ask it aloud. The answer scared him more than the not-knowing.

Oscar sat cross-legged on a blanket he'd spread near the pit and pulled off his shoes to rub his aching feet. The insides of his shoes were still damp from the Shantytown sludge, smelling like compost. Then again, everything here smelled like compost.

Nathaniel snapped some branches and twigs from the trees and started building a fire in the hole Oscar had dug. He poured a dollop of fuel on the branches, set a bundle of twigs ablaze with the lantern, and stuffed them under the larger branches. He extinguished the lamp and worked on the bonfire. Soon, it crackled and popped soothingly, radiating a subtle glow on his haggard face.

"There. Should keep us warm for the night." Nathaniel took off his shoes and settled on the second blanket.

It was full dark now. All the light left in the world seemed to originate from their modest bonfire and a few other specks flickering deep in the distance, everything else consumed by the ever-hungry dark. Oscar watched the tongues of the flames rise from the bonfire to dance their little dance, and his mind lulled into a place of absence.

Nathaniel said something, his voice muffled and far away.

"Huh?" Oscar asked.

"How are your fingers?"

Oscar inspected his hands but didn't dare remove the gauze wrapped around his fingertips. "I can't decide whether they hurt or feel numb."

"I know the feeling. You don't know whether something hurts so bad that it's making you numb, or it's so numb that it hurts."

"Yeah. Something like that." Oscar dabbed the gauzed fingertips with his thumbs.

"Are you tired?" Nathaniel asked.

"Not really."

"Good. Then you can take first watch."

Oscar sobered up. "Watch what?"

"Intruders. People. No-good sons of bitches who might get the bright idea to visit our camp."

"Wh— But I don't know how."

"That so?" Nathaniel lifted four fingers. "How many fingers am I holding up?"

"Twenty-eight."

Nathaniel shot a tired look at Oscar. "You'll take first watch." He removed a coil of rope from his satchel strap and tied it around his wrist. He passed the rest of the rope to Oscar. "If you hear those tripwires clatter, don't say anything. Don't scream, don't jump up, don't run off. Just stay still and yank this rope. Got it? I might not get up immediately, but rest assured, I will be awake and dealing with the problem in no time."

"Hold on. I—"

Nathaniel lifted a hand to silence him—a patronizing gesture that made Oscar bristle. Nathaniel continued, "If you see someone with a torch or a lantern heading this way, the same plan applies: stay still and yank the rope. I'll assess the situation and deal with it. And if you start dozing off, don't try to power through it. Just yank the rope, and we'll switch right away."

"On second thought, I do feel kind of beat."

"Nice try." Nathaniel lay his head on his satchel, using it as a pillow, and cradled his knife against his chest. "Make sure the fire stays about yay big. We gotta keep it subtle."

"Goddamnit," Oscar muttered, squeezing the rope.

"Don't worry. This is probably just me being paranoid."

"How comforting."

Oscar stared at the trance-inducing flames and listened to Nathaniel's slow breathing. An image kept creeping into his mind: Nathaniel's sliced belly, sewn with a shoelace. The grotesqueness of it had branded into Oscar's retinas like a scar. But what shocked him even more was that such an injury should have been lethal without proper medical care, and it was clear Nathaniel hadn't received any. Nathaniel should be dead. And yet, he had said that the wound was months old. He was still walking, talking, and breathing as if a fatal wound was nothing but a minor inconvenience.

Is he even human?

Oscar snapped out of his thoughts as he heard Nathaniel mumble in his sleep. The words were unintelligible, but Oscar detected desperation in his tone. Nathaniel's shoulders twitched, and the mumbles turned to whimpers, helpless and childlike. They rose in volume until the man was sobbing. Eyes still shut, he threw himself onto his back. His body went into a deadlock, and his teeth welded together, panicky breaths and cries pushing through them.

Someone's going to hear that, Oscar thought, horrified. (Then again, how was Nathaniel's ruckus any different from the other voices filling the soundscape?)

Nathaniel's eyes shot open, and he sat up with a jolt, his knife extended into the dark. Sweat drenched his hair, and his face was frozen in a grimace of horror. His helplessness and terror were so heartbreaking and out of character that, amid the fear, Oscar couldn't help but pity the man.

"Nathaniel?" he asked, throat dry.

Nathaniel flinched, whipping his knife toward Oscar. "Where am I?"

"In the desert." Oscar lifted his hands in surrender. "We made camp."

Nathaniel blinked, and a whiff of recognition returned to his eyes. "Is everything alright?"

"You tell me," Oscar laughed nervously.

Nathaniel lay back down, hiding his face under his arm. "I'm alright, I'm alright." He took a moment for his breathing to steady. "Are you tired? We can switch."

"No, I'm good." Adrenaline coursed through Oscar's veins, making the idea of sleep sound absurd—as did the fact that he was out camping with a knife-wielding, obviously unstable stranger.

Nathaniel rolled onto his side, his back to Oscar. He stayed in this position for the rest of the night. The pace of his breaths told Oscar that he was awake the whole time, merely pretending to sleep.

CHAPTER SEVEN

Dawn seeped through the cracks in the clouds, its first lights piercing the heart of darkness like copper spikes. The desert appeared from the dark like some misty castle in a feverish dream—desolate and empty, yet full of secrets and uncombed floors.

As the two travelers cleared camp, Oscar watched this eldritch landscape unfold. For the first time, he allowed himself to evaluate things. The first question that came to mind was this: *Has the world ended?* The signs were there: the vegetation was all dead, he'd seen no animals, strange clouds shrouded the sky, and all the people here, present company included, were injured and sick with something. And Oscar felt the same way. His body ached, he felt nauseated, his skin was sore and itchy, his fingernails were (apparently) falling off, a taste of rot coated his palate, and a hard lump had taken residence in his belly.

Thinking this through, Oscar's breathing turned erratic.

Is this… radiation sickness? He took another look at the desert and felt its hopelessness creep in deeper. *A nuclear holocaust?*

"Is there, like, radiation around here?" Oscar asked, trying to steady the vibrato in his voice.

Nathaniel was coiling up the tripwires. He stopped and raised an eyebrow. "Radiation? The fuck if I know. Why?"

"So… we're not in the middle of a nuclear winter?"

"A *what?*"

"Nothing. Never mind. Forget it." Oscar shook his head and went back to rolling up the blankets.

Nathaniel's response was enough to make Oscar drop the issue. If Nathaniel—a hardened and knowledgeable survivor—didn't worry about radiation and hadn't even heard about a nuclear winter, then how could Oscar's nuclear holocaust theory be right? Besides, the idea was so disturbing that he was glad to let it go.

But if this isn't nuclear winter, then what is it? Where am I? Why am I feeling like this? Nathaniel had told Oscar that he needed to figure it out himself, that otherwise Oscar would never believe him. But all Oscar had to go on were foggy memories, broken and scattered by blackouts. How much of those memories could he trust to be real? Could he rely on any of this being real?

With these questions haunting Oscar, he followed Nathaniel out of the remains of their campsite.

Later that day, Oscar and Nathaniel came upon an area where the desert plain descended into a valley filled with towering rock formations. Canyons lurked in the shadows of the rugged stone mounds, some as narrow as Shantytown's corridors, others as wide as cathedral halls.

They stopped at the top of a slope that led into the canyons.

"Goddamnit," Nathaniel muttered.

"What is it?" Oscar asked.

"I wanted to circle around this place. But we're losing too much time making camp every night, so we have to take our shortcuts where we can get them."

"So there's… something bad down there," Oscar said. He wasn't sure if this was a question or a statement.

"No, no. I don't think so," Nathaniel said but also unsheathed his knife.

Oscar tensed and took a step back, a cold ripple running through him.

"It's just a precaution," Nathaniel said, looking slightly offended.

A lukewarm redness crept up Oscar's face. He lowered his eyes to his feet.

"You should keep your knife ready, too."

Oscar took out his knife and inspected it. It sent a primitive pulse that traveled up his arm, shoulder, and neck, settling at the base of his skull, stirring some long-slumbering part of his lizard brain.

"Remember," Nathaniel said, "it's for defense, not assault."

"I'm not going to *assault* anyone," Oscar said. Something about Nathaniel's implication had struck a nerve. "I mean, I've never even been in a fight. I think."

"Let's try to keep it that way."

They descended the slope and entered the canyons. Black moss speckled the stone walls, and vines crept through the cracks in thick clusters, like tentacles of lurking sea creatures. One brushed Oscar's cheek, lifeless and soft with rot, sending shivers all over his body. In the tightest portions of the tunnel, the vines crossed between the opposing walls like sinew strung between slabs of torn flesh. The air hung damp and heavy, charged like the sultry stillness before a thunderstorm. Anticipation weighed down the silence, broken by the irregular drips of water.

They slowed their pace, their demeanor now calculated and alert. The tunnels branched, spread out, narrowed in, ascended, and descended. And soon Oscar had lost track of where they'd come from. He clutched his knife tighter.

"You sure you know where we're going?" he asked. His voice multiplied in echoes, each one a lesser whisper than the last.

Nathaniel shot him an annoyed look. "I get that you don't trust me, but dial it down, okay?"

Their path opened into a courtyard-like space where branching corridors intersected and the walls loomed as high as three-story buildings. Cave entrances gaped slack-jawed on the walls, and calcified water traces dribbled from them like foamy drool.

At the mouth of one of the caves stood a man. He was naked except for a tattered cloth draped over his shoulders. Blackened cuts and bruises scattered across his skin, and his arms, legs, and sides were pocked with scarred dents where chunks of flesh had been either hacked or gnawed off. A crown of small bones and twigs hung tangled from his matted hair. His glassy eyes fixed on Oscar and Nathaniel. His chapped lips formed a round, innocent *o*.

"Oh, Jesus!" Oscar jumped. "Who the fuck is that?"

"Just some hermit," Nathaniel said, his voice tight but even. "Stop staring. It might provoke him."

The hermit's eyes narrowed to sharp slits, and his mouth twisted into a mischievous smile. He covered his face, peeked through his fingers, and giggled—high-pitched, constant, and compulsive.

"Quite the character," Nathaniel said under his breath.

"Can we head back? I think we should head back."

"Let's just keep at it. He's seen us either way."

Oscar and Nathaniel hurried past the hermit's perch,

sticking close to the opposite wall. The hermit tracked them with his stare. His giggles turned more frantic, echoing off the jagged walls and traveling through the caves, approaching the two travelers from all around as if the canyons themselves were laughing at them.

They reached the end of the courtyard-like trench and slipped into another narrow corridor. Oscar looked back, relieved to see that the hermit hadn't moved from where they'd first seen him. He was now seated, feet dangling over the edge of his lookout.

They pressed on in tense silence. After a moment, the echoes of the hermit's giggles faded. Oscar allowed himself a quiet breath of relief. It didn't seem the hermit would engage with them.

The grounds were challenging and untamed, and the abrasions in Oscar's feet flared up. Keeping up with Nathaniel's pace only worsened the pain, but he didn't dare complain. He knew his constant distrust was riling Nathaniel up. He feared the man would grow tired of him and abandon him to this stone maze. Oscar was so dependent on Nathaniel that it was hard to breathe. Frustration burned corrosively in his throat.

They entered a narrow tunnel, and the stack of firewood on Oscar's back scraped against the walls. The bindings loosened, and the branches clattered to the ground. Oscar closed his eyes as the acid in his throat flared hotter.

Nathaniel raised his nailless forefinger to his lips, shushing at him.

Oscar gave him an annoyed look as he gathered the branches and bound them back together. He realized that with the firewood on his back and the roll of blankets under his arm, he wouldn't stand a chance defending himself.

"You know, this would be a lot easier if we'd share the load a little," he said.

"I promised to keep you safe. Can't do that with my hands

full."

"But there isn't all that much going on right now."

"That so?" Nathaniel asked. "I take it you haven't noticed that fucking hermit has been following us this whole time?"

The crammed tunnel led to a grand hallway where the walls towered thirty feet high, spotted with vine-curtained cave entrances. Some of them drooled weak rivulets of water into a ditch that ran alongside the pathway.

Oscar shot glances at every entrance, corridor, and crevice they passed. He flinched at every sound and shadow, feeling like a rubber band stretched to its limits, ready to snap. But the hermit was nowhere to be seen.

"Where is this guy?" he asked.

"I spotted him in a tunnel we passed a while back and in one of those caves. The bastard probably knows the area like the back of his hand."

"What does he want?"

"Beats me. Best case scenario, he's making sure we leave his lair. Worst case, he wants to ensure that we never do. Either way, we're mere guests here, and he's our host."

"Jesus Christ..." Oscar whispered. "Shouldn't you, like, stop him?"

"Stop him?"

"Yeah. Like, fuck him up or something."

Nathaniel halted. "We don't do that kind of shit, Oscar. I can defend us, but I'm not going to assault anyone. The hermit hasn't done anything."

Oscar lowered his gaze, ashamed.

"If violence is your first solution to a problem, I seriously have to reconsider our arrangement."

"It's not. I'm sorry. I'm just scared."

"Alright." Nathaniel resumed walking. "Come on, we're

almost through."

The hallway arched left, and a stone wall obstructed the view ahead. Somewhere up the path, something was breathing heavily, the voice raspy and pained.

Oscar's blood froze. "Oh, shit. No, no, no."

"Here we go," Nathaniel muttered.

In the ditch that ran along the path, Oscar noticed streaks of red swirling through the water. He tapped Nathaniel's shoulder and pointed at the stream.

"Yeah, I saw it. Our host's got a flair for the dramatics."

"What does that mean?"

"It means I might have to fuck him up."

The arching path straightened. Up ahead, the hallway opened into a gateway between the canyons and the desert. The stone walls loomed tall and mighty, framing the desolate desert view with an air of divine judgment.

Abandon all hope, ye who enter, Oscar thought. (He would soon realize how close to home he had hit with that reference.)

Something hunkered at the foot of the gateway. As they approached the figure, Oscar first mistook it for a torn trash bag, its contents spilled across the ground. But upon a second glance, he realized that the trash bag was expanding and deflating with labored breaths. It was the mangled corpse of a man, lying there on the stone floor. Everything from his clothing to skin to flesh was a shredded mess, all doused in syrupy blood. It spilled to the ground where it ran in heavy rivulets into the water stream by the side of the pathway. Yet, beneath this macabre display, the man still drew breath, turned his one functioning eye to them, and even tried to move his mauled arm.

"Oh God." Oscar's arms fell limp, and his knife clattered to the ground.

A high-pitched giggle burst from behind them. They turned around to find the hermit standing fifteen feet down the corridor with a wide smile spread across his face, now smeared with fresh blood. He had drawn a longbow, its string pulled tight, the arrow aimed at—

"Nathaniel!" Oscar screamed.

The hermit released the bow, and the arrow shot through the air with deadly speed. Nathaniel lifted his satchel to shield himself, and the arrow sank into it. He reeled from the impact but managed to stay on his feet.

"Oscar! Stay back!" Nathaniel sprinted at the hermit and unhooked the satchel strap, letting it fall behind him midway.

The hermit dropped the bow and went for a hatchet that hung from a rope tied around his waist. His smile turned into a panicky grimace as he struggled to get a grip on the weapon, his hands slippery with blood.

Nathaniel reached the hermit and drove his fist into his face. The punch swept the hermit's feet from under him, and he fell on his back, dazed. Nathaniel rolled him onto his stomach, jumped on him, grabbed two fistfuls of hair from the back of his head, and slammed his face into the ground, hard. The hermit went limp.

Oscar watched all this with glassy eyes, his feet rooted where he stood. His gaze flicked to the mangled mess of a corpse, then back to Nathaniel and the hermit. He wobbled drunkenly, feeling faint. Beneath all this, the thrill popped his synapses like bubble wrap—a sensation that both confused and shamed him.

Nathaniel grabbed the hermit's foot and pressed his knife against the ankle. "Don't watch, Oscar. I have to make sure this son of a bitch doesn't follow us."

But Oscar did watch. And with one swift stroke, Nathaniel sliced through the hermit's Achilles tendon. The sinew's tension released with a pop, and the hermit let out a piercing scream. Then the pain overwhelmed him, the scream faded to a whimper, and he lost consciousness.

Oscar didn't know whether it was the violence, the adrenaline, the way this scene unfolded before him, or a culmination of all these aspects, but a sobering sensation washed over him. His mind cleared, no longer convoluted by fear or confusion or denial.

Nathaniel stepped away from the hermit and slicked back his hair, hands trembling. He went for his satchel which slumped on the ground with the arrow still sticking out of it. He pulled out the arrow, and a stream of black liquid gushed from the satchel.

"What? No!" Nathaniel stuck his hand into the soggy satchel and took out a drained pouch. It had been punctured by the arrow and was now spilling what little lantern fuel remained. "Fuck!"

"Nathaniel..." Oscar's lower lip quivered, and chills raced up and down his spine.

Nathaniel ignored him. "Goddamnit, no! That's half our fuel supplies!"

"Nathaniel!"

"What?!"

The words forced out of Oscar's mouth as if they had a will of their own: "I'm in Hell, aren't I?"

CHAPTER EIGHT

Oscar and Nathaniel settled by a patch of bedrock in the desert, a covert spot a safe distance from the canyons. They would have made better time traveling while it was still light, but after everything that had happened, they needed a moment to recuperate.

Oscar sat on the ground, his shoes removed, fiddling with his knife. The bronzed daylight gleamed off the blade, dancing to the beat of his nervous twitches. Nathaniel slumped against the bedrock wall, staring at his blood-spattered hands in a daze.

A hundred questions raced through Oscar's mind, each one competing to be asked first. But it was Nathaniel who asked the first question: "How much do you remember about your life?"

The question took Oscar off guard. He tried to recall something, anything, but it was all a blank. "Nothing," he said. "I remember my name, and that I am… was… twenty-one."

"Figures," Nathaniel said. "Everyone enters Hell with amnesia. It'll pass, though. The memories tend to come back in chunks. Most of them do, anyway."

"Most of them?"

"From my experience, and from the people I've talked to, no one remembers their death or the moments leading up to it. Death is too much to comprehend, so the mind blocks it away. The same goes for the time spent in the grave."

Oscar's brow furrowed. *The grave?*

"See, when someone dies in the living world, they wake up in a coffin in Hell," Nathaniel continued. "There's six feet of dirt weighing down on the coffin, so it's safe to assume that most of us never make it out. Some of us do, though. Lucky us, right? Then there are also the grave looters. They exhume people from their graves. Most of them just loot a grave and leave the sorry bastard occupying it alone, but there are also some depraved fuckers who enslave the ones they exhume. The shock renders one an easy prey. I wasn't there to see how you made it out, but those fingernails of yours indicate you crawled out yourself. See, the ones dug up by grave looters still have their fingernails intact." He paused, then added, "Although some folks probably lose them while they're busy clawing at the coffin lid."

Oscar couldn't even begin to fathom how to take this all in. The mention of grave looters rang some distant bell, but the events at the cemetery were all a fog to him. "Wait, you're saying I crawled through six feet of dirt?"

"Probably not *quite* six feet," Nathaniel said, scratching his chin. "The earth is constantly shifting in the cemetery. You can feel the tremors there. Some say it's because Hell is expanding, making more room for the dead. But I don't know, it might be bullshit. Either way, all those earth's shifts and movements create clefts into the soil. Some of the coffins get pushed closer to the surface, some of them get broken. It improves the chances of escaping. Then again, a lot of folks probably get stuck in the dirt for the same reason. And there they remain, stuck, crushed, unable to breathe, alive—forever."

"Forever," Oscar echoed. The word took on new weight in his mind: unlimited, never-ending, infinite forever.

Nathaniel took a pack of cigarettes out of his satchel and offered Oscar one. Oscar declined and wondered where Nathaniel had found a pack of cigarettes. Then he got it: the grave looters. They robbed the dead of their belongings. *So the clothes you're wearing and the items you're carrying come with you to this world when you die?*

Nathaniel stuck a cigarette between his lips, held it to the lantern's flame, and lit it with practiced ease. He squinted at the smoke and took a long drag. "The dead can't die. Our bodies are sort of… dormant. It's like we're suspended in some sort of half-existence. Whatever decomposition we go through halts at an early stage in the grave." Nathaniel took another drag. "What else? We don't age, nor can we starve or feel hunger. We do feel thirst, but we can't dehydrate. Or at least we can't die from dehydration."

Oscar repeated Nathaniel's words in his mind several times. The hardest thing to digest was that all of this applied to him: *he* could no longer die, *he* would no longer age. "I just… I can't wrap my head around this," he said, his voice caught between a cry and a laugh.

"Well, I'm sorry to be the one to tell you this, but it gets worse. See, our bodies are dormant, so our wounds only heal to an extent. If you have anesthetics at hand—not easy to come by, by the way—you can numb the pain, but you can't escape it forever. Remember: the dead can't die. No matter how much physical trauma you go through, your consciousness never ceases. But you'll still feel pain, and you'll have to live with the repercussions for all eternity."

"Repercussions?"

"Take this gut wound, for instance." Nathaniel unbuttoned his vest and lifted his shirt, revealing the wound that crossed through his abdomen with the shoelace zigzagging over it like a corset string.

Oscar studied the wound. The awkwardness and alarm he had felt the last time he saw it were now gone.

"If I'm lucky, it'll heal shut. But whether it does or doesn't, I'll be stuck with this fucking shoelace forever." Nathaniel lowered his shirt. "Repercussions."

"I'm sorry this happened to you," was all Oscar could muster.

Nathaniel shrugged. "At least I don't have to worry about it getting infected. See, we don't get infections, either."

"So it still hurts?" Oscar asked.

Nathaniel exhaled smoke through his nose. "No, it feels great."

"Sorry." Oscar felt like an idiot. "So that guy who was all sliced up by that hermit..."

"There's nothing we could've done, Oscar. He's stuck with those wounds forever. Same story with the hermit. The son of a bitch will probably walk with a limp for all eternity."

"How does it feel... having to do that?" As the words left Oscar's mouth, his stomach churned with self-loathing. *Why am I drawn to this?* he thought. "I mean, I'm not judging. He attacked us, and you had to make—"

"It hasn't really sunk in yet. I'll have plenty of time to condemn myself later."

The admission surprised Oscar. After seeing how methodically Nathaniel had handled the hermit, Oscar had expected him to be more... hardened. But if anything, Nathaniel seemed to sympathize with his foe.

"Don't take this the wrong way," Oscar said, "but I figured you'd be more, I don't know, calloused by all this."

Nathaniel laughed, a cloud of smoke erupting from his

mouth. "I wish. It'd make everything a lot easier if I didn't have a conscience." He paused. "And then there's the part of me that's just pissed off about the lantern fuel. So maybe I *am* callous."

Oscar glanced at Nathaniel's bloodied hands, and an image flashed in his mind: a severed hand nailed to a door, its fingers still moving. The memory made his skin crawl.

"This never-ending consciousness you mentioned... Does it apply to, I don't know, amputations?"

"It does," Nathaniel nodded. "Lose a limb, and you can still feel it—even have control over it. Although from what I've seen, it's mostly just involuntary twitching."

Again, Oscar had no idea how to wrap his head around this. "That's... this is absurd."

"Absurd is good. It means all of this is still theoretical to you. You're still chewing on it, not quite ready to swallow. Most folks get all this shoved down their throats. They have to learn it the hard way, through experience." Nathaniel took one last drag and stubbed out the cigarette. "Maybe you can find some solace in that, maybe not."

More of Shantytown's horrors returned to Oscar: the mangled, animate corpses hiding in their unified misery; the manic outbursts and the psychotic chants echoing through the streets; the stench of death that made the air a humid, unbreathable vapor. If Oscar hadn't met Nathaniel at the cemetery (he realized the encounter itself was still a blur), he probably would have stumbled to Shantytown by himself and, as Nathaniel put it, learned Hell the hard way. It would have been shoved down his throat. All things considered, Oscar had gotten off lucky, and he had only Nathaniel to thank for that. He felt a stab of guilt for constantly doubting him.

Nathaniel studied Oscar. "Now do you understand why I didn't tell you what this place was?"

Again, the man had a point. Oscar couldn't have imagined

having this conversation in the state he'd been in earlier. He would have thought Nathaniel was insane. He probably would have ended their collaboration right then and there. Oscar now saw how it had been essential for him to recognize this place for what it was at his own pace. Allowing Oscar to reach this catharsis by himself had been another empathetic gesture from Nathaniel.

"I understand," Oscar said. He fixed his eyes on Nathaniel. "Thank you."

Nathaniel raised his water canteen in a silent toast and took a swig.

But still... Oscar thought. *Can I* really *trust him?*

As Oscar and Nathaniel recuperated and discussed Hell, the day waned to dusk. They decided to set up camp at their current location by the patch of bedrock for the night. Oscar dug a hole in the gravel for a bonfire and spread blankets on either side. Meanwhile, Nathaniel set up tripwires around the camp, just as before. There weren't any trees nearby, so they used firewood from the stack Oscar had been lugging around. Nathaniel managed to get a modest smolder going with flint and kindling. They gathered around the fire, settling on their blankets.

"How are you feeling?" Nathaniel asked.

"Like I'm having every hangover I've ever had at once. Does this ever get better?"

"Afraid not," he said. "But once you forget what being alive feels like, you sort of grow numb to it. You no longer have anything to compare it to."

Once you forget what being alive feels like, Oscar recited. If his hunch was correct, he had died at twenty-one; he'd barely had the chance to experience life, and now it turned out it'd be better to just forget all of it to "sort of grow numb" to feeling dead. It just wasn't fair. He had no recollection of his life, but he still remembered how it *felt* to be alive. And he missed it. He missed it so bad that he couldn't breathe.

Oscar felt the sting of tears behind his eyes. He pressed his hand to his chest and began rubbing it. A circular motion to soothe the heart and relax the lungs. Then he stopped, eyes wide. He had just remembered something: his sister used to comfort him like this. The memory was clear and clean, as if it had never been gone. Like finding something you've lost exactly where you left it.

In this memory, Oscar was a little boy, probably around seven years old. He sat on his bed in a dark room, legs crossed, rocking back and forth. His sister sat next to him, ten years old at the time, squeezing his shoulder and rubbing his chest. Oscar was having trouble breathing, and this was the only way his sister knew how to calm him.

Mom had had one of her tantrums again. She'd gotten insulted by something not worth getting insulted about and let the feeling fester in her mind until it bloated out of all proportion. Usually, something as small as forgetting to thank her, not returning a smile, or not hearing what she'd said was enough to set off a tantrum. Whatever it had been this time, it had sent her spiraling down a rabbit hole of self-pity and provocation, eventually causing her to isolate herself in her bedroom, slamming the door shut behind her without a word.

Both Oscar and his sister knew that tonight there would be no dinner, no screen time, no bath, no bedtime stories. Sure, they could do all that by themselves, but if they made so much as a peep, Mom would storm out of her room and conduct these chores with such passive-aggressive fire that being near her felt dangerous, like she might erupt at any moment. The guilt trip she'd take them on would be so full of venom that going to sleep hungry, dirty, and miserable felt like the better choice.

Sometimes, Oscar wished Mom would never come out of her room. In his juvenile mind, he believed he and his sister would do just fine without her. His sister knew better, though, and after nursing Oscar through the anxiety fit, she'd often go to their mother, begging for forgiveness. Oscar doubted his sister even knew what she was apologizing for most of the time. By the time Mom forgave her—usually well past their bedtime—she herself probably didn't even remember what had upset her.

For the time being, Oscar could only remember events from his childhood, but in all of them, he'd been terrified of his mother. Even her good moods felt over the top and outright manic sometimes. Balance, moderation, mildness—these words didn't fit into the vocabulary of her emotional range.

This wasn't to say that there were no good memories from Oscar's childhood. There was a lot of playing and laughter, and the one constant in all the good memories was his sister. The two were inseparable. She was his guardian and caregiver and, as far as young Oscar was concerned, the only real family he had. She was also his best friend. They would go on adventures around their neighborhood, watch funny videos and laugh until their sides hurt, and read books together that they lent from the library.

But something about the memories felt off. No matter how hard Oscar tried, he couldn't recall the names of his sister or mother, nor what they looked like. Where their faces should have been, only a blind spot remained. And now that he thought about it, he couldn't remember his own last name, either. It was like noticing a book had gone missing from a shelf, only he couldn't remember which one.

Nathaniel snapped his fingers at the base of Oscar's ear. "Everything alright?"

"I just remembered stuff from when I was a kid."

"The memories tend to rush back in clusters," Nathaniel

said, nodding.

"I remember my mom, and I know I had an older sister... *have* an older sister." Oscar didn't know whether to use the present or past tense for people who were still alive while he was the one dead. The English language, or any language for that matter, wasn't designed for dead tongues. "But I can't remember their faces or names."

"We all forget," Nathaniel said, resigned. "I know I had a wife and two little girls. I remember the time we had together clear as day, but now I couldn't pick them out of a line. They're probably here somewhere—" his voice broke, and he drifted off.

"So we can't reunite with our loved ones," Oscar said quietly.

Nathaniel nodded.

Oscar realized he had lost his sister and mother in much the same way they had lost him. Though they were still presumably alive and well, he would, in his own way, mourn losing them as they must be mourning him.

All he could ask was, "Why?"

"The whys are a whole other can of worms," Nathaniel said. "We'll get back to them. Don't you have enough on your plate already?"

More than enough, Oscar thought. If he received anything more to process, he feared he might have a nervous breakdown. He already felt himself teetering on the edge of one.

But still, that same old doubt crept through the heartache: an argument could be made that Nathaniel was holding back information to keep Oscar dependent on him. Maybe Oscar was paranoid, maybe not. Either way, it seemed every assessment he tried to make of the man was gnawed by distrust. No matter how much understanding and thoughtfulness Nathaniel directed toward him, Oscar simply couldn't silence the suspicions. Here he realized that he couldn't breathe freely or think clearly until he knew for sure that Nathaniel wasn't planning something against him.

Nathaniel lay by the fire, eyes closed. Oscar knew from the pace of his breathing that he wasn't asleep yet.

He waited, staring at the flames.

I can't die because I'm already dead—it was such an alien thought, so contrary to everything it meant to be human, that Oscar now had to regularly repeat this phrase to himself. His body felt like a foreign artifact, as if he was controlling a doppelgänger of his former self. He wondered if his constant itching and discomfort weren't only the banes of death, but because his soul was rejecting his body. Like a parasite trapped in a host it didn't want to depend on. Like a ghost that couldn't move on.

As if in response to these thoughts, the lump in his belly broadcast aching pulses through him. He slid his hand under his shirt and pressed the spot where the signals originated. He could actually feel the lump, stiff as a flexed muscle, throbbing against his skin.

Did I have cancer? Is that what killed me?

Oscar snapped out of it at the sound of Nathaniel's mumbles. The man had finally fallen asleep.

His anxiety ebbed, replaced by determination. He might be powerless against Hell, against endlessness, against his malfunctioning body—but he refused to be powerless against Nathaniel. He was entitled to know if the man had something planned for him.

Oscar got up quietly and sneaked over to the other side of the campfire. He eyed Nathaniel's satchel, tucked under his arm. He could, in theory, access its contents without touching or waking the man. Maybe he would find evidence of Nathaniel's plan, maybe he wouldn't. At this point, the act itself felt more important than its objective. He had no trouble admitting this to himself. This was, in his opinion, the only way to regain control over his fate and balance the power between himself and Nathaniel. Oscar wanted to trust the man, but he had to reach that trust on his own accord and not by anyone else's dictate.

Nathaniel's lantern was attached to the satchel strap. Oscar moved it out of the way, but as he did, it slipped from his sweaty palms and hit the ground with a clatter. Nathaniel flinched, his brow furrowing. Oscar tensed, his accelerated pulse throbbing in his temples. He waited for Nathaniel's eyes to open, but the man remained lost in whatever nightmare was haunting him.

Oscar opened the satchel and spread it wide. The contents were still sticky from the spilled lantern fuel. He reached in and felt a water canteen, strips of rags, rolls of gauze, and a small sewing kit.

"Back the fuck up," Nathaniel said, his voice low.

Oscar turned to him with the grace of a creaky door. Nathaniel's eyes remained closed. He repeated the threat, this time with more fear and fragility.

Oscar exhaled silently and continued navigating his hand deeper into the satchel.

Then, a spasm stung Oscar like a taser, causing him to nudge Nathaniel's side with his elbow.

Fuck.

Nathaniel's eyes shot open, and a wild scream tore from his throat. He swung his knife which Oscar barely evaded. Before Oscar had a chance to recuperate from almost being sliced in half, Nathaniel tackled him to the ground, jumping on top of him. He forced Oscar's arms to the ground with his knees, grabbed his hair, and pushed the knife's tip against his throat. One firm thrust would send the knife through the floor of Oscar's mouth and skewer his tongue. Nathaniel carried out the movements with terrifying efficiency, all the while screaming in sheer horror.

"Nathaniel, calm down!" Oscar cried.

The knife pierced his skin. The pain was sharp and jarring, but he didn't dare react.

Nathaniel kept screaming, his breaths laborious and uneven. His eyes were unfocused, as if he was somewhere else entirely.

"Nathaniel. I'm Oscar. You're in the desert with me," Oscar stammered, trying to sound calm. "We're looking for Dean Theodore. No one's trying to hurt you. You're safe."

Nathaniel's screams faded into guttural breaths. The mist in his eyes began to clear.

"It's okay. Put the knife down. Please."

"Oscar…?" Nathaniel's trembling eased, his breaths now long and drawn out. He released Oscar from his grip and dropped the knife to the ground. "I'm… I don't know what came over me."

Oscar crawled back to the other side of the campfire, holding his bloodied throat, gasping.

Nathaniel dropped his head into his hands as whatever demon of his past he'd just confronted retreated into the dark of his mind.

CHAPTER NINE

Oscar pressed a bundle of fabric to his throat, waiting for the bleeding to stop. Somehow, the wound didn't feel all that important because, much to his surprise, the worry he felt for Nathaniel exceeded it. He couldn't trust Nathaniel due to his instability and their unfair power dynamic, but this didn't mean he didn't care for him. He did. How could he not after everything Nathaniel had done for him? And, in a sense, Nathaniel's instability only made Oscar care about him more. It shattered the image of cunning Oscar had suspected the man to possess. It made him more human.

Nathaniel clung to his water canteen with shaking hands. The bonfire's embers lit his pale face, reminding Oscar of a ghoul emerging from the dark. His absent stare gave his features a lingering sadness.

"What was that?" Oscar asked.

"I don't know," Nathaniel said, avoiding eye contact. "Just a nightmare."

"That wasn't just a nightmare. You were awake."

"Sometimes the nightmares follow me beyond sleep, I guess."

"What are the nightmares about?"

"I'm not ready to go there, Oscar," Nathaniel muttered, rubbing his brow.

"You're asking me to cross a desert with you," Oscar scoffed, "but you're not ready to tell me what you were dreaming about while you stuck a knife to my throat? You have to meet me halfway."

Nathaniel considered this. He sighed. "They're… about things that have happened here. Things that were done to me. Things that I've done."

Oscar didn't need to know more to understand—nor did he want to. In a dog-eat-dog world like this, a place where everyone is out to get everyone… what else could it offer but experiences you'd rather forget but can't because they refuse to leave you alone, haunting even your dreams?

"You know," Nathaniel said, "I've been thinking about what you said about callousness, about expecting me to be more callous toward violence."

"Yeah?"

"I think it's a belief people learn in the living world. Callousness comes easier when you're under the impression that death is the ultimate escape. The living believe that death ends all pain, that suffering can be stopped"—he snapped his fingers—"just like that. Whether the pain is directed at you, your loved ones, or your enemies, the assumption is that there's only so much a person can take and once it ends, it's over. That's callousness."

"So… you're saying there's a kind of messed up mercy in callousness?"

"Exactly. But that kind of mindset doesn't really apply in Hell. No one can die and the pain never ends here. If you hurt someone, you can't stop their hurt. Callousness in Hell isn't based on mercy. It's based on sadism and cruelty. That's why turning callous is not as common here as a newborn such as yourself might expect."

Oscar assumed that by "newborns" Nathaniel meant the recently deceased.

Nathaniel broke a stick in two and fed it to the fire. The flames devoured the wood and flared higher.

"That said," he continued, "there *is* a threshold to all this shit. I've seen people cross over to the other side, but I've never seen one of them come back. This world tries to push you over that threshold, so you have to push back."

An image flashed in Oscar's mind: an emaciated man with a lizard-like leer slicing someone's face open with a razor, then jumping up and down in excited triumph. The teardrop-shaped wound on his cheek itched at the vision.

"Maybe your nightmares mean you haven't crossed that threshold," Oscar said. "Your moral compass still works. When you start sleeping just fine—that's when you should start to worry."

A tired smile spread across Nathaniel's face. "Well, there's a fucked up silver lining if I ever heard one." He paused for a beat. "Remember when I told you I was looking for someone to help me with this journey?"

"Yeah. Logistics. Carry your stuff and whatnot."

"Well, I was also scouting the cemetery because I needed a newborn. I wouldn't have been able to trust anyone who knew the lay of the land. I'd have been stabbed in the back the moment the opportunity rose." Nathaniel paused, assessing his words. He continued, "But I guess that's only part of the truth. See, I figured maybe if I could spare just one person from the experiences I've gone through, from what Hell has to offer… I don't know, I thought it might be worthwhile. There's no real salvation here, but at least some horrors can be avoided. I wanted to give that chance to someone Hell hadn't yet corrupted."

Oscar stared at his lap, soaking in Nathaniel's words. The fire crackled, its warmth brushing Oscar's cold cheeks. He wanted to thank Nathaniel and apologize for constantly doubting him, but a sting in his throat kept him silent.

The following morning, Oscar and Nathaniel set out further east. The day reached its peak soon, and the infernal clouds blossomed amber and orange, the spectacle like something from a doomsday prophecy. The temperature remained bland, and the air was windless. Outcrops jutted from the desert plains, creating rocky hillsides and stone formations. Some were stained with a psoriasis of moss, veiled with vines, and shaded by trees and shrubbery, while others lay bare as bone beneath Hell's skies. Clouds of dust rose from the gravel with every step forward, and that day, many steps were trod.

During this time, Oscar counted seeing six of the dead in the distance. Their dark figures slouched through the desolation—three together in a group, the others wandering alone. Oscar and Nathaniel kept a close eye on them to ensure they kept their distance. But none approached. They were on their own nomadic journeys and, in all likelihood, as averse of uninvited company as the two men.

Now that Oscar knew the people here were dead, every one of these strangers evoked a new kind of dread in him. Talking about death with Nathaniel had felt almost abstract and hypothetical. But seeing it here, moving and undeniable, felt more concrete. Of course, Oscar knew that Nathaniel and he himself were also dead, but somehow it wasn't the same. In Nathaniel, he saw a person, not a walking corpse. It made Oscar realize just how well Nathaniel had fulfilled his role in keeping him both safe and secluded.

Somewhere in the wasteland, Oscar and Nathaniel came upon a grave. A cross of branches leaned to the side with a patch of mulled gravel at its base. Oscar slowed down, but Nathaniel advised him to keep walking.

"There's someone buried there?" Oscar asked. "And they're, like, still alive?"

"It's more likely a trap," Nathaniel said.

"A trap?"

"The idea is to get a passerby curious, get them digging in hopes of finding a companion or a supply stash. Once the passerby has worn themselves out, you make your move. Maybe the goal is to rob them, maybe something else. Might be the passerby has been digging their own grave the entire time."

"You'd think there were less time-consuming ways to ambush someone," Oscar said.

"The more time-consuming, the better. Remember, we're stuck here forever. You want to have as many ineffective and arduous steps as possible."

Oscar looked over his shoulder at the receding grave, and his thoughts drifted back to his sister. Sooner or later, she too would enter this world, and this is what would be waiting for her—an unmarked grave with six feet of hard ground above her. She would be trapped in a coffin, in the dark, unable to breathe, unable to die, with little to no chance of getting out. And if she did get out, what preyed above ground was an eternity of suffering, danger, and insanity. And Oscar could do nothing to help her. The true essence of Hell was dawning on him.

Was there any way to avoid this? Could she, what, repent for her sins, lead a righteous life, and end up in Heaven instead of Hell? After all the things Oscar had learned here, the idea of an eternal paradise felt impossible. Wouldn't the same rules of infinity apply there? Wouldn't the never-ending feel just as pointless? Wouldn't endlessness become just as much of a torment as it did here in Hell? Humans would still be humans there and sooner or later lose their minds in the face of eternity. Only somehow it would be... better? Besides, wouldn't the knowledge of Heaven also entail the knowledge of Hell? What kind of paradise would that be, knowing someone you loved was suffering in Hell?

"Does everyone end up in Hell?" Oscar asked. "Not just the, I don't know, sinful?"

"Everyone ends up here," Nathaniel said. "How so? Are you a religious man?"

"I'm not."

"An atheist, then? You believe Darwin?"

"I do. Did. I don't know," Oscar sighed.

"The evolutionary theory still applies—to an extent, at least," Nathaniel said. "Might need some expanding on account of all this, though."

"So if this place is not Hell in a religious sense, why do people call it that?"

"What else would they call it?" Nathaniel shrugged. "Even you, a non-believer, said it yourself: 'I'm in Hell.' I understand Hell's religious connotations are stronger for you newborns. But I, for one, rarely even think about them anymore. The afterlife—this realm—is just a natural part of existence. But all the horrors out here, the stuff of Hell, that's on us. There's no one else to blame for it. No demonic overseers or vengeful gods here. Just humans being humans, stuck forever in a desolate, dead realm, unable to cope or find peace because we're not wired to understand eternity. We make our own Hell."

"We make our own Hell," Oscar echoed.

"Are you familiar with Maslow's hierarchy of needs?"

"Yes." Oscar recalled the hierarchy visualized as a pyramid, divided into five horizontal segments. These segments listed different human needs for survival and fulfillment. At the base of the pyramid were the basic physiological needs: air, light, water, food, shelter, and so on. Once these needs were met, a person could aspire to the next segment: safety and security. And once the safety and security needs were met, the person reached for the higher levels of the pyramid, one segment at a time: love and belonging, self-esteem, self-actualization. In Oscar's understanding, that was the gist of it.

"The basic needs, the ones at the base of the pyramid, are welded into our core," Nathaniel explained. "Life taught us they're essential for survival. They drive and define us. But death renders these needs useless. The dead don't need to breathe, eat, drink, or worry about getting sick. The dead can't die. So everything that made us what we are no longer applies to us. When our basic needs are erased from the bottom of the pyramid, it inevitably affects everything higher up on the hierarchy as well—love, happiness, fulfillment, all that. Can you imagine what's even left of a person after that?"

Oscar pictured the pyramid crumbling, its collapsing base dragging the entire structure into the rubble. Or maybe the pyramid transformed into something more twisted and complex—a crooked horn, perhaps? Whatever the image, the outcome was the same: the total destruction of the human psyche.

"Hell," Oscar said, breathless. "That's what's left."

"We make our own Hell," Nathaniel nodded.

Oscar's eyes, half-glazed, swept over the wasteland. The empty desert stretched beyond sight into never-ending oblivion. Paradoxically, the vastness made Oscar feel almost claustrophobic—like a cornered animal scratching frantically at a brick wall.

The day faded, the amber lights dimmed. Weary from the day's journey, they made one last push up a hill and set camp at the top. Black-leaved dead trees and wilted shrubbery shaded the hill's crown, offering a secluded place for a rest.

Oscar had recited everything he'd learned from Nathaniel, mulling it over in his head until Hell's absurdity didn't seem quite as absurd. The living world was beginning to feel distant and foreign, like a fictional place from a dream. He understood, at least in theory, how this posthumous world worked and how the human beings trapped here functioned. But to think that none of this would ever end didn't seem any less absurd than the first time he'd heard it. He tried to push the thought away, but it always crept back in like a compulsion.

Nathaniel sat down by the bonfire, holding a stack of branches he'd gathered from the surrounding trees. "You look troubled. More so than usual, I mean."

"It's the infinity part I can't wrap my head around," Oscar said, his chin resting on his hooked knees, eyes fixed on the flames.

"Don't even bother trying." Nathaniel peeled strips of bark from the branches and braided them together—binding rope, Oscar figured. "My theory is that the human mind has a limited capacity when it comes to time. If you spend enough time here, the past begins to fade. Take that hermit in the canyons, for example. You think someone that far gone even remembers they were once alive?"

To be dead for so long that you forget you were once alive. Just the mere thought made Oscar feel blank, empty.

"Don't look so glum, kid. I think there's a certain comfort in knowing that whatever happens, two hundred years from now you're probably not going to remember it." Nathaniel tugged at the braided rope, testing its endurance, but it tore in two. "Goddamnit," he muttered, tossing the experiment into the fire.

Oscar furrowed his brow. "Is that supposed to make me feel better?"

Nathaniel shrugged.

The thought of a never-ending future evoked nothing but anxiety, so he turned to his past for comfort. But try as he might, no new memories surfaced. Mostly, he just wanted to know what'd happened to his sister, and regaining his memories was his only chance of finding that out. If she had outlived him, she'd now be in her mid to late twenties—depending on how long Oscar had been in the ground (one more thought to shudder at)—so she still had plenty of time to live a good, long life. If her love and care from his childhood memories still applied after all these years, Oscar's untimely demise would probably never cease to burden her. But this didn't mean she couldn't still find happiness, stability, and love. Then again, the longer she lived, the more challenging it would be for her to crawl out from her grave once it was time to enter Hell.

So the sooner she dies, the better, said a voice in Oscar's head. Pressure tightened his chest, and the lump in his belly responded by hardening into a cramping bundle. The sensation forced Oscar to lean forward.

"You okay?" Nathaniel asked.

"Do you ever get these cramps?" Oscar huffed through gritted teeth.

"Not really. Death symptoms vary between people, though."

Oscar took some deep breaths and shook his head. "Why… why can't the dead remember the names and faces of their loved ones?"

"You sure now's the right time to get into it?" Nathaniel asked with a worried frown.

"Please. I need to know." The pain in Oscar's stomach unraveled like a loosely bound knot, easing his discomfort. "I'm okay. The cramp's passing."

"Alright. Why can't we remember the names and faces of our loved ones?" Nathaniel paused, gathering his thoughts.

"There are a lot of theories—some decent, most bullshit. I'll tell you the one I'm most inclined to agree with. Human beings are social animals. We've survived as a species by sticking together. Therefore, humans naturally gravitate toward love, care, and nurture. But because survival no longer applies to us dead—because we're past survival, so to speak—our minds sever all ties with the people we loved. We forget their names and faces. Life was a social phase where we needed loved ones and a tribal mindset to survive. Death is a different phase, a more solitary phase. Maybe this face-and-name blindness is some deeply ingrained instinct in our genes trying to help us let go of life. See, this happens to everyone here. Systematically. Without exception. It must be somehow embedded in the core of humanity. *Species-typical behavior* is what they call it. It's fucked up and cruel, but if you dissect it with cold logic, you can't deny its efficiency."

Oscar was quiet for a long time, feeling a sort of horrified awe. "So… the reason I can't remember my sister's name or face is that some innate part of me is, I don't know, *orienting* me to Hell?"

"That's the theory," Nathaniel replied. He took out his knife and picked dirt from under the few fingernails he still had left. "Or you can just interpret it as God's wrath. Plenty of people do. But follow that line of reasoning, and pretty soon you'll hit a brick wall."

Oscar didn't need to follow "that line of reasoning" because another forgotten image flashed in his mind: a woman in Shantytown cradling a baby, its skin as pale and lifeless as its round, unfocused eyes. This memory was all it took for Oscar to conclude that there was no God. He shook his head, trying to erase the image.

"Does all this have something to do with Dean Theodore?" Oscar asked. Saying the name out loud triggered a peculiar tingling sensation on his tongue, like licking a battery. "I mean, you said he's studied Hell and gathered rare information."

"It does, in a sense," Nathaniel said, nodding. "We share the same school of thought about the nature of afterlife. But I can't go into specifics about him."

"Why?"

"Because you seem to have a pretty good head on your shoulders. You might figure out my discovery. I've gotta be careful for both our sakes, Oscar. See, others would benefit from the discovery, too. What do you think would happen if you knew my secret, and someone tried to get it out of you by any means necessary?"

By any means necessary? Oscar thought, shuddering at the implications. "Probably wouldn't go too well."

"You're probably right." Nathaniel blew the dirt from his fingers and sheathed his knife.

"Have you met him?" Oscar asked. "What's he like?"

"Haven't had the pleasure," Nathaniel said. "But I hear he's calm, intelligent, considerate. He's warm. People have told me they've felt at peace talking to him."

Oscar listened, mesmerized. He could hardly wait to meet this man.

CHAPTER TEN

The following days burned long. The wasteland stretched forth, its gravelly plains and rocky hills observing their doomed subjects in quiet indifference. The dead slouched through the barren desert in sparse numbers, their presence no more than distant silhouettes by day and blips of light by night. Even the screams and howls had muted, now only rare interruptions in the silence.

A handful of shacks lay scattered across the desolation. Their rickety, branch-woven structures sagged like scarecrows kneeling in prayer, held together by fraying rope and clumps of dry mud. Each time Oscar and Nathaniel saw one, they veered off their path to check it for supplies—primarily lantern fuel. They would study each shack from afar and if it looked unoccupied, proceed to rummage through it; if it didn't, they would leave it and move on. They never found anything worthwhile, though. The unoccupied ones had all been picked clean. With each failure to replenish their fuel, Nathaniel's shoulders stiffened a little more and the grinding of his teeth grew a little louder.

During this time, they had one encounter with a stranger—though calling it an encounter might be debatable. This happened one night while Oscar was keeping watch. He was sitting by the campfire, rocking back and forth, trying to ignore some random pain coursing through his body. Nathaniel slept with a rope wrapped around his wrist, the other end clutched tightly in Oscar's hand.

A tripwire went off in the dark, its metal shards rattling together in alarm. Oscar flinched out of his stupor, and a chill like no other washed over him. He gave the rope a discreet tug. Nathaniel remained still, lying on his side, but Oscar noted a new tenseness in his figure. He was now awake, aware something was wrong. The metallic chimes quieted, and silence followed, stretching the atmosphere taut with suspense.

After a beat, footsteps. It sounded like the intruder was retreating. The shifting of gravel softened with each step until the sounds disappeared into the darkness from which they'd come. Oscar figured the intruder must have been as startled by the tripwires as he was.

"Kill the fire," Nathaniel whispered, his back still turned to Oscar.

"What? Why?"

"The intruder could have been a scout. They might come back with a larger posse. If we kill the fire, they can't find us unless they have a light of their own. In which case, we'll see them coming."

Oscar did as told and kicked gravel into the fire. The night devoured everything so completely that its mass felt almost tangible. It settled on Oscar's skin, pushed through, and seeped into his core as though he himself had dissolved into the dark.

"And now we'll be absolutely silent," Nathaniel whispered, his voice quieter but also clearer in the pitch black darkness.

Oscar remained frozen in place for the rest of the night. He feared the tiniest of movements might summon the intruder. The logic was similar to that of a child who believed being tucked under a blanket was enough to keep the monsters at bay.

The next night, they made camp in the shade of some bedrock when the exhaustion that'd been creeping up on Oscar over the past few days finally reached its peak. To the best of his recollection, he'd been awake ever since he'd crawled out of his grave. The uneven day-and-night cycles didn't help. He felt like they'd cast him into a kind of perpetual jet lag.

He was still hesitant to let his guard down and fall asleep in Nathaniel's company, but staying up simply wasn't an option anymore. Nathaniel agreed to keep watch for the night, and Oscar lay down on his tattered blanket. He closed his eyes, and sleep took over almost instantly.

But after what felt like only few minutes, he awoke with a start, drenched in sweat, fighting to breathe, his muscles locked by some claustrophobic nightmare. Once he calmed down, Nathaniel explained that this was a common symptom among newborns, their time spent in the coffin still a fresh wound. After that, Oscar knew he could trust Nathaniel enough to sleep in his company. Then again, he no longer knew if he could trust himself.

He began to experience similar sensations even while awake. Intense anxiety attacks and uncontrollable crying fits would strike him out of the blue. For whatever reason, these episodes only happened at night, after Nathaniel had fallen asleep. In those moments, all Oscar could do was struggle through the episode and hope he wouldn't wake the man.

Sure, Nathaniel would probably understand and support him, but the root of Oscar's anxiety couldn't be fixed—not unless Nathaniel could revive him and send him back to the living world—so he had no use for Nathaniel's words of empty comfort. The purpose of such words, Oscar figured, was to get him to adapt to Hell, to accept it. But Oscar didn't want to adapt. He didn't want to accept it. He wanted out. But of course, there was no escaping this place. And to this, his body responded with another anxiety attack.

With each step forward, the monolithic mountains rose higher and higher from the desert plains. The tallest mountains punctured the drooping clouds, and their stone faces basked stoically in the afternoon light. Oscar and Nathaniel marched forth in humility at the feet of such grand apparitions. They were still a few days from reaching the mountain range but close enough to distinguish a vast forest covering its base, its foliage lush and black.

"What happens after the desert?" Oscar asked.

"We'll cross that forest, find a mountain pass, and cut through it. Hold on... I have a map." Nathaniel produced a folded piece of paper from his chest pocket and passed it to Oscar.

Oscar studied the map, his eyes squinting from sleep deprivation after another restless night. The map's illustrations depicted a cluster of mountains encircling a valley. A forest covered the left-hand side of the map—the same forest that now loomed in front of them—and landmarks drawn out of proportion lay scattered here and there: clearings, swamps, rivers, rock formations. A red line traipsed through these landmarks, dividing the map in two, starting from the western forest and leading east where the map ended unillustrated.

Nathaniel's finger traced the red line across the paper. "We'll follow this safe passage through the forest, the mountain range, and the valley. We'll continue following it until we reach the other side of the valley. Somewhere by the edge of the forest up ahead is a tree with an X carved into it. That and these landmarks will tell us we're on the right track."

Oscar rubbed his eyes, nodding, trying to stay focused. Then: "Wait. A safe passage from what?"

Nathaniel hesitated a moment, then sighed. "Some people call them the mountain folk. There are two tribes that reign over the area depicted in the map. They don't want to start a conflict with the other tribe, so they've divided the area in two to keep a respectful distance from each other's territory. The safe route represents their border, their no man's land, a place where we won't run into either tribe."

"And what happens if we end up on either one's territory?"

Nathaniel hesitated some more. "They, uh, they hunt people. Then they eat them. That's what's in store for us if we—"

"Whoa, hey, fuck no." Oscar was suddenly wide awake. "I'm not going there. No way."

"We'll be fine. Their border has remained the same for probably hundreds of years."

"'Probably?' I'm not going to some fucking cannibal lair. Can't we just circle around the forest and the mountains?"

"That would take ages. Didn't I tell you already that we're on a schedule? Dean Theodore is on the move. We have to get to him before the trail goes cold. Besides, circling the mountain range would entail a whole other world of dangerous shit I haven't prepared for. At least with the mountain folk, we know what's what."

"Goddamnit, what's wrong with this place?" Oscar asked, his jaw clenched tight.

"Where do I begin?" Nathaniel countered, resigned. He took back the map and folded it. "Do you trust me?"

The question threw Oscar off guard—not only because it felt like an ultimatum, but also, he realized, because he no longer knew the answer. But then again, did his trust even matter at this point? He certainly didn't want to be alone in this death-ravaged world, and Nathaniel had offered him safety and camaraderie in a place where only despair and violence thrived. He was tired of looking for signs of distrust that simply weren't there. The only conclusion he could come to was this: as of now, whether he trusted Nathaniel or not wasn't important.

"Well?" Nathaniel asked.

"I mean, sort of."

"'Sort of?'" Nathaniel laughed. "Either you do or you don't."

"I do. Mostly."

"And that's the best I'm going to get?"

Oscar hesitated. "For the time being."

"You have a very indecisive way of talking, you know that?"

"I guess so."

Nathaniel gave him a tired look.

"Fuck it," Oscar said. Then, with more conviction, "Fuck it. Let's go to cannibal hunting grounds. Let's go boil in a pot. What do I care? Lead the way."

"That's the spirit." Nathaniel slapped Oscar's chest with the folded map. "But first we need more fuel. Most of the safe route goes through an overgrown thicket, I hear. We won't be getting any daylight there. We'll need to use my lantern the entire way, and our current fuel supply won't get us far."

"Jesus, how many abandoned huts have we scavenged so far?" Oscar sighed. "Honestly, I don't think we're going to find anything with this approach. You got a plan B?"

"I saw a hut over yonder. Looked abandoned. We'll give plan A one more shot, and if the place is dry… shit, might be I have to break into an occupied house."

"Like, rob someone…?"

"Yes. And you're staying back. I'm not letting you

participate in that shit."

"I don't know about this."

"Me neither," Nathaniel muttered, securing the map back into his pocket.

The shack slumped in the desolation with only a few boulders in the near vicinity keeping it company. Vines and twined branches held its shoddy walls together, and its gabled roof was padded with patches of shrubbery and moss. Stone ornaments and stick figurines perched on the walls like small animals left to bleed out.

Oscar and Nathaniel hid behind a nearby rock, scanning the shack and its surroundings for signs of life. Oscar already knew there would be no fuel stashed inside. He could feel it. *So we're going to have to rob someone.*

"I'll go see what's what," Nathaniel said. "You wait here."

"There's nothing there."

"Yeah, well..." Nathaniel sighed.

Nathaniel approached the shack and circled behind it. He soon emerged from the other side, waving at Oscar to join him.

The entrance was located on the shack's far side, shrouded by a cloth hanging from the doorframe. A three-legged stool lay tipped over next to the entrance. Nathaniel positioned it upright and wiped the seat.

"Planning on staying here?" Oscar asked.

"Figured might as well reap some benefit out of this goose hunt," Nathaniel said. He uncovered the entryway and urged Oscar to enter. "It's getting dark. It would be nice to have a roof over our heads for once."

The waning daylight filtered through the shack's musty air. A thick layer of dust covered the flat rock floor, and a pile of ragged clothes lay in one corner. Lifeless vines and withered patches of shrubbery drooped from the ceiling, and weird silver-tinted poppy flowers hung amid the black foliage like constellations in the night sky. Their buds and wrinkled stems reminded Oscar of yanked-out eyeballs. The flowers and their incessant stare made his skin crawl, and he forced himself to look away.

"Rustic," he said.

"And dry as bone." Nathaniel folded the cloth at the doorway to air out the place. "Looks like we're going to have to go with plan B."

"So we're going to steal the fuel?"

"*I'm* going to steal the fuel. We have a pretty good view up here, so we'll keep a lookout for light sources once it gets dark. Where there's fire, there's bound to be fuel."

"And then?"

"And then we'll head out and assess the situation. It all depends on what we're dealing with."

Oscar figured "what we're dealing with" was a euphemism for "what kind of person we're going to rob." He cursed under his breath. On one hand, being an accomplice to robbery terrified him; on the other, he felt too tired to care.

Without realizing it, he had resumed staring at the poppies hanging from the ceiling. It felt as if they were staring back at him. "What are those?"

"They're called mold poppies," Nathaniel said.

"Those things only grow in Hell?"

"Well, they're dead like everything else here, so the matter of growth is debatable. I'm sure some botanist—or mycologist—could offer a more well-versed theory. But no, they exist in the living world as well. Or at least they used to."

"Weird."

"Depends on whether you're observing it through the parameters of life or the parameters of death."

Parameters of death? Oscar didn't have the energy or the

willpower to ask what Nathaniel had meant by that. He sat down on the floor, closed his eyes, and rubbed his temples.

"You okay?" Nathaniel asked, sorting through the pile of clothes in the corner, trying to find something worth scavenging.

"I need to sleep," Oscar said. "I can't think straight."

"The room's yours. I'll take watch for the night and stay on the lookout for—oh, shit!"

Oscar jolted and looked up, eyes wide.

Nathaniel held up a cognac-colored tweed blazer, an impressed look on his face. The jacket had frayed here and there, but by Hell's standards, it was still in mint condition. He patted the dust off and put it on. "What do you think? A size or two too big maybe, but still..."

Oscar let out a long breath, a wave of relief washing over him. This seemed to amplify his fatigue tenfold, and he succumbed deeper into the cozy, warming exhaustion. "Looks good," he muttered, nodding, barely awake. "Dope."

"Dope, huh?" The word didn't quite fit Nathaniel's mouth, as if this was the first time he had used it in such a context. "Dope," he repeated, giving the word another taste.

A small bonfire crackled in the center of the room, casting light on the poppies hanging from the ceiling. They stared blindly at Oscar, lurking amid the black shrubbery as if the darkness above had sprouted eyes. From outside, the sluggish rhythm of squeaks carried over as Nathaniel rocked back and forth on the three-legged stool. Tobacco smoke drifted through the wicker walls, mingling with the charred scent of the fire.

Oscar awoke to this setting and found himself unable to move. At first, he thought it was another deadlock following some claustrophobic nightmare, but he soon realized this paralysis held a deeper grip—a grip that seemed to reach the deeper depths of his very essence.

Something had changed, or was about to.

He sensed something else, too. A presence. A figure sat in the corner of the room. It was the size of a small child, sitting motionless, holding its breath. Its round eyes were fixed on Oscar, glistening obsidian in the firelight, radiating what Oscar interpreted as excitement. The creature was smiling, its grin stretching from ear to ear, revealing a mouth filled with rows and rows of tiny, needle-sharp teeth.

Cold sweat soaked Oscar's clothes, and his breathing quickened to a panicked beat. Apparently amused by this, the creature began to cackle. It was a rattly sound, ugly and constant, like the wind-up mechanism of an old toy.

"Ke ke ke," the creature cackled, its hideous laughter punctuated by the clattering of its teeth.

It slid its bulky figure across the room toward Oscar, its hunched movements like those of a small primate. The bonfire glowed behind it, shrouding its features in shadows—all except for those glistening nocturnal eyes. Cackling without pause, the creature climbed on Oscar's chest and sat down, heavy and robust like a gargoyle. Its weight pressed Oscar's ribcage against his lungs, forcing out what little air there was left. Tears streamed from his eyes, blurring his vision.

The creature grabbed Oscar's head with a scaly, dry hand, its talons long and cracked, its grip unyielding. The nails sank into Oscar's scalp, and with it came an odd warmth, euphoric in its own way, the sensation vivid and unmistakable. It seeped through his skin, pushed past bone, and invaded his mind.

From that warmth, a vision took shape. Oscar was drifting down a dark cave, its walls crowded with mold poppies, their stems bent under the weight of their silvery buds, as if bowing to him. The creature's cackles faded behind him, growing softer as he drifted further. Soon, all he could hear were the nervous beats of his heart.

The vision carried him to a bonfire at the cave's end. Its tangerine light glistened on the damp walls thick with those silver flowers. A naked man knelt before the fire. He breathed in the bonfire smoke, swaying from side to side with his arms spread wide like some shaman casting a spell. Gradually, his movements slowed to a halt. He lifted his head and turned toward Oscar.

The man's face didn't belong to him—nor did his long, blood-slicked hair that draped over his shoulders. He wore the face of a woman, peeled from someone's head and pulled over his own like an ill-fitting mask. The mask's eyelids drooped over empty slits, and its gaping mouth hung paralyzed, the face looking as if it were slowly melting. Beneath that drooping sack of skin hid another face, its eyes fixed on Oscar. He could feel the masked figure assessing him.

And somewhere at the mouth of the cave, the creature cackled, "Ke ke ke."

CHAPTER ELEVEN

When Oscar awoke, the bonfire was down to its last embers. His exhaustion was gone, but all the symptoms of death were still very much present. He paid them less mind than before, though—the way an alcoholic might consider hangovers as the status quo. He sat up and stretched, grunting at the sharp pain in his chest and neck. He felt out his messenger bag in the dark, pulled out a water satchel, and took a long swig.

"Nathaniel?" he called, surprised at the hoarseness of his voice.

"Yes?" Nathaniel answered from outside.

"I'm coming out."

"You don't need to tell me. Just come out."

Oscar got up and pulled aside the cloth covering the entrance. Nathaniel was still sitting on the stool, his back against the wall. Two cigarettes lay stubbed out at his feet.

"How'd you sleep?"

“Can’t remember.” Oscar crossed his arms and leaned on the doorframe, rubbing his brow.

“Means you must have slept well,” Nathaniel said absently, his eyes fixed on the dim landscape.

Darkness still reigned outside although the pitch-black night had softened, hinting at the beginnings of a slow dawn. It was the kind of brisk morning when time stands still and you feel like you’re the only person awake in the world. Their current shelter was set against the side of a gently sloping hill, offering a decent view of the land stretching between them and the forest at the base of the mountain range. Oscar scanned the scenery and spotted a light source not far from them. Based on the obscured shapes it illuminated, it looked like some kind of a cabin. A large yard surrounded it, enclosed by a stone fence and a ring of trees and shrubbery.

“You noticed it too?” Nathaniel asked. “Been staring at it all night.”

“That’s a lot of light.”

“A lot of unnecessary light. There’s fuel there. Has to be. You’ve had enough sleep?”

“You want to head out *now?*”

“Dawn’s breaking, but it’ll take a while before the daylight blows our cover,” Nathaniel explained. “We can get close to the cabin without having to use a lantern and give ourselves away. I don’t like to use words like *ideal* or *optimal* in Hell, but”—he nodded at the cabin—“this is as good as it gets.”

“Right.” Oscar felt nervousness tug at the bottom of his stomach. “I’ll pack up my stuff.”

Some half an hour later (a wild estimate since his grasp of time was slipping), Oscar’s back rested against the stone fence that surrounded the cabin’s yard. He hid under the shade of the thick shrubbery, hugging his messenger bag and waiting for Nathaniel to return from scouting the cabin. The roll of blankets, the stack of firewood, and Nathaniel's satchel lay in a pile next to him.

On the other side of the fence, some forty yards ahead, loomed the cabin. A branch-woven slate roof perched over its walls that were a mishmash of rock, wood, and mud. Light seeped through the windows draped with torn fabric, painting the stagnant desert air around the cabin with a feverish glow. Its warmth was almost hypnosis-inducing, like a haunted house trying to lure in strangers.

Oscar wasn't sure how he felt about this venture to break into someone's accommodations. He knew it was dangerous and morally questionable, but beneath all that doubt, the thrill pulsed through stronger than before. It was the same thrill that had crept up on him at times when he should have felt the most appalled. Other than feeling ashamed by it, he didn't know what to make of it. He didn't know what it meant. He asked himself how he would feel if Nathaniel came back from the scout to say the burglary was a no-go, and the answer came to him clear as day and without hesitation: he would feel disappointed. He wanted to go through with this.

This line of thought carried Oscar back to the night when the campsite intruder had set off one of Nathaniel's tripwires. Although fear had been the dominant sensation then, Oscar had also felt a similar disappointment after he realized the intruder wouldn't return.

Did I want the intruder to attack? he thought. *Why? Just so that I could see Nathaniel fuck somebody up?*

Oscar wondered whether he had always been like this, and, as he did, another cluster of memories of his past life returned unannounced. The memories extended to his teenage years. His sister had gone off to college, and Oscar lived alone with his mother.

His sister had always been a straight-A student. They were

a low-income family with a single mother and no savings, so she had to fight for a scholarship if she'd ever want to escape their dysfunctional household and build a decent life for herself. However, for reasons Oscar could never fathom, it seemed that his sister's biggest motivator wasn't her future but to make their mother proud. He never understood how she couldn't see that Mom was incapable of feeling pride when it came to her children. Mom was the master of erratic pessimism, but it seemed his sister was dead set on taming her through overachievement and excellence. As far as Oscar knew, she never received the praise she yearned and undoubtedly deserved.

The interesting thing was that whenever Oscar's sister wasn't around, Mom used her stellar grades as a weapon to criticize and shame Oscar. It seemed that her goal was to get the siblings to turn on each other, but all she ever managed to do was make her children team up against her and drive them further away.

After his sister had gone off to college, their mother complained daily that she had abandoned her and Oscar. Oscar was glad that things were working out for her, but deep down he also felt like Mom was right. She had abandoned *him* to save herself. The thought was irrational, intrusive, and toxic, but there it lay, in his heart of hearts, refusing to leave.

This was around the same time Oscar started drinking heavily. He'd gotten drunk before and, up until this point, had been as occasional a drinker as any teenager. But after his sister left, Oscar's drinking escalated from once a month to once a week, and eventually to two or even three times a week.

And when he got drunk, he always ended up hurting himself. He would climb to the rooftop of someone's house, get the attention of the other kids, and jump down with dramatic flair. He rarely bothered to check where he'd land—a bush, a tree, someone's lawn, or the curb of a sidewalk. It didn't matter. As long as he got a reaction, any reaction, from the audience, the stunt was a success. He would also invite the other kids to line up and take a swing at him, seeing how many punches he could take before he hit the ground. He would ride home on his bike, blackout drunk, his eyes closed, hands off the handlebars, hoping someone would catch him.

Once the kids Oscar hung out with noticed his knack for self-harm, they provoked him just to get some cheap entertainment out of him. Oscar would always deliver, and the other kids would get their laugh and post videos of the stunt on social media.

The reason these memories returned to him *now*, he figured, was that they made him realize that all the pain he had ever wanted to cause was solely directed at himself. He didn't want to hurt people. He didn't want conflict with anyone. In fact, considering how much he'd avoided Mom once his sister moved out, one could argue that Oscar was an exceedingly non-confrontational person.

But now Hell made him wonder what he had *really* been avoiding when he fled conflict. Had the thrill of hurting others always been there? Or was it something Hell planted in all of its subjects? Oscar wasn't sure which option frightened him more, but the thought gnawed at him nevertheless.

"Oscar," a voice whispered from somewhere close by.

He turned toward the voice but couldn't see anyone.

"It's me. I'm back." Nathaniel emerged from behind a nearby tree and crouched his way to him.

"Man, you're quiet," Oscar whispered. "What'd you find out?"

"I have to appreciate the homeowner's craftsmanship," Nathaniel said. "The cabin's sturdy. He's probably been lugging lumber from the forest over yonder. I heard a man's voice, but it didn't sound like he was talking to anyone—just a lot of grunting and the like. I think he's alone in there."

"So... we're doing this?"

"Yes. At first, I was hopeful the cabin would be empty because I didn't see any movement, but I think the lights are arranged so that you can't see inside."

"What else did you see?"

"The yard's full of shoddy booby traps. I figure their function is more to deter intruders than to hurt or capture them. I think that's why he's also keeping the lights on—he's not trying to hide; he's trying to keep people away. Whatever the case, I can get through the traps."

"And then?"

"Get in, steal some fuel, get out. I know the guy's awake, so I might have to rough him up. I'll—"

"Wait a minute," Oscar said, louder than he had meant to.

"I won't do anything excessive. I'll hide by the front door and throw a rock into one of his traps. He'll come out running to see what's what. I'll knock him out, tie him up if I have to, get in, steal the shit, and get out." He paused, hesitating as if knowing what came next would sound foolish. "And I need you to do something. When the trap goes off, I need you to, uh, scream."

"Scream?" Oscar's brow furrowed.

"Yes. Scream like you're in agony, like you're caught in a trap. Once he comes out, it'll take a moment for his eyes to adjust to the dark. He'll try to source the screaming. During all that confusion... that's when I'll strike."

Something in Oscar's gut bubbled nervously—stage fright. "I'm... I'm not much of an actor."

"I don't expect you to be. And *he*"—Nathaniel pointed toward the cabin—"sure as shit doesn't expect you to be. You just have to scream. Simple."

"What happened to violence being the last resort?"

"This is the last resort, Oscar," Nathaniel said, resigned. "I don't have to remind you how much we need this fuel, and knocking on a neighbor's door to borrow sugar isn't really customary in Hell."

Nathaniel had a decent plan and solid reasoning, but Oscar still found himself stammering for a counterargument. Before he could come up with one, the cabin's front door creaked open.

The two men tensed up. They peeked over the fence. A man stood by the entrance. Even with his head tilted low and his back arched forward, his enormous figure dwarfed the porch like an adult's foot in a child's shoe. Warm light spilled through the open door and silhouetted his features, but Oscar saw a big bushy beard droop from his face like a ball of tumbleweed. A bucket hung from his hand, and something thick and clumpy leaked from it like a gluey paste.

"Now what?" Oscar hissed.

"Let's just see how this plays out," Nathaniel whispered, his eyes locked on the man.

The homeowner descended the porch steps into the yard, and the wooden structures groaned in dismay. He stared in Oscar and Nathaniel's general direction, seemingly unaware of them. He turned another way and headed across the yard, each movement heavy and deliberate. The bucket swung in his hand like a pendulum, its gooey contents splattering with each swing. The man seemed unconcerned about the mess. Reaching the yard's edge, his shadowed figure disappeared behind the fence and shrubbery.

"Okay. Our chances don't get any better than this," Nathaniel whispered. "I'll head in, grab the shit, get out. Stay here. If you see him heading back to the cabin while I'm still inside, throw rocks until you trigger one of the traps. Then scream. I'll come running and knock him out cold. Then we get the fuck out of here."

"No, no, no. Hold on," Oscar stammered. Now that the mission was moving from planning to execution, insecurity overrode the thrill. Reality flooded in and drowned the fantasy.

Nathaniel ignored him. He rose to his knees. He adjusted the shoelace under his shirt with a pained grimace as he took out his knife.

"Can't you just wait?" Oscar demanded.

"No, I can't." And with that, Nathaniel was off. He picked up a fist-sized rock, climbed over the fence, and crept through the yard.

Oscar took a few deep breaths and gathered rocks from around him, piling them up in case he had to start hurling them into the yard. He peeked over the fence to get a better look at the traps but found himself none the wiser: he could see the cabin because it stood on elevated ground, but the yard below was hidden behind the fence. To get a better look, he would have to climb over the fence. Oscar was dead set on not doing so unless he absolutely had to.

He fixed his eyes on the cabin, unblinking, watching Nathaniel as he reached the foot of the porch. Nathaniel inspected the entrance, apparently checking it for traps or unexpected occupants. Without realizing it, Oscar dug his hands into the gravel, squeezing clumps of dirt with trembling fists.

Something rustled behind him.

The tension in his body dissolved to ooze. He turned around.

The homeowner loomed above him, face shadowed by the branches and black leaves of the surrounding trees, stoic and massive like a statue of some ruthless conqueror. A butcher's apron covered his barrel-like torso, its fabric stained with dried blood and streaks of a thick grayish paste. A utility belt hung from his hip over dark trousers, holding an unlit lantern and a machete crafted from scrap metal.

Before Oscar had a chance to react, the homeowner leapt at him and swung his bucket in a wide arc, bringing it down on

Oscar's face like some mighty hammer of judgment. His nose cracked like a chestnut, and searing hot pain exploded across his face. He slammed against the stone fence and collapsed to the ground. Blood pulped from the bridge of his nose, spilling over his eyes and gushing down his gullet. He doubled over, coughing and gagging.

The homeowner rolled him on his stomach, ripped off his messenger bag, and twisted his hands behind his back. A chain clattered, a ratchet rattled, and cold metal snapped around Oscar's wrists. The homeowner had cuffed him.

Oscar's blood-smeared face twisted into a pained grimace as the homeowner yanked him up by his hair. Next, he fired up his lantern and brought it close to Oscar's face to get a better look at him.

"Well, isn't this something," the homeowner said, his voice a low, rumbling baritone.

I know that voice. Oscar blinked the blood from his eyes and immediately recognized his captor.

"And so the prodigal son returns," Heinrich said.

CHAPTER TWELVE

Up until this point, the events at the cemetery had been a murky haze, but now they rushed back to Oscar like a sharp surge of adrenaline. He remembered the two grave looters, Ernie and Heinrich, and their two prisoners. He remembered stumbling to their convoy, the weight of the noose around his neck, and the jarring pain on his cheek when Ernie branded him with the razor, claiming him as his property—"family," as he'd called it. He remembered Ernie's unhinged behavior, how he had cut Son Number One's face on a sadistic impulse, while Heinrich had watched from the sidelines, cold and indifferent. He also remembered Nathaniel's conveniently timed entrance and how he knocked Ernie out with a shovel, sparking the chaos that ensued.

But what burned brightest in these memories was the young woman with the messy bob cut. She stood in the center, a focal point, taking Oscar's hand to share the diminishing warmth of their deceased bodies—a calming gesture to ease his distress. Her worried, empathetic eyes comforted him despite her own turmoil.

Next came an abrupt shift to those same eyes, now laced with disbelief and disappointment when Oscar couldn't save her—when he had abandoned her. Of all the horrors that had taken place at the cemetery, that stare haunted him the most.

Daughter. They named her Daughter and me their Son.

Heinrich tossed Oscar into the yard like a sack of garbage. He slammed on the hard ground, hands bound behind his back. He grunted through gritted teeth and, in between raspy breaths, coughed up blood that had gathered in his throat. Heinrich pulled Oscar up on his knees and pressed the machete against his throat. Oscar tried to steer away from the blade, gasping in panicky staccatos.

"Nathaniel!" he cried out.

Up on the porch, Nathaniel's silhouetted figure turned in surprise.

"Stranger, I have your boy!" Heinrich's voice boomed across the yard with stern authority. "Drop your weapons and step down from the porch."

Nathaniel froze. Oscar could almost hear the cogs churning in his head as he tried to devise a way out of this. Whether the plan involved saving or abandoning his protégé, Oscar had no idea.

Stop it. If abandoning you were an option, he would just run. He's trying to save you.

"Do it, or I'll cut his head off!" Heinrich barked.

"Fucking goddamnit." Nathaniel tossed away the knife and the rock, then stepped down from the porch. "Don't hurt him."

"Raise your hands above your head and do not move," Heinrich said, pulling Oscar to his feet.

Oscar now had a full, unobstructed view of the yard, and contrary to Nathaniel's claims, it contained much more than mere booby traps. Across the yard, stakes jutted from the ground, and on these stakes perched severed human heads. The stakes rammed through the victims' dissected windpipes, some so deeply embedded that they protruded from their mouths, forcing the heads to stare slack-jawed at the sky, a never-ending gag reflex itching at the back of their throats. Most of the faces remained motionless and paralyzed like clumps of melted cheese, but a few followed Oscar and Heinrich with their mad, glassy-eyed stares, faint croaks and gurgles echoing from their midst.

Upon seeing this, Oscar's energy drained like a candle out of wick. His knees buckled. It made sense now why Nathaniel had been so quick to resort to violence after scouting the cabin: a person who decorates their yard with severed heads would probably not be open to negotiate.

Heinrich slapped Oscar to the side of the head. "Do not pass out."

Oscar shook his head, sobering just enough to keep going. Heinrich marched him toward the cabin, past the poorly covered tiger pits, tripwires, and those macabre, croaking scarecrows. They reached Nathaniel, and as the cabin's glow unveiled Oscar and his captor from the dark, Nathaniel's alarmed expression dissolved into hopeless dismay—he, too, must have recognized Heinrich from the cemetery.

"Lace your fingers behind your head." Heinrich's tone was serious, tense, and stripped of theatrics. He stated what he wanted with harsh efficiency, wasting no words.

Nathaniel did as told. "This is really unnecessary. We just wanted to trade—"

"Face the wall. Now."

Nathaniel shuffled closer to the cabin. Heinrich shoved Oscar to the ground and moved behind Nathaniel. He grabbed him by the back of the head and smashed his face into the wall three times in rapid succession.

"Wh— Stop!" Oscar stammered helplessly.

Nathaniel crumpled to the ground. A black dent gaped from the corner of his eye, spilling a rivulet of blood down his face. Heinrich whipped out a pair of zip cuffs from his utility belt and bound Nathaniel's hands behind his back with the swift precision of an assembly line worker.

Nathaniel grunted in protest but otherwise remained docile. Oscar hoped Nathaniel was so compliant because he already had an escape plan in mind and not because the hit to the head had given him a concussion.

Heinrich pulled Nathaniel's staggering figure upright and ushered him up the steps and into the cabin. As they disappeared inside, Oscar's disbelief morphed into sheer terror.

"Why are you doing this?" he cried. Each word sent a pulse of pain through his broken nose, his speech slurred by the blood gathering in his throat and sinuses. "Please don't hurt him! Nathaniel? What's happening? Nathaniel!"

No response. Oscar tried to push himself up but managed only to flounder in panic, his hands bound and the rest of his muscles deadlocked with fear.

Heinrich returned, his expression blank with indifference. He grabbed Oscar by the ankle and dragged him to the porch. Oscar writhed and screamed, but it was useless—he felt like a worm on a fish hook. Heinrich dragged him inside and slammed the door shut.

Oscar shuffled to his knees, his gaze darting around the brightly lit cabin. A lantern burned on a table in the center of the one-room dwelling, and oil lamps molded from clay perched between the barred windows. The lighting felt harsh and sterile, like in an operating room; as Oscar associated this image with Heinrich's bloodied apron, his stomach churned.

His eyes snapped to a line of six nooses hanging from the wall. Dark, rust-colored blood smeared the floor beneath each noose with drag marks leading to a sturdy trap door in the corner of the room. It looked like the entrance to a storm shelter. Or a dungeon.

Or a torture chamber, Oscar thought.

Nathaniel was slumped against the wall, his hands bound behind his back, one of the nooses biting into his neck. His bloodied face bore a sullen, exhausted expression.

"Nathaniel, are you okay?" Oscar wept.

"No talking," Heinrich said.

He shoved Oscar against the wall, forced him on the floor, and fastened the noose adjacent to Nathaniel's around his neck. The rope pressed against Oscar's Adam's apple, turning his breathing into a high-pitched wheeze. He felt the dried blood on the floor stick to his pants.

How many before him had been held captive on this very noose, choking on their own blood, waiting to be dragged to whatever horrors lay behind those trap doors? And, more importantly, how many of them had escaped? A handful? Two? Just one? Somehow, Oscar felt the most likely answer was none.

This is real, he thought. The realization felt crushing, its weight beyond comprehension. *This is real.*

Heinrich patted Oscar down, snatched his knife, and tossed it on the table. He headed for the door and glanced around the room one last time, ensuring his prisoners had no means to escape. Then he exited the cabin, leaving the door behind him open.

Oscar turned to Nathaniel, his throat scraping against the rope as he moved. He shifted his weight, trying to ease its grip. "Please tell me you have a plan to get us out," he said, voice cracking.

"I'm working on it," Nathaniel grunted.

Heinrich returned a minute later with Nathaniel's satchel,

Oscar's messenger bag, and the roll of blankets they'd left behind the fence. He tossed the blankets into the corner and took a seat by the table, dumping the contents of Oscar and Nathaniel's bags on it.

"Traveling light," he said. "Very light."

"All our good shit is stashed close by," Nathaniel said. "We were hoping to trade it for some fuel."

"So you say." Heinrich sorted through their belongings—water canteens, a nearly dry oil pouch, a collapsible spade, rolls of gauze, a sewing kit, tripwires.

He looked at Oscar. "I know you remember me from the cemetery, boy." He turned to Nathaniel. "And you. Ernie told me about you. You were watching us, waiting for me to leave. I know you remember me too."

Nathaniel remained silent.

"And now you say you're here for oil." Heinrich clicked his tongue, shook his head.

"Coincidences happen," Nathaniel said, trying to sound calm. "What happened at the cemetery… that's water under the bridge as far as we're concerned—"

"Quiet!" Heinrich snapped, and Nathaniel's lips pressed tight.

Oscar couldn't hold it in anymore. "What are you going to do with us?" he asked, sobbing.

A smirk peeked through Heinrich's scruffy beard. "Me? Not much. But I imagine Ernie has a thing or two he'd like to do."

CHAPTER THIRTEEN

The long dark dawn had given way to a flame-hued noon by the time Oscar, Nathaniel, and Heinrich exited the cabin. The skewered heads sprouted around the yard like grotesque fungi, their strained croaks echoing through the air. The only reason Oscar could bear to look at them was because they were all facing away from the cabin. *Just clumps of hair perched on stakes*, he told himself. *Nothing more.* He tried counting them but stopped after reaching twelve, deciding he didn't want to know the full number.

In addition to their hands being bound, both Oscar and Nathaniel now had nooses hanging around their necks. Heinrich latched their ropes to two separate wooden beams supporting the porch, then disappeared behind the cabin, leaving them alone.

Oscar immediately began pulling at his noose, his movements frantic and desperate. The rope wouldn't budge, and with his hands cuffed behind his back, he couldn't muster enough strength to make a difference. The beam might as well have been made of solid concrete.

He looked around for something, anything, that might aid their escape. A little ways from the porch lay the charred remains of a bonfire. Empty cans and a pot fashioned from a metal helmet leaned next to it. A wireframe sieve, a wooden ladle, and a spatula made from scrap metal rested on a piece of board. Oscar couldn't reach them—not that they would have been of much use anyway.

"We need to get out of here, Nathaniel," he whispered.

"I'm aware." Nathaniel sat on the edge of the porch, making no effort to escape.

Oscar detected something uncharacteristic in Nathaniel's tone. It was a tremor, a little more than a micro-expression, but still enough to make Oscar uneasy. Of course Nathaniel was afraid—who wouldn't be?—but for him to be *so* afraid that he could barely hide it was something new. It unnerved Oscar. He knew the man's stoic demeanor was just a mask, but seeing it slip, even a little, spoke volumes.

He tried to calm himself by clinging to Nathaniel's promise: he would keep Oscar safe and use his experience, cunning, and everything else in his power to do just that. It might have been childish to hold on to a promise, but what other choice did Oscar have? Lose all hope? He wasn't quite ready to go there yet.

Heinrich returned, pushing a wheelbarrow that clattered and squeaked like a rusty merry-go-round. Oscar remembered seeing the sorry contraption back at the cemetery. It had looked pitiful then, and it looked pitiful now. Heinrich parked the wheelbarrow at the foot of the stairs.

"No sitting," Heinrich ordered, his eyes on Nathaniel.

Nathaniel didn't move a muscle. Heinrich grabbed him by the hair and yanked him up. "You are my property now, and you will do exactly as I say. Understand?"

Nathaniel bared his teeth like a cornered dog but didn't resist further. Heinrich studied him, scoffed, and released his grip.

Heinrich re-entered the cabin and emerged a moment later with a lapful of supplies. He loaded the cart with a couple of oil pouches (Oscar noticed a thief's greedy glare in Nathaniel's eyes), a coil of rope, two water canteens, a lantern, a duffel bag, and Nathaniel's satchel. He removed his butcher's apron, hung it on a rack by the door, and slipped on the trench coat and brimmed hat he had worn at the cemetery. Finally, he tied Oscar and Nathaniel's nooses to the front of the cart as if they were a couple of plow horses.

Oscar stared down at the setup, feverish anger igniting inside him. The humiliation felt so visceral and tangible that Oscar wanted to grab it by the throat and squeeze all life out of it.

"We can be civil and cooperate." Heinrich unlatched a whip from the handle of the wheelbarrow. "Or I can use this. Your choice." He pointed at a set of wheel tracks leading to a gate by the side of the yard. "We follow the road."

"Civil?" Oscar asked. His face tingled with frustration, the anger like an irritant simmering under his skin. "This is your idea of civil?"

"Oscar," Nathaniel warned. "Just do what the man says."

But the itching got so bad that Oscar wanted to peel his own face off. "How can you do this to people?!"

Heinrich lashed the whip at him. An explosive crack pierced the air like a gunshot, and a searing pain ripped across Oscar's back from shoulder to waist. He screamed in agony.

"That's how. Now pull. You too, thief." Heinrich cracked the whip again, this time on Nathaniel's back. Nathaniel grunted, but managed to swallow most of the pain.

Heinrich pushed while Oscar and Nathaniel pulled, and the wheelbarrow crept forward with a spine-tingling squeal.

The noose tightened around Oscar's throat. He strained his neck muscles, but it did nothing to ease the choking. He was gagging and sobbing now. His sinuses were clogged with coagulated blood, so breathing was already a struggle, even without the noose and the weight of the wheelbarrow constricting him.

Oscar looked over at Nathaniel. He had grabbed the rope with his cuffed hands, twisting his body into an awkward position. But at least the pressure on his throat seemed to have eased, letting him breathe more freely. Oscar followed suit, relieved to draw in air again.

They reached the gate at the edge of the yard, and already Oscar's back and arms ached like they'd been injected with something corrosive. But what burned worse was the humiliation. The physical pain bore no match to it. Heinrich had taken away their human value without blinking an eye. Oscar fantasized about escape, but instead of focusing on the freedom that'd follow, he indulged in the part where he'd get to exact revenge on Heinrich. *Just wait, you deranged piece of shit.* He used these violent daydreams as fuel to plow forth.

Beyond the gate, the desert stretched wide, a dark planar field beneath a bed of smoldering clouds. Up ahead, the forest loomed like a black barricade between the desert and the mountains; it seemed Heinrich was herding them straight toward it. Dread crept up on Oscar. According to Nathaniel and his map, that area was cannibal territory.

"Where are we going?" Oscar asked, each word a strained sputter between the pulls.

Nathaniel shot him a fiery glance: *Stop. Talking.*

"I told you," Heinrich said.

To Ernie? Oscar wondered. Did Ernie live in the forest? How could he survive in cannibal territory? Maybe he was holed up somewhere along the safe route Nathaniel had mentioned? Oscar could have asked, but he figured the less

Heinrich knew about their plans, the better. Nathaniel had signaled as much. Whatever schemes Nathaniel had in the works, Oscar didn't want to ruin them by blabbering to their captor.

"You two think there are no consequences in Hell," Heinrich said. "You think you can assault anyone, steal their property, disrupt their business. But consequences still apply—even to the dead."

To Oscar, Heinrich seemed the kind of man who'd rather give lessons than take them, so he likely never stopped to wonder what the consequences for enslaving and torturing people were. Even if he'd get what he deserved, he probably wouldn't see it as the result of his own horrid actions. In Heinrich's mind, no matter how many people he hurt, he would always be the victim, and the day he finally got what was coming would only serve to confirm it.

A more hopeful thought struck Oscar: maybe the woman with the bob cut and the teenager with the broken glasses, Daughter and Son Number One, were being held at Ernie's place. Hadn't Ernie mentioned something about "keeping the pretties to himself" back at the cemetery? Then again, Oscar also recalled Ernie and Heinrich talking about selling their captives to a "client."

Oscar didn't have enough information to form a solid guess, but the idea of reuniting with his fellow prisoners seemed possible. If that happened, they'd have the numbers to overpower Ernie and Heinrich. They would show the grave looters the consequences of treating people like this. And then Oscar could explain to Daughter why he hadn't been able to save her at the cemetery, how the memory still haunted him. Maybe she would listen. Maybe she would forgive him. And whatever horrors she had endured in Ernie's hands, he would help her get through them. They would share their warmth again, and it would be enough to hold Hell's frigid darkness at bay.

The convoy trudged along. With his posture forced to a hunch and his arms bent backwards, Oscar felt like a rag being wrung dry. Even when the rope didn't choke him, it scraped his skin raw. Adjusting his position to ease one ache flared another, and this was how he plowed forth, seesawing between different kinds of pain. The path they followed looked worn and trodden—this wasn't the first time Heinrich had herded prisoners through here. Oscar figured neither he, Nathaniel, nor the countless Heinrich's previous victims could have completed this hike alive—the breathing was that disjointed and grueling.

They were nearing the edge of the desert. The tree line grew with each step, and beyond the forest, the mountains rose black, crooked, and colossal like the horns of Satan, their tips cloaked in the clouds.

What little doubt there'd been in Oscar's mind now disappeared completely: Heinrich was leading them to the woods. A violent shiver took hold of him, and the lump in his stomach burned as if he'd swallowed hot coals.

"Why are we going to the woods?" he asked, voice cracking.

"No talking. Pull."

"But don't you know what's in there? The—"

Heinrich yanked the wheelbarrow, and a brutal force jerked Oscar and Nathaniel by their throats, throwing them on their backs, gasping for air. Heinrich strode over to Oscar and kicked him in the stomach, knocking the wind out of him. He pinned him down by planting a knee on his chest, then drove his thumb into the bridge of his broken nose. He pressed down hard, and a series of cracks followed as the bone snapped further. A wildfire of searing agony spread through

Oscar's skull, locking his body in place. He couldn't even scream—the pain was so intense, so paralyzing. He feared he might pass out which, then again, didn't sound all that bad.

"Don't you fucking touch him, you son of a bitch!" Nathaniel wheezed on the ground. "Punish me! I'm responsible for him!"

Heinrich ignored him. His cold eyes locked with Oscar. "Do you know what happens to children who misbehave? They get taken to the woods."

"Please… stop…" Oscar managed to sputter through the pain.

"I know the forest, and the forest knows me," Heinrich said. He pulled out his thumb from the bloody crater. "And soon so will you."

CHAPTER FOURTEEN

The group soon reached the border between the desert and the forest. Here the tallest trees stood three stories high and formed a canopy of intertwining branches and black leaves that blocked out all natural light, plunging the forest below into an eternal night. Smaller trees sheltered beneath them in scoliotic postures, their spindly limbs twisted in complex deformities.

Heinrich halted the wheelbarrow without warning, sending a sharp tug on Oscar and Nathaniel's throats. He opened an empty duffel bag, transferred the supplies from the wheelbarrow into it, and slung it over his shoulder.

Anger flared inside Oscar. Heinrich could have carried the supplies himself this whole time, yet he'd forced them to drag the wheelbarrow through the desert. All this had been nothing but a cruel, pointless display of power. Oscar scoffed to himself. *Just wait, you fucking piece of shit.*

Heinrich then pulled a long shepherd's crook from the

wheelbarrow and attached his lantern to it. He tied Oscar and Nathaniel's ropes around the crook, pushed the wheelbarrow into the thicket, and hid it with some loose shrubbery.

While Heinrich was busy, Nathaniel clicked his tongue to get Oscar's attention. He nodded toward the trees. Oscar followed his gaze and spotted one of the trunks had been marked with an X, the carving dyed with a deep red. He remembered Nathaniel mentioning this when they'd studied the map: X marked the start of the safe route.

So Heinrich wasn't leading them to the cannibals—not yet, at least. A smile forced itself on Oscar's face. It drove a spike of pain through his broken nose, but he didn't care. There was still hope. Pain caused by hope he could endure.

The group crossed the tree line, and the forest swallowed them whole, pulling them from the desert's desolation into a world of its own. Its nocturnal chambers stretched ahead like the great halls of a forsaken tomb buried deep underground. Ancient dust hovered in the air, thick and heavy. The silence hummed a different tune here—more private, more solemn than out in the open desert. And in between that silence, the forest conversed in its secret language: dead wood creaked like an old door, underbrush cracked and rustled, and the leaves above ruffled their black mass as if struck by a shiver. Every sound felt intimate, like a whisper at the base of one's ear.

Oscar and Nathaniel led the way while Heinrich herded them from behind. His lantern hung from the shepherd's crook, casting a dim halo over the group and rendering the surrounding branches with a skin-like texture. A narrow path peeked through the foliage, and the group followed it faithfully. Pale roots slithered in and out of the soil, and twigs snapped under the group's feet like bones in the nest of some predatory bird.

Oscar flinched at every sound, and his eyes darted from one suspicious shadow to the next. He acknowledged he must have looked like a paranoid rodent—admittedly, he felt like one. Nathaniel exhibited none of Oscar's fidgety fear, but the sharp clench of his jaw, the bulging veins on his neck, and his tightly welded fists told Oscar the man was just as scared as he was.

They continued along the path. Soon, the canopy of birch and leaf thinned, letting diluted daylight filter through. Beams of bronze light pierced the foliage like rays from a mirror ball, casting a dreamy haze over the musky air. A half-withered swamp came into view. What little water remained was thick like tar and veiled in a thin sheet of mist. A congregation of trees hunched in the muck, threads of moss dangling from their branches like unkempt hair.

Despite the situation he was in, Oscar still found himself marveling at Hell's nature. The vegetation was either blackened with death or withered gray but otherwise didn't deviate from the broadleaf forests or forested wetlands of the living world. And yet, there was something more there that Oscar couldn't quite put his finger on. The tallest trees looked like beeches but weren't; the smaller ones like swamp cypresses and alders but weren't. It was as though different climates and their verdure had tangled together to create an ecosystem both familiar and alien. These species didn't exist in the living world nor did they seem to follow its natural law. Different laws governed this realm, laws that didn't require organisms to be alive to draw breath.

The path followed the swamp shore then veered back into the forest. Soon, the path merged with a dry creek, and the group climbed in. The trees bent over the creek in arcs, forming a tunnel draped with wads of moss. Pebbles coated the creek bed and shifted under their feet with soft clatters that echoed in the tunnel's faint hum.

Eventually, the thicket to their left thinned out, and a clearing came into view through the sparse alignment of trees.

Heinrich yanked the shepherd's crook. "Turn left here."

They climbed the bank and stepped through the tree line. The clearing basked in the noon glow, its knee-high grass carpeting the ground all the way to the surrounding thicket. Up ahead, the mountains loomed over the trees like giants peeking into a courtyard.

Oscar studied the setting. He remembered Nathaniel saying the safe route was an overgrown thicket where a constant light source was required, but so far, their path through the forest had been nothing of the sort. From this, Oscar could draw only one conclusion: they were no longer on the safe route. His stomach twisted at the realization.

"Halt," Heinrich ordered. He walked past the prisoners and scanned the surroundings, his back turned to them. "Not much further now."

Not much further, Oscar thought. Not much further until they would reach whatever hole Ernie called home. Not much further until Oscar would find out if Daughter and Son Number One were alright.

A sharp snap jolted Oscar from his thoughts. He turned to Nathaniel and, for a moment, couldn't comprehend what he was seeing. Nathaniel's hands were unbound. And what's more, he was clutching a knife. Oscar's eyes widened. Nathaniel was free.

Nathaniel slipped the noose from his neck, his face twisted with rage-fueled resolve. He took a deep breath, readied the knife, and sprinted toward Heinrich.

This is it, Oscar thought.

Nathaniel leapt at his target, but before he could strike, Heinrich spun around and drove his elbow into Nathaniel's face. A loud crack discharged like a revolver, and the blow sent Nathaniel crashing to the ground. Oscar gasped in dismay.

Heinrich gazed down at Nathaniel with a sullen, unsurprised expression. He grabbed Nathaniel by the throat, took hold of his knife-wielding hand, and lifted him off the ground so that his dangling feet barely grazed the grass.

Oscar stood by, his heart pounding. He tried to twist and strain his cuffs, but they wouldn't budge.

"I was wondering when you would make your move." Heinrich squeezed Nathaniel's wrist, trying to force him to drop the knife. Nathaniel's jawline hardened in defiance. He wasn't going to let go.

"I saw you pick up the knife from the porch, you know," Heinrich continued. "'Let him have his toy,' I thought. I figured the trip would go smoother with some false hope in you. It worked longer than I expected. Now, drop the knife."

The porch? Oscar thought. He remembered Nathaniel dropping the knife on Heinrich's porch after the ambush, but that was the last time Oscar had seen it. Nathaniel must have pocketed it later—probably when Heinrich had left them unattended to fetch the wheelbarrow?

"Drop the knife," Heinrich repeated, calmer now.

Nathaniel's eyes burned with fury. He tried to fight back, but it was no use—Heinrich's grip was too strong.

Heinrich didn't bother telling him a third time. He squeezed harder and harder until Nathaniel's wrist broke with an audible snap. His face contorted in agony, and his grip on the knife faltered. The blade fell to the grass.

"Fucking son of a bitch," Nathaniel snarled, voice breaking.

"Quiet. I— What's this?" Heinrich interrupted himself as something caught his eye—a folded piece of paper peeking out from Nathaniel's chest pocket. He plucked it free.

Nathaniel's face went slack with dread.

Heinrich tossed him to the ground like a toy that no longer interested him. Nathaniel landed on all fours, only to receive a vicious kick to the stomach. He gasped in pain and collapsed onto his side, curling into a tight ball.

"Stop it, Heinrich. Please," Oscar pleaded, thrashing

uselessly against the handcuffs. His wrists were raw from the effort, but so far he had made zero progress.

Heinrich planted his boot on Nathaniel's throat, pinning him to the ground. He unfolded the piece of paper and studied it. His eyebrows lifted in surprise as he recognized the area depicted on the map.

"Well, well," Heinrich said. "We can't have you carrying this around."

Nathaniel writhed beneath Heinrich's boot like a wolf caught in a trap. He tried to reach for the knife, but it was well out of his reach.

Oscar spotted the blade glimmering in the grass and took a step toward it.

"One more step, and I'll break his neck!" Heinrich barked.

Oscar froze. The man's command had cut deep into his bones.

Heinrich rolled up the map and dipped it into his lantern's chamber. The flames licked the paper then devoured it whole. And so, Oscar and Nathaniel's only assurance of a safe passage through the mountain folk's lair was gone, reduced to ashes.

Heinrich removed his boot from Nathaniel's throat. Nathaniel cradled his broken wrist and focused his fevered eyes on his captor. "You're a fucking pathetic degenerate," he snarled through clenched teeth.

Heinrich seemed genuinely taken aback. He clearly wasn't used to such defiance from his "property." After the initial surprise, a darkness fell upon his face. "You're beginning to be a lot more trouble than you're worth," he said quietly.

He pulled out his machete and knelt over Nathaniel, his legs squeezing Nathaniel's arms to his sides like a straitjacket. Nathaniel wriggled helplessly as Heinrich brought the blade close to his face.

"I'll make the boy drag whatever is left of you the rest of the way," Heinrich said. Then, with a steady hand, he raised the blade high over his head.

Nathaniel stopped squirming. His eyes went wide with horror.

Oscar's mind raced in circles. *What do I do? What do I do?*

But even as he was asking this, his body had already launched into action. He sprinted toward Heinrich and drove his knee into Heinrich's jaw. Oscar felt the impact reverberate through his knee and up his thigh, but Heinrich's head barely jerked back. The grunt he made wasn't any louder or more pained than his usual talking voice.

Still, it was enough to steer his attention away from Nathaniel. Slowly, he rose to his feet, his morose gaze fixed on Oscar.

"I… I'm sorry," Oscar stammered, stumbling backward.

Without a word, Heinrich stomped his boot down on Nathaniel's face. A horrible crack followed, and for a second, Oscar thought Nathaniel's head had split in two. Then he realized half of it had sunk into the dirt. Nathaniel's eyes rolled in his head, and his body went limp.

Before Oscar could react, Heinrich lunged at him, teeth bared in a snarl. His iron body slammed into Oscar like a freight train, sending him to the ground with violent velocity. Oscar's world spun, and stars exploded behind his eyes.

Heinrich placed a knee on his chest and leaned in with his whole weight. At the same time, Oscar felt the noose tighten, cutting off his air. Not that it mattered—he still hadn't caught his breath from the tackle.

Oscar didn't need to breathe, but the lack of oxygen, the pain in his windpipe, and the adrenaline rushing through him with no outlet to discharge drained all strength out of him. His vision blurred, darkened.

Where will I wake up? he wondered. *And in what shape?*

He couldn't die a second time, but the choking sure made it feel as though he could. His body knew what dying felt like, and now, on the verge of passing out, it seemed to mimic the sensation. In this never-ending afterlife, this simulated death felt strangely… peaceful.

Until it ended abruptly. A muffled thud cut through the haze, and the pressure on his chest lifted. The rope loosened.

No, don't stop.

Oscar's vision cleared, and he saw Heinrich kneeling over him, gasping. His cold stare now looked confused and lost. An arrow stuck out of his chest. Heinrich looked down, saw the arrow, and the reality of the situation flooded over him.

"*Nein, nein, nein,*" he repeated in accelerating panic.

Oscar heard rapid footsteps, growing louder, approaching.

Three figures charged at Heinrich like a pack of wildcats. They jumped on him simultaneously and toppled him over. Oscar's eyes widened—the attackers were children. Two preteen girls and a boy, all dressed in ragged clothes, their hair tangled and messy like tumbleweed.

Each of them gripped a rusty shiv and stabbed Heinrich with the pace of a sewing machine. Heinrich screamed and thrashed, but the children didn't relent. One stabbed his chest, the two others his stomach and sides. Blood sprayed and scattered in fine droplets, cloaking the chaos with a red mist.

The attack was fast and efficient. In mere seconds, this tower of a man was reduced to a blood-gushing heap of dead mass, riddled with dozens of stab wounds. His shrieks tapered off into wheezes and gurgles. The children's eyes were hollow, staring into some manic void as they continued plunging their blades into him.

Oscar crawled away from the slaughter, his movements stiff with terror. He reached Nathaniel and collapsed next to him. "Nathaniel, please wake up," he cried.

Nathaniel moaned in a daze, his face a blood-splattered mess, his sharp features swollen like a lump of spoiled dough.

A short yelp, strangely uncontrolled and primal, echoed

from across the clearing, drawing Oscar's attention. More children emerged from the thicket, moving their way. There were nine of them. The oldest, a girl of around fifteen, led the pack while the youngest, no more than four, rode on the shoulders of one of the older children, wearing a mask made of tree bark. The rest of them looked like they'd died in their preadolescent years. Their scarce, tattered clothing revealed withered bodies marred by deformities and half-healed wounds. Patches of skin had been flayed, only a few pairs of hands still bore all ten fingers, and wounds, both old and new, ran deep and dark.

Save for the four-year-old, all the children carried crude, makeshift weapons: shivs, spears, hatchets, and bows.

But what terrified Oscar the most was the disconnected look in their eyes. He saw no humanity there, no hint of intellect—only a predatory sharpness. Every glance was an assessment of potential danger, as if their lizard brain had taken over entirely. Fear and heartbreak formed a knot inside Oscar, and he didn't know whether he should run away or hug them.

"Nathaniel, snap out of it," Oscar whispered. "There's people here."

The three preteens who had attacked Heinrich stood around his convulsing body, out of breath, staring at the mess they had made. One of the girls shook off her daze and turned to the approaching group. She pointed at Oscar and Nathaniel, yelping in alarm.

Two boys and the fifteen-year-old—whom, judging by her commanding presence, Oscar assumed to be the leader—rushed toward them. One boy leveled a spear at Oscar, while the other nocked an arrow and aimed it at Nathaniel. The leader brandished her shiv, ready to strike.

Oscar hunkered closer to Nathaniel. "No, no, no. Wait."

The spear-wielding boy pulled back his weapon, gathering momentum. But before he could thrust it into Oscar, the leader yelped and raised her hand, stopping him. The boy suspended the spear in midair. He looked at her, waiting.

She tapped her cheek, yelped again, and pointed at Oscar.

Oscar blinked, holding his breath. The leader repeated the gesture: she tapped her cheek, then pointed at him.

Oscar's mouth went slack. He understood now. A scar shaped like a teardrop marked the girl's cheek. It was all but identical to the scar Ernie had branded on Oscar back at the cemetery. What's more, the boy with the spear had one too. As did the boy with the bow. Slowly, they lowered their weapons.

Something between a sob and a laugh escaped Oscar's lips.

The girl's owlish eyes locked on Oscar. She placed her thumb on her cheek and swiped it across the scar. The two boys mimicked the gesture, then looked at him expectantly. Oscar realized he was supposed to return the salute, but his hands were still bound behind his back.

"Hey," Nathaniel said, awake now, steering their attention to him. He saluted them on Oscar's behalf.

Apparently satisfied, the three children backed away and rejoined the group gathered around Heinrich. Past their circle of skinny legs, Oscar could see Heinrich lying in the tall grass, twitching and gurgling, his hands contorted into half-made fists over his chest. The children stared down at their victim in a heavy, solemn silence.

After a beat, the teen leader yelped with animal authority and entered the thicket, leaving the clearing. One by one, the others left the circle and followed their leader into the dark of the forest.

And soon, Oscar and Nathaniel were left alone with Heinrich's carcass.

The reality of everything that'd happened washed over Oscar, and suddenly the grip of his bindings felt tighter. "Get me out of these cuffs. Get them off. Now."

Nathaniel sat up with a groan and examined the cuffs. He

produced a bobby pin from inside his shoe and began picking the lock. A series of clicks and rattles followed, the cuffs loosened, and then… Oscar was free. He yanked the noose from around his neck and tossed it into the grass as though it were a poisonous snake.

"Sorry for the wait." Wincing, Nathaniel dabbed at the wounds on his face, assessing the damage. "The bastard stayed behind us the whole time. I couldn't get to the knife any sooner. You okay?"

"We have to get out of the open," Oscar whispered. Although he'd just been freed, he didn't feel free—on the contrary, his skin felt tight and suffocating. "The kids might change their minds, or someone else might show up."

"Calm down. We can take a moment," Nathaniel said. He grabbed Heinrich's duffel bag lying nearby and pulled it on his lap. "We *need* to take a moment."

Oscar got up and paced back and forth, arms wrapped around his sides. He scanned the tree line, eyes burning wild, while Nathaniel sorted through the contents of the duffel bag. "The son of a bitch stole my cigarettes," he muttered. Oscar had a thousand questions swirling in his mind—about Heinrich, the children, and these woods—but they would have to wait until they found someplace more secure.

A frail whisper caught Oscar's attention. It was Heinrich.

His eyes locked on his former captor lying in the grass. Unaware of himself, he moved closer.

"Oscar," Nathaniel warned.

But Oscar ignored him. The ground around Heinrich had turned to a bloody sludge, and Oscar had to tread carefully to avoid slipping. He knelt down, studying this blood-soaked human pincushion from head to toe. He noticed one of the children had left a shiv sticking out of his belly.

Oscar was relieved to notice no trace of that shameful thrill. Instead, a sort of impending sickness bubbled in his gut, as if he were in a dream teetering on the edge of a nightmare.

Heinrich whispered something again.

"What?" Oscar asked, leaning closer. "What did you say?"

"*Mutter,*" Heinrich wheezed, his unfocused eyes staring up at the sky. "*Mutter.*"

Something snapped inside Oscar. He recoiled, his face twisting in disgust. His breathing quickened, tears blurred his vision, and his body felt as strung as a piano wire. His hand reached for the shiv still lodged in Heinrich's belly. He yanked it free.

"*Mutter. Mutter. Mutter,*" Heinrich whimpered.

Oscar's drove the blade in Heinrich's throat, pulled it out, then drove it in again. And again. Blood pulsed in thick rivulets, soaking Heinrich's beard like an oily rag. Heinrich churned with weak gasps, but that was all the retaliation he could muster anymore. Oscar wailed like a child, his voice loud and uncontrolled. There was no thrill, no morbid curiosity—just pure, visceral horror and revulsion. And yet he couldn't stop himself. It felt like his knife-wielding hand had complete autonomy.

"Oscar!" Nathaniel shouted, staggering toward him.

Oscar's eyes squeezed shut as he sobbed and screamed, his arm still swinging wildly even though most of the strikes were only cutting through empty air now. Nathaniel wrapped his arms around him and pulled him away.

"No! Fuck you!" Oscar thrashed, trying to kick Heinrich's convulsing corpse as Nathaniel dragged him out of reach. "Why won't you die, you piece of shit?! Why?!"

Nathaniel held him tight, enveloping him in an all-consuming hug, the kind that could only be shared between open hearts. "It's alright, Oscar. It's alright now."

Whatever had activated inside Oscar now collapsed and withered. He sank into Nathaniel's embrace, his sobs turning into soft whimpers. The tears flowed freely, cleansing him. In its own self-destructive way, the rage had felt good, but letting go felt better.

CHAPTER FIFTEEN

Oscar and Nathaniel had moved beyond the hearing distance of Heinrich's rattly wheezes and now crouched under the trees just outside the clearing. The ashen light of dusk settled through the shrubbery into their hiding place. Nathaniel's satchel and Heinrich's duffel bag lay slumped on the ground, the latter containing two water canteens, Heinrich's makeshift machete, a coil of rope, and three pouches of lantern fuel—"At least we got what we needed out of this shit show," Nathaniel remarked.

Nathaniel had already patched himself up. His battered face was now stitched together in three places, and his broken wrist—"Just a hairline fracture," he'd said—was secured with a splint and strips of fabric.

Now, he was tending Oscar's broken nose. Red-eyed and wincing from the sharp pain, Oscar sat still as Nathaniel cleaned the broken dent, examined it, and set it straight. He placed a splint on the bridge of the nose and secured it with gauze that he wrapped around Oscar's head.

"There," Nathaniel said. "You'll probably have a hump on your nose from now on. Better get used to it."

Oscar didn't respond. He stared down at his hands. They were slathered in blood and trembling uncontrollably. Strands of Heinrich's beard stuck out of the blood smears like insect antennae.

The shaking spread from his hands, climbed up his arms, and soon overtook his entire body. He began to sob, drained and exhausted, tears wetting the gauze wrapped across his cheeks. Without a word, Nathaniel soaked a rag in water and began wiping the blood from Oscar's hands.

"Back in the desert, you said there's a threshold you shouldn't cross," Oscar said, watching the blood wash away. "Does this mean I've crossed it?"

Nathaniel considered the question for a moment, then said, "What this means to you… that's only for you to decide."

Oscar wiped away his tears, rubbed his eyes, and let out a long, tired breath. "What are we going to do? We lost the map."

"That fucking map." Nathaniel's head sank. He gathered himself and continued, "We already established that circling the woods and the mountain range isn't an option. I don't know if there's anything else to do but push forward. Head east. Get past those mountains. There's that valley on the other side—it's still mountain folk territory, but I guess we'll have to push through that as well."

"How are we supposed to do that?"

"We'll need to be stealthy, stay hidden, play it smart. We're dealing with hunters, though, so we're also going to need a lot of luck."

"What about Ernie?" Oscar asked. "Maybe he knows about the safe passage. I mean, how else could he hole up in their forest? Heinrich said we're close to his place, and I saw where the path picks up from the clearing. That's got to lead to Ernie, right?"

"And who's going to make him talk? You?" Nathaniel asked.

"I was thinking you might be more persuasive in that department."

"Figures," Nathaniel scoffed.

"I mean, it's a lead, right? It's either that or we go in blind into the hunting grounds."

Nathaniel mulled it over, then sighed. "Goddamnit, alright. I'll get him to talk if it comes to that."

"Good." Oscar cleared his throat and tried to steady his voice, hoping it would sound firm and unyielding. "I have one demand, though."

"Do you now?" Nathaniel raised an eyebrow.

"The woman and the kid from the cemetery—the ones who'd been imprisoned by the grave looters. I think they might still be with Ernie. If they are, they get to come with us."

Nathaniel was silent for a moment, a calculating look showing beneath his bruises.

"I'm serious," Oscar pressed. "I remember what happened at the cemetery now. You were always kind of vague about it, and I think you did that on purpose. I'm guessing you didn't want me to remember that we abandoned them."

"I don't have the capacity to save everyone, Oscar. I—"

"I'm not holding it against you," Oscar interrupted. "I mean, I get it. Your plan was to save someone who fit your needs. Fine. Whatever. It's messed up, but I understand. But now we have a chance to do right by them. We owe them that. And you owe it to *me.*" His voice trembled with resolve. "You already saved someone. Give me a chance to do the same."

Nathaniel thought about it for a moment. "If they're still with Ernie, if there's still something left worth saving, and if they're willing to follow us—all big ifs—then, fine, they can come."

Relief swept through Oscar like a cool breeze. "It's settled then. Are you good to walk?"

"Other than feeling like someone blasted me in the face with a shotgun, I'm fine. Let's take it slow, though."

The trail picked up at the eastern edge of the grassy clearing. Oscar and Nathaniel re-entered the black crevices of the forest and followed the snaking path illuminated by the faint glow of Nathaniel's lantern. The woods grew thicker here. Roots pierced through the soil in tangled, tentacle-like clusters, and the moss-covered birches drooped low, forcing them to walk with hunched backs. Yet despite the overgrowth, the trail remained well-trodden and clear.

Though the scenery stirred fear in Oscar, he wasn't worried about running into the mountain folk here. The thicket was simply too dense for even the most skilled hunters to move through unnoticed, and chasing prey without getting tangled in the branches would be next to impossible.

"Just so we're clear on Ernie... You do realize he's not just going to hand over the information?" Nathaniel said. He was leading the way, pushing aside drapes of moss. "It might get rough while I interrogate him. You're okay with that?"

"After seeing what he did to those kids? Yes," Oscar said. "I mean, they were Heinrich and Ernie's prisoners, weren't they? They all had that scar. Same as Daughter, Son Number One, and me."

"That's the impression I got," Nathaniel nodded.

"What do you think happened?" Oscar asked. "How'd they end up at the clearing? Why now?"

"I'll be sure to ask Ernie about that."

"Did Ernie and Heinrich dig them up from the cemetery? They weren't, like, born here, right?"

"We're barren, Oscar. The dead can't breed life. Those kids ended up in Hell like everyone else—through the cemetery. Some grave looters prefer capturing children because they're easier to control. Cowards."

Oscar felt a sting of anger and disgust. He shook his head to calm down. "And all those animal noises? That yelping? What was that?"

Nathaniel scratched his chin, careful to avoid the stitches. "You know, someone once told me about this other group of kids. 'Feral children,' he called them. Kids don't stand much of a chance getting out of the ground by themselves, so the ones you see in Hell were probably dug up by grave looters. They were subjected to exploitation from the moment their coffins were pried open. Well, this particular group found kinship through shared trauma. They teamed up to defend themselves from all the abuse they'd suffered at the hands of adults."

"If this story turns into a *Lord of the Flies* situation and the kids turn on each other, I'm not sure I want to hear it."

"All groups turn on each other over time. But that's not the point of the story. See, the kids came from different cultures, different eras. They had a deep sense of camaraderie, but they couldn't really communicate—not with words, anyway. We stop developing once we die, so we're stuck with whatever brain capacity we had when we passed. For these kids, that meant a limited set of wits. They couldn't create a common language together—not a complex one, at least. Words became useless. Enough time passed, and eventually, they forgot the language they'd learned in the living world."

"Civilizations wouldn't exist without language," Oscar said. "I think I read that somewhere."

"Exactly. They forgot their mother tongue and, as a result, lost their civility, their culture—in essence, their humanity. They went feral. I'm not saying this is exactly what happened to the kids *we* encountered, but when someone as sadistic and unhinged as Ernie imprisons a bunch of children and treats them like animals… well, let's just say there are many roads to regression."

"In a place like this, maybe going primal is the way to go," Oscar said quietly.

"I'm sure we'll all get there someday," Nathaniel said, a bitter smile on his face.

CHAPTER SIXTEEN

The terrain grew hilly and uneven as they got closer to the mountains. They climbed up a steep slope by gripping to exposed tree roots, then hoisted themselves onto a stable patch of ground. Here they discovered talisman-like contraptions dangling from the trees, crafted from small bones, wads of hair, and strips of skin. Seeing these macabre ornaments made Oscar's insides churn.

Nathaniel unsheathed his knife. "I'm starting to doubt this trail leads to Ernie."

"What do you mean?" Oscar stammered.

"I mean Heinrich might have fucked us over. He might've been leading us straight to the mountain folk the whole time."

"We don't know that," Oscar countered weakly.

"And therein lies the problem."

"What are you saying?" Oscar asked. "You want to bail *now?*"

"No, I'm saying we should get off the trail and approach

with more discretion. Keep an eye out for traps. We're close to wherever the fuck it is we're going."

They strayed from the path and shadowed it from a distance. Even here in the dense thicket, the human-based ornaments infested the trees like some invasive species.

Firelight flickered through the trees ahead. Nathaniel quickly extinguished his lantern.

"Careful," he whispered. "I'll take the—"

He stopped mid-sentence as a familiar voice broke out in song:

From the morgue I was towed to the old moor road,
But this old moor road leads nowhere at all.

It was Ernie. His voice, slurred and drunken, drifted from the direction of the lights. He trailed off, then started over from the first line.

Excitement flared inside Oscar. He pulled Heinrich's machete from the duffel bag Nathaniel had assigned him to carry and, without a second thought, sprinted toward the voice.

"Oscar!" Nathaniel spat and ran after him.

The trees parted, revealing a small clearing in the deep of the forest, isolated from its surroundings by a wooden fence. Oscar vaulted over the fence and stopped. A bonfire crackled in the center of the clearing, and oil lamps hung from the few trees scattered around it, their glow pushing back the dark. A dry creek bordered one side of the yard, running downhill; the forest circled the rest of the yard.

A windowless cabin slumped by the creek, gray and sad, as if weighed down by the horrors it held within—a house haunted by its subjects. Shoes, most of them children's, had been stacked against the cabin wall like firewood. Littered throughout the yard were empty cages, the largest ones waist-high to Oscar, the smallest reaching only his knees. Shackles were bolted to the trees, nooses hung from the branches, and a boulder stained with dried blood sat beside a wooden workbench cluttered with rusted tools.

But Oscar barely registered any of this. His eyes were fixed on the figure sprawled on the ground by the bonfire: Ernie. The man's emaciated body twitched with lazy spasms, his moony eyes were wide and unblinking, and a thin cord of drool trickled from his mouth. The swelling on the side of his head where Nathaniel had struck him with the shovel had subsided, but the skin remained bruised and discolored like an overripe prune.

"*From the morgue I was towed...*" Ernie slurred disjointedly.

Nathaniel caught up with Oscar and grabbed his shoulder. "I told you to stay back."

Even Oscar was surprised by his own impulsiveness. He'd wanted to see if Daughter and Son Number One were still here, but of course that didn't excuse his recklessness. He lowered his gaze and muttered an apology.

Nathaniel approached Ernie, knife drawn, with Oscar looming close behind. He knelt beside Ernie's unresponsive body, the ground beneath his weight slick with blood.

"The blood's fresh," Nathaniel said. "Keep that machete ready."

"Heinrich?" Ernie sputtered. "Have you brought me gifts?"

"Snap out of it, you son of a bitch. What happened here?"

Ernie's eyes rolled sluggishly in their sockets. Nathaniel slapped his cheek, but there was no reaction. He slapped him again.

"They take the meat. You take the blubber," Ernie mumbled. A twitching smile spread on his face. "But ya'll will never take my children."

Nathaniel slapped him harder this time, jerking Ernie's head to the side. The movement revealed a deep cavity in the back of his skull. His head had been cracked open.

"What...?" Oscar whispered, peeking over Nathaniel's shoulder.

Nathaniel grabbed what few strands of hair Ernie had left and lifted his head for a better look. A heavy rivulet of blood and brain matter sloshed to the ground. Ernie's lazy spasms escalated into a full-blown seizure, and his mouth began to foam.

"Woah, okay," Oscar stammered. All the color drained from his face, his knees buckled, and the machete slipped from his grasp. Trying not to pass out, he shook his head and steeled his focus.

"So much for a safe passage." Nathaniel stood up, letting Ernie's head drop into the bloody dirt.

They left Ernie by the fire, circled the house, and arrived at the front door. Nathaniel cracked the door open, and something clattered overhead. They paused and glanced up: a chime made from hollowed bones hung above the doorframe. They stood still and listened. Nothing stirred inside.

They stepped into the one-room cabin. The walls and ceiling were draped with strange, larval-white cloths that hung in lumpy, ill-fitted layers, their texture waxy and semi-transparent. A bone chandelier hung from the ceiling, its lit candles illuminating a long table in the center of the room. The table had belt-strap restraints dangling from each corner, and its surface was stained maroon with dried blood.

On the back wall, knives, a pair of scissors, an ax, and a plastic bag with a hole chewed through it hung from hooks, the arsenal arranged like the devil's cutlery. Two weapons were missing—a hatchet and a hammer, judging by the faint imprints left on the wallpaper behind them.

The horror of the room struck Oscar with such force that

he felt breathless. But before the feeling could spiral, a familiar numbness cocooned him, like a protective membrane. He remembered this shield from the cemetery and Shantytown. To his surprise, he realized he had missed it. The void it pulled him into was cold and dark, but at least here nothing could hurt him.

"There's nothing here, Oscar," Nathaniel said, tense.

Nathaniel didn't seem to have a cocoon of his own to retreat into. Maybe, Oscar thought, he'd worn it out a long time ago.

A dresser stood to the left of the table with a small mirror mounted on the wall above it. Atop the dresser sat a pink satin box decorated with delicate rose gold etchings. Oscar picked up the box and opened it. A plastic ballerina figure rose slowly, then twirled in place as the music box played an off-key lullaby.

"Turn that off," Nathaniel said. He tried to sound stern, but his voice was breaking.

Oscar snapped the lid shut. The melody cut abruptly, and the ballerina folded back into her slumber.

"I'll wait outside," Nathaniel said, already halfway out the door, his face wan with nausea.

Oscar set the music box back on the dresser and surveyed the room. He noticed cobweb-like irregularities beneath the wallpaper's waxy texture—thin, tangled threads of black and blue. Some sections of the wallpaper even had fine, translucent hairs growing from them. He traced a finger along the wall, and the wallpaper *shivered* beneath his touch, its waxy texture now uneven with goosebumps.

A nightmarish realization crashed down on Oscar. His protective cocoon dissolved. The walls and ceiling were covered with human skin—strips of it sewn together and nailed into place.

"Oh, sweet Jesus." Oscar's hand shot to his mouth.

Right then, he saw something move in the mirror above the dresser; behind him, the padded skin wall was peeling open like a slowly widening wound. A figure slipped through the gap.

Before Oscar could react, the figure screamed and hurled something at him.

He dove behind the table just as the mirror shattered with a loud crash. A hammer clattered to the floor amid shards of glass. Oscar had only caught a glimpse of the attacker, but he already knew who it was.

He sprang up without a second thought, hands raised in surrender. "We're not here to hurt you!"

His instincts were right. It was Daughter. She stood there on the other side of the table in a defiant, alert pose. She was holding a hatchet, wads of hair hanging from the bloodied blade. Her eyes screamed fury, fear, and exhaustion, and violent shivers shook her body. She wore an oversized sleeveless shirt that hung halfway down to her thighs, revealing bruises on her arms and legs. Dark indentations and abrasions circled her neck and wrists, and a black eye bloomed above the teardrop-shaped scar. Her face, hair, and shirt were specked with red drops as if she'd strode through a mist of blood.

Despite everything, her physical injuries seemed mercifully minor. Oscar knew mental wounds could cut just as deep, though, and those she undoubtedly had plenty. Even so, he thought it fair to conclude that she was alright. He had found her, and she was alright.

Nathaniel burst through the door, his bruised face contorted with tension, his eyes wild and charged. Daughter screamed and retreated into the corner. She pointed the hatchet at them like a loaded gun, switching her aim between the two men.

"Wait. Nathaniel, stay back." Oscar threw his machete to the floor and turned back to Daughter. "We came to save you.

You're safe. We just want to help."

Daughter swung the hatchet as if swatting at invisible flies. "*Ni! Poshol na khuy! Trymaysya podali!*" she screamed, her voice shifting between rage and panic.

Nathaniel held up his knife in a non-threatening manner. "*Tovarishch. Tovarishch.*"

"*Tovaryshu?*" Daughter scoffed, her voice dripping with contempt. "*Ya ne rusnjá, suka khuylo.*"

Nathaniel spread his arms in a gesture of *I give up*. Apparently, that was the extent of his multilingual skills.

"Please... Just let us help you," Oscar pleaded, his voice cracking.

Daughter's bloodshot eyes measured him suspiciously.

"I'm Son Number Two," Oscar said, trying a gentler tone. "Remember? From the cemetery?"

"Son... Two?" she echoed.

"Yes, Son Two." Oscar could sense her struggling. She wanted to drop her guard, but she wasn't quite there yet.

"She can't recognize you, Oscar," Nathaniel said. "Remove the gauze."

Oscar unwrapped the gauze crossing through his face and removed the splint pressed against the bridge of his nose.

He looked into her eyes, and she looked into his. Oscar wasn't usually big on making eye contact, but with her, it felt different. It reminded him of the only other person whose eye contact had never felt intrusive to him—his sister's. He couldn't remember her eyes anymore, though.

"*Tse ty...*" Daughter whispered. Recognition flickered in her eyes, and her gaze sharpened, locking onto him in a new way. Her mouth twisted downward, and her chin began to tremble. The arm holding the hatchet slowly fell to her side.

"I'm sorry. I'm so sorry I abandoned you," Oscar pleaded. He took a cautious step forward, but she lifted the hatchet again, warning him to stop.

"Give her space," Nathaniel said, sheathing his knife. "Probably not a big hugger after whatever the fuck happened here."

Oscar stood back, fighting the urge to close the distance between them, to reach out and make sure she was real. Hell had rooted its claws deep enough inside him to make him doubtful if something felt right. And this moment did feel right, like a missing piece finally falling back into place.

In the end, he didn't have to go to her. She came to him.

And slapped him across the face.

"*Poshol na khuy! Yak ty mih zalyshyty nas?! Ty znayesh, cherez shcho my proyshly? Pizda!*" she yelled, punctuating each phrase with another slap.

Although the swings made Oscar's ears ring and his cheeks burn, he stood still and took it all in without protest. Strangely, he felt relieved by Daughter's violent response. She was on the same page with him about what had happened. They both agreed that he deserved to be punished for abandoning her. And maybe there was also a chance she'd eventually be willing to move on. After all, what is punishment if not a promise of forgiveness?

CHAPTER SEVENTEEN

Oscar, Nathaniel, and Daughter had moved outside, positioning themselves on the far side of the cabin, away from the sight of Ernie's convulsing corpse. The two men sat on the ground. Nathaniel was readjusting the splint and gauze on Oscar's face while Oscar kept a wary eye on Daughter, hoping she wouldn't run off. He knew it was unlikely, but still.

She had found a pile of clothes behind the cabin and was now dressed in a dark oversized T-shirt and a pair of stone-washed jeans. Leaning over a water barrel by the cabin wall, she rinsed the specks of blood from her face. A backpack she'd retrieved from inside the cabin's skin wall rested close at her feet. Everywhere she moved, she kept the backpack within arm's reach, ready to bolt at any given moment.

When she'd finished cleaning up, she settled on the porch, twiddling at the strap of her backpack. Her calculating gaze was fixed on the two men, her face half-hidden behind her tucked knees.

After Nathaniel had finished patching him up, Oscar got up and approached her cautiously.

"What's your name?" he asked.

"Name?" Daughter's intonation carried a strong Slavic accent. "Daria."

"Daria," Oscar repeated. A small smile spread across his face. "Daria. I'm Oscar. He's Nathaniel."

"How do you do?" Nathaniel muttered.

Oscar sat on the porch steps, keeping a respectful distance from her. "What happened here? What happened to Ernie and the kids?"

"I kill Ernie. Now, kids free," Daria said firmly. Her eyes sharpened, as though assessing Oscar's reaction to her confession.

But Oscar didn't really react to it; he was more surprised at how neatly the pieces fell into place. It was Daria who'd bashed Ernie's head in. She must have let the children out of the cages who had then taken off and crossed paths with Heinrich and his prisoners at the clearing. Oscar guessed Daria had been getting ready to leave when he and Nathaniel had arrived here. She must have heard them approaching and hidden inside the wall.

Oscar turned to Nathaniel, eyes wide with realization. "She saved us."

"So it seems." Nathaniel's gaze now held the same calculating sharpness as hers. "Daria, did Ernie mention anything about a safe passage? A trail? No man's land? Any of those sound familiar?"

Daria shrugged and shook her head, looking lost. Even if she'd heard Ernie mention the safe passage, Oscar doubted she understood anything Nathaniel had just said.

Nathaniel cursed under his breath.

"I need help Yung," Daria said.

Now it was Oscar and Nathaniel who were looking lost.

She twirled her hands as if trying to summon the right words. "Son One, okay? Son One is Yung. Ernie sell Yung. They go—" she waved toward the mountains. "We help Yung, okay?"

So Ernie has already sold Son Number One—Yung—to this "client" of his, Oscar thought. But why hadn't he sold Daria? Maybe he'd taken a shine on her and kept her for himself?

"Here's the thing, Daria." Nathaniel cleared his throat. "These lands are full of dangerous people, and we can't stay here much longer. Me and Oscar here are heading east. Over the mountains. You're welcome to join us. We can look out for each other until we get someplace safe. I can't guarantee we'll find Yung along the way, though. It's a tough call, but it's one you'll have to make right now. What do you say?"

"*Ya nichoho ne zrozumiv, shcho ty skazav,*" Daria said, shaking her head.

"Uh-huh," Nathaniel nodded. "Oscar, she's your responsibility now. Translate what I just said."

The next fifteen minutes passed with Oscar painstakingly explaining their situation and her possible involvement in it while Nathaniel rummaged through the yard and cabin for supplies. Daria listened carefully, repeating a few words in English here and there, then trying to translate them in her own language. She nodded encouragingly whenever Oscar stumbled through a phrase, urging him on.

The exchange was clumsy with both sides tripping over language barriers and piecing together the shared information bit by bit. Still, Oscar cherished the moment. Their time at the cemetery had been brief and wordless, yet he felt like he was catching up with an old friend. Whatever horrors Ernie, Heinrich, and Hell itself had inflicted upon her had changed her, but beneath the high-strung and exhausted demeanor, the person who had shown Oscar the power of compassion and simple decency was still there.

Eventually, the message got through, but still she remained hesitant.

"You don't trust us?" Oscar said, half-asking, half-stating.

Before she could reply, a shriek tore through the forest—a shrill, ugly sound seasoned with hate and primal bloodthirst. Oscar and Daria sprang to their feet. Nathaniel appeared from behind the house, a wild look in his eyes, knife already in hand.

"What was that?" Oscar asked.

"We have to go," Nathaniel said. "Right now."

Oscar swung the duffel bag over his shoulder and pulled out the machete. "Come on, Daria. Let's go."

Daria hesitated a second, then made up her mind. "*Suka blyat,*" she spat through gritted teeth. She grabbed her backpack and ran after her new companions.

They followed the creek bordering Ernie's yard upstream. They hurried along the embankment, moving east and up the base of the mountain. A shallow trickle of water wound its way between the stones at the bottom of the creek. The first light of dawn filtered through the sparse treetops, casting a bronzed glimmer on the water.

There had been no follow-up to the visceral scream, and after fifteen minutes of hasty trekking up the creek, Oscar summoned the courage to open his mouth.

"That scream... It was the cannibals, wasn't it?"

"*Kanibaly?*" Daria cut in, her eyes wide.

Oscar and Nathaniel both nodded. She scoffed and ran her fingers through her hair, trembling all over.

"It sounded like some sort of battle cry," Nathaniel said. "I don't think it was meant for us. We'd know by now if it was."

"So... we're not on the safe passage anymore," Oscar said. "Nor were we at Ernie's."

"I reckon you're right," Nathaniel nodded.

Oscar's insides churned; he'd hoped he was wrong. "How could Ernie stay here if it's not safe?"

"Remember those ornaments hanging from the trees?" Nathaniel said. "I don't think they're meant for just deterring outsiders. They're symbols of immunity. One of the cannibal tribes must be Ernie and Heinrich's client. They let Ernie stay on their grounds in exchange for something—meat, probably."

Oscar repeated the words in his mind: *Their client is one of the cannibal tribes.* Now that Nathaniel had said it, the answer felt so obvious.

"So Ernie and Heinrich fed a whole tribe?" Oscar asked. "How big are these groups?"

"Someone told me the tribes have close to fifty members each. Considering the land they have to patrol, that estimate seems kind of low. So no, I don't think they fed a whole tribe. Maybe they just served a small group—a nearby outpost, perhaps."

"Huh." Oscar said. He turned to Daria. "Did you see Yung's buyers?"

She looked at him blankly, waiting for clarification.

"Ernie sell Yung… to who?" Oscar asked, hoping his broken English wouldn't sound patronizing.

"No see. They hide," she replied.

They hide, he thought, a shudder running through him. "Great. Like all this wasn't creepy enough already."

The creek led them to a plunge pool at the base of a rocky cliff. A weak trickle of water fell from a cave halfway up the rock wall, forming a modest puddle at the bottom. It looked like the remnant of an old waterfall. Oscar recalled Nathaniel's lecture on the subterranean sewer systems back in the desert, back when they'd discovered the spring. Applying that information here, he figured the underground tides surged out of the cave above in irregular intervals, leaving the plunge pool dry most of the time.

They drank from the shallow pool, filled their canteens, and found a spot where they could scramble to the top of the cliff.

They zigzagged from one boulder to the next and soon reached a rocky crest that jutted from the mountain base like a terrace alongside some grand gothic castle. The mountain towered above, black and judgmental, disappearing into the sandy clouds like a ghost ship drifting into mist. The forest stretched partway up the mountainside before thinning into a barren, obsidian stone expanse.

Nathaniel slumped to the ground to catch his breath. He slipped his hand under his shirt and tugged the shoelace suture tighter, sucking air through his teeth.

"Safe?" Daria asked, eyeing Nathaniel's lounging pose skeptically. "Is safe?"

Nathaniel made a *so-so* hand gesture. Daria shook her head, unsatisfied, but also sat down.

"Why are they doing this?" Oscar asked. "Hunting people, eating them. I mean, it can't be for sustenance, right? We can't starve or feel hunger."

"Maybe it's some kind of a ritual. People here have some fucked up beliefs," Nathaniel replied. He paused, considering something. "Remember when we discussed how the dead can't die?"

"How could I forget?" Oscar scoffed.

"Let's say you devour someone. The victim feels all of it—during and after. Their consciousness remains. I can't even begin to imagine what kind of existence that might be, but that's how it is."

Oscar thought about Ernie and Heinrich. What was the state of their consciousness now—one stabbed hundreds of times, the other with his brains splattered on the ground? Their wounds and pains would be their burden for the rest of eternity. Their fates felt incomprehensible, let alone the fate of someone who'd been cannibalized.

"One could argue that once you devour someone," Nathaniel went on, "their consciousness becomes a part of you. Knowing what we know about never-ending consciousness, I can understand the logic of that argument. And I can imagine especially these warrior-types getting off on it."

"So they think they can gain their opponent's power or something," Oscar said. He felt absorbed by the theory on an intellectual level, though he realized he should probably be appalled and afraid; after all, this hypothesis could become his reality at any moment.

"Or something," Nathaniel said. "But here's what I don't get: the cannibals had the grave looters traffic newborns all the way from the cemetery. Why? If you're looking to absorb someone's power, wouldn't it make more sense to choose someone actually... powerful? Someone who's survived here?"

"In the cemetery, Heinrich mentioned something about the client liking them 'fresh,'" Oscar countered. "Maybe newborns are somehow purer. They've been dead for a shorter time, so they might have more, I don't know, vigor? Maybe that's what the mountain folk are after instead of strength."

"Huh. Could be." Nathaniel scratched his chin.

"I guess Heinrich developed a taste for human flesh, too," Oscar said.

"How so?"

"I mean, there were cooking appliances in his yard."

"I saw them, too," Nathaniel said. "He didn't use them for cooking."

"What, then?" Oscar asked. "Or... do I even want to know?"

"You don't."

"Okay." A pause. "Except now I sort of do."

Nathaniel sighed. "He used them to render fat." He looked at Oscar, waiting for a reaction, but all he got was a confused stare. "Where do you think we get the oil for our fires?"

Oscar furrowed his brow and shrugged. "I hadn't really thought about it."

"Heinrich abducted people, skimmed their fat, and rendered it to produce oil that could be used as fuel," Nathaniel said. "Not many people are willing to take on that kind of task. Most people probably don't even know where the oil comes from. Or maybe they know but refuse to acknowledge it. And then there are people who have no problem manufacturing and selling it. People like Heinrich. They make sure that the oil business in Hell is thriving."

Oscar stared at Nathaniel's lantern in horrified disbelief. He could feel the oil pouches sloshing sickeningly in his duffel bag. The realization settled in, evoking nausea and dizziness. He dropped his head between his knees. *The fires of Hell burn on human-based oil.*

"There's not much else you can do but not think about it," Nathaniel concluded grimly.

During their conversation, Daria had taken her hatchet out of her backpack. She'd rinsed it clean of blood and tied a lock of hair around the handle—hair which Oscar recognized as Ernie's. She tinkered with the hair absent-mindedly, an unfocused, thousand-yard stare in her eyes.

The two men looked at the wad of hair coiled around her finger. Oscar turned to Nathaniel and saw a disturbed expression on his face, very much mirroring his own reaction.

"Right," Nathaniel said. "We might want to start being more careful around her."

"What do you mean?" Oscar stammered defensively.

"Think about it," Nathaniel said. He leaned closer and lowered his voice. "She was captured by two grave looters who had successfully enslaved, sold, and tortured people for who knows how long. She managed to outsmart, defeat, and escape Ernie with barely a scratch on her. We don't really know what kind of person she is, do we? We have to be careful."

Oscar scoffed, shaking his head. "Ernie got sloppy. It was only a matter of time before he got what was coming to him. Ditto for Heinrich."

"Sure, they were sloppy," Nathaniel agreed, "but look how long they got away with it. Now, I might be wrong about her, but maybe not. I'll be keeping a close eye on her, and I expect you to do the same. Keep it in your pants and tread lightly."

"'Keep it in your pants and tread lightly,'" Oscar echoed, eyebrows raised. "Wow. This is turning into a very strange father-son talk."

"If you're looking for a father figure, you're talking to the wrong guy," Nathaniel said dryly.

"I know." Oscar's mouth curled into a small smile—a smile he himself didn't quite understand. "I'll be careful."

Oscar joined Daria at the edge of the crest, watching the dawn light spill across the landscape. Below, the treetops formed a dense, black tussock, and beyond them stretched the desert, desolate and still like the ocean floor. Further in the distance, the clouds still wore their night cloak, and there, Shantytown's tangerine glow burned a lone hole through the darkness.

"So," Oscar began, hoping to steer the conversation away from Daria's mental state, "we have oil manufacturing, a black market, cults, human trafficking. But no communities, no real societies or civilizations. No, like, infrastructure. You'd think someone would have built something here by now—something more organized than Shantytown, I mean. But instead, there's nothing. Just… desolation."

"The feral children I told you about are a community. So are the cannibal tribes," Nathaniel countered. "But they won't last. Even if they manage to stay out of harm's way, which is highly unlikely, apathy and depression will eventually take over, destroying whatever camaraderie they mustered. Sure, small communities are easy to uphold for a time, especially if they have a common cause. But societies, civilizations, infrastructures… Do you know what something that complex requires in order to work?"

"I don't know. Rules? Laws?" Oscar guessed.

"Exactly. But how do you get people to follow those same rules, to submit to laws? Well, the first emperors and kings told people that God—or gods—spoke through them. 'Follow these rules, submit to these laws, and you will walk a righteous path which will lead you to fortune in life and—'"

"And in death," Oscar finished. "I see. I think I know where this is going."

"Societies, civilizations—the entire success of our species in fact—was largely built on stories, especially stories about the afterlife. What's more universal, more unifying, than the fear of death, right? But in Hell, those kinds of beliefs don't take root—not on a scale large enough to make a difference, anyway. So what's left? Apathetic, cynical, hopeless anarchy." Nathaniel nodded at the bleak landscape below them. "Desolation."

Oscar crossed his arms, mulling it over. "I read somewhere that human inventions have developed so fast that our species hasn't been able to keep up. Like, our DNA still assumes we're living in hunter-gatherer times. So, genetically speaking, we're not wired for something as complex as society." He paused, reflecting on his own words. "In a way, Hell seems more fitting to a hunter-gatherer than to someone from the modern world, doesn't it? So maybe we're actually better suited to this place than to the living world."

How do I know that? Oscar wondered. His last real memories were from his teenage years, which had been occupied by budding alcoholism, self-harm, and skipping classes. Then again, despite being a poor student, he'd always been an avid reader.

"Interesting," Nathaniel said, his brow raised in surprise. "Maybe that's also why people submit to Hell instead of trying to recreate the systems they had before. We are home, so to speak."

Oscar imagined an ancient creature, deep within the cave of his subconscious, waking from hibernation. It sniffed at the stench of violence drifting from the surface and crept toward it, ready to take control. He shuddered at the image.

Oscar and Nathaniel turned silent, and the group continued gazing over the barren view. None of them noticed the five strangers skulking under the nearby tree line. They studied their prey from the shadows, taking in every detail, then slipped back into the forest soundlessly, their smiles wide, joyless, and unchanging.

CHAPTER EIGHTEEN

The group climbed through the thinning woods at the base of the mountain and soon arrived at a rise where their way forward shot up into a near-vertical wall. They stopped and studied the setting. A few trees clung to the stone wall, their roots twisting in and out of its cracks. Further up, a narrow platform ran laterally along the cliff—a steady stretch of ground winding along the side of the wall.

"We need to get up there," Nathaniel said, his eyes fixed on the platform. "We can use the visibility to our advantage and probably walk along it for a while. It's safer up there." He unlatched the coil of rope from his satchel. "But I don't think I can climb this without some help. Think you could get up there and secure this rope?"

Oscar eyed the wall, sizing up the climb. "Uhh…"

"I go," Daria interjected. She took the rope from Nathaniel and looped it over her shoulder. She measured her options, picked a sturdy-looking tree, and climbed it up until she reached a branch thick enough to hold her weight. Using the branch for leverage, she sprang to a ledge on the rock wall. Feeling out the roots and cracks for footing and handle, she shimmied her way up with what looked like little to no effort.

"Careful!" Oscar hollered.

Daria reached the top, pulled herself over the edge, and vanished from sight. Nathaniel's silence suggested he worried she might abandon them, but Oscar wasn't concerned. He had already decided to trust her. His experience with Nathaniel had taught him that trust was a choice and doubt was nothing but indecisiveness. Besides, he had a gut feeling about her.

After a moment, Daria peeked over the edge and tossed down the rope. Nathaniel tested its strength, then gestured for Oscar to go first. Oscar climbed without much hassle and soon reached the top. He crawled onto solid ground as Daria held the rope steady.

"Thank you," he said.

She responded with a finger gun and a click of the tongue. Oscar thought she was the only person, alive or dead, who could make such a goofy gesture look cool.

Nathaniel followed after, mumbling a breathless thanks to Daria before readjusting the shoelace beneath his shirt.

The platform stretched along the mountain face, a narrow trail etched into the obsidian rock. The forest was now behind them, no longer disrupting the view of the surroundings. The mountainside curved over them like a stone canopy, and far below lay a mountain pass—a stretch of thick, nigh-impenetrable forest separating this mountain from the next.

Oscar didn't normally suffer from vertigo, but staring down at the steep drop into the mountain pass and realizing how unprepared they were for this kind of climb made his insides twist into a knot. He tried to calm himself with the notion that Nathaniel wouldn't have led them here if it was too dangerous. He repeated this in his mind until he believed it to be true.

He checked on Daria following close behind him. The look in her eyes said, *Are we seriously going to do this?* Oscar nodded and forced a smile, hoping it would come across as reassuring. Her expression stayed the same, not looking reassured one bit.

The trail led northward along the mountainside, and the group followed. Ideally, it would bring them all the way to the other side, but they had no such luck; after a while, the trail sloped uphill and faded into a rugged, complex terrain where tall and taller boulders jutted out from the bedrock. The deeper they drifted into this cabinet of stone, the poorer the visibility grew. Mist, as if straying from the clouds, wandered down the slopes like a lost specter, blurring all sense of distance and space. Oscar tasted ash and copper in the air. Their combined tang made his gums tingle.

"Do you know where we're going?" he asked.

"Yes," Nathaniel said after a beat.

That was a long pause, Oscar thought.

The poor visibility and thickening mist stirred a nagging feeling of being followed. At first, it was just an itch in the back of Oscar's mind, but soon he could practically envision legions of blood-starved predators circling them, drooling and snarling, preparing to tear them to shreds. He pictured the cannibals stalking their every move, studying their patterns, searching out weaknesses—a psychotic foreplay before massacring them on these isolated hills. They probably weren't called the "mountain folk" for nothing, so they likely knew these lands like the backs of their hands. They would find their prey if they wanted to—Oscar was sure of it.

Being at the mercy of something he had never seen felt frustrating and unfair. Oscar almost wished they would find some evidence of the mountain folk's presence up here—at least then his terror would feel more grounded, more justified. He tried to pry more information about the cannibals from Nathaniel, but Nathaniel couldn't provide much. He only knew that the title "mountain folk" stemmed from their worship of the mountains, which either meant they never set foot on their holy ground or that they occupied it constantly. This notion offered no comfort or practical value.

Soon, the mental and physical strain caught up with Oscar, and exhaustion took over. His feet pumped acid through his veins, and his stomach flared with cramps that spread feverish chills all over his body. The adrenaline that had carried him ever since Heinrich's cabin had shoved his chronic aches into the background, but now his body's complaints could no longer be ignored.

A thought occurred to him: maybe Hell's denizens were so prone to psychotic outbursts and violent altercations because adrenaline was the only available anesthetic—and intoxicant—here. The dead needed distractions from their broken bodies and minds, so they surrendered themselves to the whims of adrenaline.

"How about a break?" he suggested.

"Sure," Nathaniel said. "We're secluded enough, I think."

Oscar glanced at Daria. "Rest. Sleep. Okay?"

Daria nodded slowly, a trace of suspicion in her eyes.

They spotted a dried-up creek, followed it uphill, and discovered a small cave at the end. Nathaniel illuminated the dark hollow with the lantern, and the group peered inside. The cave stretched deeper into the mountain but was blocked by murky floodwater. At the far end where the tunnel sloped downward, the water gleamed faintly, as if squinting back at the lantern like a one-eyed spider. Oscar figured the tunnel, just like the waterfall at the base of the mountain, must connect to Hell's subterranean water network.

"As far as holes in the ground go, I've seen worse," Nathaniel commented.

They settled in, and Nathaniel offered to keep watch while Oscar and Daria rested. Daria, though, seemed too wired to sleep. She isolated herself in the farthest corner of the cave, hatchet in hand, hugging her knees, her eyes sharp and watchful. She looked like an alert animal studying another, unsure whether it would bite or not.

Oscar remembered behaving the same way with Nathaniel at the start of their journey. He felt sorry for her and wished for some magic combination of words that might ease her distrust. But no such spell existed, and he figured the best way to win her trust was simply by doing nothing at all.

And so, exhausted and crashing from adrenaline, Oscar closed his eyes and let sleep take over.

Oscar awoke to a bubbling sound. He blinked the sleep from his eyes and saw air bubbles surface in the water at the back of the cave, like black eyeballs rising from the depths, each one bursting open to make way for the next.

"There's something in the water," he said, then realized that no words had come out. Had his lips even moved? He tried to sit up, but his muscles refused to respond.

The memory of the cackling nightmare creature rushed back to him, and he realized that what had happened at the abandoned cabin in the desert was about to happen again.

As if summoned by Oscar's fear, an oversized, bald head crowned from the bubbling pool, followed by a pair of round, unblinking eyes. The bubbles stilled as the creature's nose surfaced, sniffling and snorting water with strings of snot dangling from its nostrils.

As its mouth rose above the water, the creature began cackling that hideous rattle in a nonstop loop.

"Ke ke ke."

A smile stretched from one stub of an ear to the other, lined with hundreds of tiny teeth that clattered like keys on a typewriter.

The creature crawled out of the water, moving its small, bulky body with surprising slyness and grace. It advanced toward Oscar, cackling, cackling, cackling forever, and rolled him on his back. The change in position allowed Oscar a view of his companions. Daria hunkered in the corner, her head resting on her tucked knees, eyes closed. Nathaniel sat by the entrance, looking out.

Only now did Oscar notice the dead flowers. Their silvery heads poked from a crack above the cave's entrance, right above Nathaniel. What was it that Nathaniel had called them? Mold poppies? Oscar remembered seeing the same flowers for the first time back in the abandoned cabin. Or was that the first time? He wasn't sure.

The creature climbed on Oscar's chest, and he felt his ribcage creak under its weight. He tried to scream but managed only a sad, wheezy whimper. But it was enough to gain Nathaniel's attention. He turned to Oscar. His puzzled yet subdued expression made it clear that he couldn't see the creature. Apparently, only Oscar could.

The creature grabbed Oscar by the hair, twisting his head to face its leering smile. But instead of the creature, Oscar now saw another familiar figure: the man with the woman's mask. The drooping bag of skin and hair hovered above him like a pillowcase on a drying rack, its slack mouth trickling spit, its pearly skin webbed with blue veins. The mask's long black hair fell over Oscar's face like the legs of dead spiders, trailing thin streaks of blood across his cheeks. Through the mask's holes—the mouth, the eyes, the nostrils—Oscar saw only darkness but felt a gaze drilling deep into his bones.

"Oscar," a voice called out, distant and muffled. Then,

clearer and closer: "Oscar!"

Oscar jolted awake, screaming. The first thing he saw was Nathaniel kneeling next to him, a firm grip on his shoulder, a worried frown on his face. Oscar sat up and backed away, pressing himself against the wall. Daria stared at him from her corner, and Oscar felt a sting of embarrassment. He didn't want her to see him like this. But her eyes held no ridicule or discomfort—only a sad, quiet understanding. The look told him that she, too, often woke up screaming. His breathing slowed, his shivers subsided.

"Do you know where you are?" Nathaniel asked.

"I... I think so."

"Tell me."

Oscar let out a long breath, feeling the edges of his anxiety soften. "We climbed the mountain and found this cave."

"Good. That's good." Nathaniel patted his shoulder. "What were you dreaming about?"

"I can't remember."

They left the cave and descended to an altitude where the visibility was clearer, less obscured by the fog. They continued along the mountainside. Rugged slopes led to dizzying cliffs, and the dizzying cliffs led to more rugged slopes.

With Nathaniel in the lead, they opted for longer, more arduous routes over risky shortcuts. They steered clear of slopes scattered with loose rocks where a single misstep could result in getting shredded by a landslide. They turned back from trails that tapered a little too thin and a little too close to the edge. Their overcautiousness was well founded: in addition to lacking proper equipment for the climb, their dead bodies were also prone to sudden convulsions, which could prove fateful while trekking the mountainside.

They traveled in short intervals, resting frequently to save their strength in case they were attacked. Most of their time on the mountain was spent outdoors, but whenever they spotted a nearby cave, they'd duck inside for a break. They learned that each cave led to a water-filled tunnel. Speculating that the tunnels must overflow sporadically, they made sure not to get too comfortable in case they had to escape a sudden flood.

During their downtime, Oscar and Nathaniel (mostly Oscar) got better acquainted with Daria. It often took a few tries to get her attention before she'd snap out of her disconnected daze. Her hollow smile would turn into a warm one, and Oscar would always return the gesture, even when smiling was the furthest thing from his mind. It was hard not to; she had a casual charm about her that Oscar often found himself mimicking. She was an easy person to look up to.

They befriended through broken sentences and clumsy gestures. At first, Oscar felt awkward when their attempts at communication fell short, but he was motivated to get to know her, and she seemed to share his sentiment. Gradually, they adjusted to the misunderstandings, the long silences, and the frustrated pantomimes. The relief when something finally broke through the language barrier felt like a reward worth pursuing. Once they got used to this mode of interaction, nothing felt awkward anymore—they even found it amusing. It was a strange way to bond, connecting over the inability to connect, but somehow, that was what happened.

Sometimes Nathaniel would chime in, especially if the conversation touched on practical matters of survival. Mostly, however, he stayed on the sidelines, observing their exchanges, occasionally chuckling at their absurd gesturing. Other times, he'd simply ignore them, isolate to the sidelines, and brood over whatever men like him brooded about.

Oscar learned that Daria, like him, had spotty amnesia. Trying to translate her fragmented recollections into a language she barely knew seemed to agitate her, so they didn't delve deeply into her past. He did find out that she was from Ukraine where she had grown up in a small town, the name of which Oscar could only mumble and hope it sounded right. She'd left home at sixteen and scraped by on her own for the next nine years, moving from one battle to the next. At the age of twenty-five, the world finally got the better of her. As with Oscar, Nathaniel, and everyone else in Hell, the details of her death were a confusing, chaotic blur; it was a topic not worth prodding and one the dead instinctively avoided.

Despite their budding connection, Daria always kept her hatchet close and would tense up whenever Oscar came within a few feet of her. She probably had plenty of valid reasons to act like this, but Oscar also reminded himself not to see her only as a victim—bashing Ernie's head in had been self-defense, sure, but collecting a trophy for the effort… that was something else. She had a darkness to her. But then, who didn't?

CHAPTER NINETEEN

The group had spent the entire night observing the valley from a vantage point along the mountainside. Save for a single loud bang echoing in the dark ("Must have been a landslide," Nathaniel had speculated), they hadn't witnessed any activity in the valley. There were no tortured screams of cannibalized victims, no blood-crazed shrieks of the mountain folk, not even a distant flicker of firelight to suggest anything dwelt here. So far, the infamous cannibal valley was nothing but a quiet, isolated stretch of land.

"What are the chances the person who sold you the map was just bullshitting you?" Oscar had asked at one point.

"Moderate," Nathaniel had admitted. "But it's considered common knowledge that this place belongs to the mountain folk."

"Some would consider superstitions 'common knowledge.' That doesn't make them any more real. I mean, we should have at least seen some lights by now, right?"

"Maybe they hunt in the dark. Maybe they only build fires in places where they can't be spotted from afar. They've had time to figure this shit out, Oscar."

Oscar had resumed staring at the great lake of darkness below, frustrated by the unknowing.

Now, the morning clouds cast a muted light over the valley as they prepared to descend the mountainside. Mountains surrounded this hidden land like barriers around a derelict fortress, and rivers slid down their black cliffs and converged in the valley like snakes gathering in a nest. Mist rose from the swamplands and spun a silken web over the fields and forests, lending a ghostly sheen to the quiet terrain.

Now that they could finally see the valley in its entirety, Oscar explained the situation to Daria as best he could: the valley was still cannibal territory, but once they made it past the mountain range on the other side, they'd be safe.

"How find Yung?" she asked.

"I don't know," he admitted. "The most important thing for us is to get to safety. But we'll only be safe after we reach—"

"After mountains," she nodded, waving him quiet: *I got it, I got it.*

She resumed staring at the valley, a frown on her face, biting her nails. Oscar could barely imagine the three of them making it to the other side in one piece, let alone finding Yung unharmed on the way there. But more importantly, could Daria imagine it? And would she be willing to let go of such hopes? Seeing the size of the valley ought to have lowered her expectations. It sure had lowered his.

"It's a big place, though," he added, hoping she'd get the message.

"Big," she agreed.

Oscar turned to Nathaniel. "Did I miss anything?"

"I don't think so," Nathaniel said. "We'll talk more strategy along the way. There's still so much we don't know. Those bastards hide themselves well."

"And once we're past those mountains, what then?" Oscar asked. "Regarding Dean Theodore, I mean."

At the mention of Dean Theodore, Daria's worried frown turned into a curious one.

Nathaniel shot Oscar a chilling look. "Do not mention that name around other people."

"Other people?" Oscar scoffed. "It's just Daria, and she's with us. Besides, she barely understands a word we're saying. You're being paranoid."

"Being paranoid is what has gotten me this far," Nathaniel shot back.

This far? To a valley full of cannibals? Oscar thought. He wasn't sure what frustrated him more: Nathaniel's discriminatory behavior toward Daria or the fact that discussing the goal of their journey had suddenly become taboo.

But instead of prodding the topic further or picking a fight, Oscar muttered, "Congratulations," and swung the duffel bag over his shoulder, getting ready to leave their vantage point.

So began the trio's descent into the valley.

The mountain face sloped down smoothly, and the group climbed down its bare bedrock hills with ease. The mountain base gave way to a rocky hillside riddled with pits, ditches, and trenches. Visibility was poor, and the terrain offered countless hiding places—for both travelers and those hunting them.

Perfect for an ambush, Oscar thought, shuddering.

They crept through the trenches and entered a pit where the path widened, intersecting with several other pathways.

Here they stumbled upon two strangers.

A man, dead in his thirties, and a woman, dead in her fifties, rested in the shade of the stone walls. The woman lay on the gravel, a crudely sutured stab wound glaring on her exposed belly like an infected eye, still bleeding. The man slumped beside her, a bloodstained scarf wrapped around his head like a turban.

The woman was the first to react. "Gustavo," she gasped.

The man lifted his head and spotted the trio. "*¡Puta madre!*"

He staggered to his feet, pointing a rusty shiv at them. His movements were both hyper-alert and exhausted. Every fiber of his being seemed ready to give up save for that stubborn instinct that forced him to keep fighting. Running into strangers seemed to be the last straw in a long series of unfortunate events.

Nathaniel raised his knife and held up his free hand to show he meant no harm—a mixed message if ever there was one. Daria lifted her hatchet and took a defensive stance. Following the lead of his companions, Oscar unsheathed his machete but wasn't exactly sure what he was supposed to do. He certainly wasn't about to attack injured people.

Please, don't try anything, he thought, hoping the request would mentally transmit to the strangers.

Nathaniel and Daria, however, projected a more menacing demeanor, one that expressed a willingness to attack. Watching them act this way made Oscar's skin crawl. Perhaps choosing an odd time to do so, he wondered just what kind of people he'd fallen in with.

Hypocrite, Heinrich's voice echoed in his head, and an image of his maimed carcass flashed before his eyes.

"Do you speak English?" Nathaniel asked.

The two strangers looked at each other, as if exchanging a wordless conversation. The man turned to Nathaniel. "I can do the talking," he said, tense.

"Good," Nathaniel said. "Then let's sit down and talk. We're not here to harm you."

"Never heard that one before," the man said dryly.

"Look, we have the upper hand. If we wanted to hurt you, we would have done so already." Nathaniel lowered his blade. "We just need to know how long it's been since you ran into the mountain folk."

"How did you—"

"Please." Nathaniel raised a hand to cut him off. "You're deep in their hunting grounds, and you look like you've recently been through all kinds of shit. We need to know if we're talking to a marked target. This is for our safety, too."

The man sighed, his defenses loosening. "It happened last night. If they were still after us, they would've found us by now."

"Okay, good," Nathaniel said, nodding. "How about you tell us your story? We're heading into whatever storm you just escaped, so your experiences might prove valuable for us. We'll pay you. We have water and fuel, and we can exchange information."

The two strangers shared another glance; she shrugged, he nodded. The man sat down, and Oscar and Nathaniel followed suit. Daria remained standing but lowered her hatchet. This was all the diplomacy she was willing to extend.

Nathaniel introduced their group: "Nathaniel, Oscar, Daria."

The man nodded his greetings. "I'm Gustavo. This is Yvonne."

Yvonne motioned for Gustavo to lean closer and whispered something in French, her voice parched and frail. Gustavo nodded. A floral-patterned tote bag slumped on the ground, holding whatever few items the couple had left. Gustavo pulled an empty canteen from it and gave it to Nathaniel.

"Fill it with water. We also want a pouch of fuel."

Nathaniel began pouring water from his canteen, but Gustavo motioned for him to stop. "First, you drink."

Nathaniel took a sip, then resumed filling the canteen. He passed it to Gustavo, who helped Yvonne take a drink. Oscar produced an oil pouch from the duffel bag and handed it to the pair.

"Just start from the beginning," Nathaniel said.

Gustavo took a moment to gather his thoughts, then began telling their story.

CHAPTER TWENTY

Gustavo and Yvonne had heard of the cannibals long before they'd set foot in this place. They knew the horror stories about the countless travelers gone missing in the mountains, the skin-and-bone talismans found strung up in trees, and the vagabonds who'd stumbled upon abandoned campsites littered with gnawed human remains. They also knew the mountain folk had once reigned over these lands as a single group but had since divided into two factions following some kind of schism.

But what really intrigued them was the rumored safe passage said to have opened after the tribes brokered a truce. Gustavo and Yvonne had business west of the mountain range, and cutting through the passage would save them months of travel. Naturally, this was something they wanted to investigate.

They asked around the villages east of the mountains for directions, but most people offered only warnings and folklore.

Eventually, though, their persistence paid off: they learned of a man who knew the route and offered guided trips through the mountains in exchange for a payment.

After weighing their options and assessing the guide's legitimacy, they concluded he was their best chance to reach the other side. They gathered items—oil, scrap metal, drugs, and so on—as payment and prepared as thoroughly as possible for a journey that would place their survival in the hands of a stranger. They were careful. They were cautious. But, of course, none of it mattered in the end.

They traveled to a town near the eastern mountains where the guide was said to reside. It was like any other town in Hell that had been built by nomads who'd grown sick of wandering the desert. The couple's brief stint there was tranquil and quiet. This wasn't so much a reflection of the town's character as it was just good timing on Gustavo and Yvonne's part: anyone who'd spent time in Hell's isolated towns knew these communes always teetered on a razor's edge. They were just one altercation, one violent visitor, one psychotic meltdown away from being reduced to a pile of rubble.

They asked around town and got a local man to take them to the guide's tent in exchange for filling his lantern's oil chamber. The local said they were lucky; the guide had returned to town only a few nights ago and was on the market for new customers.

They met with the guide, who introduced himself as Nobu. He was a pleasant man with a bulky build. Well-mannered. Easygoing. His left arm was missing from the bicep down; he later explained he kept it hidden somewhere out of harm's reach.

One thing about Nobu unsettled them, though: he spoke and acted as if there were someone else in the tent with them—someone named Fumi-chan. He communicated with Fumi-chan in Japanese.

Once Nobu noticed Gustavo and Yvonne's unease, he addressed the issue right away: "Do not worry about Fumi-chan. I know she is not real, but I like having her around. She comforts my homesickness. By chance, do either of you speak Japanese?"

As it happened, Yvonne did. She had spent her first years in Hell surviving alongside a Japanese companion. She wasn't going to reveal their only trump card, though.

"No," she said. "We both speak Spanish, French, and English."

"Well, I speak English, Japanese, and a little bit of bullshit," Nobu said with a wink. "Maybe it is best we stick to English."

"And Fumi-chan?" Gustavo asked.

Nobu studied him for a moment, then burst into a deep, sincere laugh that rose from the pit of his stomach. "Fumi-chan is the only one who can tolerate my bullshit."

"The four of us make a good team, then," Gustavo replied.

The group laughed some more at that, and whatever unease Gustavo and Yvonne had felt about Nobu and his imaginary friend lifted right then and there. For a moment, it seemed this trip might not only be convenient but also an enjoyable one.

Nobu took half of his fee upfront and told Gustavo and Yvonne to meet him at his tent at dawn. They didn't worry too much about the request; if Nobu were planning to betray them and run off with the loot, it was better he do it now than in the mountain folk territory. In hindsight, Gustavo thought a part of him had almost hoped Nobu *would* run off; this would force them to find another route west, and they wouldn't have to worry about the cannibals. Despite all their preparations, the gathering of information, background checks, and cross-examinations, the upcoming journey still made Gustavo nervous. It made them both nervous. *Then again,* Gustavo remembered telling himself at the time, *so does everything else in Hell.*

When they returned to Nobu's tent at dawn, he was already outside, finishing up packing his backpack.

"*Ohayo gozaimasu!*" Nobu greeted them cheerfully. His good spirits seemed slightly forced, but they still appreciated the effort.

"Good morning," Yvonne said. "Ready to go?"

"Ready, madame," he grinned. "*Ikimashou!*"

The group left town and headed for the black mountains hulking over the western view. They hiked through a rural wasteland until the land rose to a hillside, guiding them into a narrow, shadowy pass—the way into the valley.

During this time, Nobu told them about his occupation as a guide and how he came to be one: "I won a map of the mountain range safe passage in a card game from a traveler in Shantytown. I had never been to this side of the mountains, so I decided to follow the map and travel here. Once I got over the fear of the tribes, I found the journey through the valley a calming experience. Yes, you might hear the horns of the tribes sometimes, but they are distant and rare. Otherwise it is very quiet. People avoid this place like a disease, so there is a good kind of loneliness here. I reached this side of the mountains without a problem and found myself wanting to travel the same path again. Before I traced my steps back west, I met a small group who were desperate to get to the other side. I said to the group, 'You pay me this and that, and I will guide you to the other side.' And this is what I have been doing ever since. I go east of the valley, visit old friends there, wait for customers, take them west, visit other friends there, and so on."

"Are you not afraid to be alone with your customers in such seclusion?" Yvonne asked. "What if they try to hurt you?"

"Then they are without guidance in a place full of cannibals. Good luck. Rest in peace." Nobu shrugged innocently, then burst out laughing.

He didn't show any interest in who Gustavo and Yvonne were, how they had gotten here, or why they were eager to get to the other side. This suited them fine because they wouldn't have been keen on sharing this information about themselves, anyway.

Sometimes Nobu spoke to his imaginary friend, Fumichan. Yvonne, understanding Japanese, quietly translated these exchanges for Gustavo in Spanish, keeping the translations brief and hushed to avoid raising Nobu's suspicions. But Nobu's mutterings were casual and harmless: offhand remarks about the trail, complaints of the phantom pain in his missing arm, curses for forgetting his deck of cards in town.

By the time they emerged from the mountain pass and into the valley, night had settled in. They made camp in a small forest close to the pass. The valley's silence set Gustavo and Yvonne on edge, and they remained wary of Nobu, so they rested huddled close together, both cradling a knife under their blankets. Thankfully, Nobu snored louder than a hippo, so at least they knew when he was asleep. His not-so-subtle sleeping habits were also reassuring—anyone this noisy wouldn't have crossed these lands repeatedly had the mountain folk been nearby.

The group carried on at dawn. Nobu led them through the forest to an open field. The dark grass rose to their waists, thick and wild, untrodden by the dead. They crossed the field, entered another forest, and followed a softly streaming creek winding under the lush canopy of trees.

When Gustavo asked Nobu what he knew about the mountain folk, Nobu was reluctant to discuss the topic. Whenever he crossed these lands, he explained, he tried to block out all thoughts of the cannibals. In his mind, he was simply hiking a secluded, peaceful trail. And sure enough, Nobu's behavior in the valley was that of someone at ease and absorbed in nature. His easygoing attitude was refreshing—contagious, even.

Things changed soon after that.

After a productive day of crossing halfway through the valley, dusk settled, gradually melting into night. The couple's torches and Nobu's lantern lit their way through yet another patch of forest. Fog drifted from nearby swamplands, glowing crimson and orange in the firelight.

They came upon a small clearing and discovered a pagan installment: a skeleton, its skull cracked open and its lower half missing, dangled from a tree like a broken piñata. Scraps of flesh and sinew clung to its bones, and its ribcage was stuffed with wilted flowers. Fist-sized stones, each dyed red, formed a circle around the horrifying figure.

Gustavo and Yvonne unsheathed their knives and braced themselves. Gustavo kept his eyes on Nobu while Yvonne scanned the surroundings, moving cautiously around the clearing, just as they'd practiced for situations like this.

"Nobu, what is this?" Gustavo asked, his voice tense.

Nobu didn't reply. He stood there, his back to Gustavo, eyes fixed on the skeleton hanging from the tree. He sighed and murmured something in Japanese, speaking to Fumi-chan.

Yvonne froze. Her eyes narrowed with fury, staring at Nobu.

"Yvonne?" Gustavo asked.

"He betrayed us," Yvonne whispered in Spanish, her words quick and cold. "We're his sacrifice for the cannibals."

Perhaps the reasonable choice would have been to interrogate Nobu or use him as leverage against the cannibals. Maybe they should have used those precious seconds to just run. But what Gustavo had just heard pushed him beyond reason.

He strode to Nobu, wrapped an arm around his neck from

behind, and drove his knife into his side.

"*Traidor de mierda,*" he hissed in his ear.

He yanked the blade out and stabbed him twice more. Nobu fell to his knees, mouth agape, his face frozen in surprise and terror. That was how they left him there.

They ran, their torches lighting the way through the dark forest. They didn't know where they were headed; they only knew they had to get as far as possible from Nobu, from the sacrificial site, from the ambush waiting for them.

Their escape led them to an open field. A cloak of fog settled over the tall grass, wrapping the space in a hazy cloud. Suddenly, a choir of strange screams exploded around them. The screams rose higher and higher, reaching a pitch that was shrill, inhuman, and unbearable. The cacophony made Gustavo feel dizzy, disoriented, and terrified beyond words.

Nobu had led them quite far north in the valley. They figured that if the valley was indeed divided in two by the tribes, their best chance of reaching the safe passage was to head south.

And so they did. They darted back into the forest to hide their torchlights and veered sharply southward, chased by the horrible battle cries. The valley's acoustics amplified the mountain folk's cries, turning them into a haunting, omnipresent threat. But soon Gustavo sensed they'd gained some distance from their pursuers. The screams sounded weaker, their vigor fading. Gustavo and Yvonne were getting away.

They fumbled into a hollow beneath a tree and waited there as those ferocious cries faded into the fog from which they'd come.

Furious for the betrayal and ashamed for their own naivety, the couple speculated on Nobu's schemes. They'd heard from enough independent sources about the safe passage to still believe it existed. Maybe Nobu truly knew the trail by heart but had made a deal with the mountain folk. Maybe he provided them with travelers to hunt, since so few dared to cross here anymore—the mountain folk's reputation had seen to that.

Following this line of logic, they realized a crucial oversight in their preparations: they hadn't found any of Nobu's former customers to verify his legitimacy. The townsfolk who vouched for him probably assumed the people they'd sent his way had reached the other side safe and sound. They'd been completely oblivious to the fact that they were sending travelers to the slaughter.

After mustering enough courage, Gustavo and Yvonne crawled out of their hiding place. They'd come too far to turn back, so they continued west through the valley. Things quieted down as the day wore on, and they began to entertain a fragile hope: maybe they had made it to the safe passage after all, maybe they had escaped the mountain folk for good.

At dusk, this hope was shattered. They were crossing through the sludgy pits of a swampland when the mountain folk confronted them. But instead of announcing themselves with a battle cry as they had the previous night, a horn rang through the swamps, its ear-splitting note like a famished shriek.

Up ahead, four tribespeople emerged from behind a muddy rise. They didn't resemble humans so much as some kind of grotesque mud creatures risen from the swamp: they wore little to no clothing, and their bodies were coated head to toe in dry mud that cracked and split like bark. Ropes wound around their bodies in intricate patterns and knots, securing their equipment and weaponry. One of the tribesmen raised his horn and blew into it, releasing another blood-freezing screech.

Gustavo and Yvonne stumbled through the slush, but each step was a battle, every movement heavy and useless. They'd barely managed half a dozen paces before something struck the back of Gustavo's head, and a numbness spread inside his skull. The last thing he remembered was falling facedown into the swamp. Then, darkness.

When Gustavo regained consciousness, he found himself trapped in a wooden cage. The cage slumped at the edge of a small camp in a forest clearing. A large bonfire roared in the middle of the camp, casting its light over a handful of tents scattered around the clearing.

Ten mud-covered cannibals huddled around the fire, roasting chunks of meat on skewers. Still dazed, Gustavo watched their blackened teeth sink into the charred meat, grease and fluids dribbling down their chins.

A wave of horror washed over Gustavo. Yvonne. They were eating Yvonne.

A voice whispered Gustavo's name. He turned around with a start and just barely managed to stifle a cry of relief: it was Yvonne, locked in a cage beside his, unharmed. He let out a wavering breath, eyes brimming with tears. They reached through the cage bars and found each other's hands. Yvonne told him not to give up, promising they would make it out somehow.

As they comforted one another, they felt eyes on them. The cannibals around the fire were staring at them, their expressions indecipherable under their crusted mud masks. They conversed in low murmurs in their private language, their eyes fixed on their captives.

Then, four of the cannibals rose and marched toward the cages. Two came for Gustavo, two for Yvonne. They unlocked the cells and dragged the prisoners out, all the while beating them with sticks. Gustavo and Yvonne tried to fight back, but their resistance ended abruptly when the guards pulled out knives made from bone and pressed the blades to their throats.

They were hauled across the yard toward the bonfire where the other cannibals waited, laughing and making animal noises. On the way, they passed one of their previous victims, sprawled on the ground like a fish prepared for a banquet. His limbs were missing, and his face was a bloody, shredded mess. His ribcage had been split open, exposing his lungs, still pumping air, expanding and collapsing like a bagpipe.

Upon seeing the maimed victim, Yvonne began thrashing around. She screamed, cursed, and fought back at every push and shove, refusing to move further. She spat in her guard's face and received a punch to the mouth in return.

Suddenly, Gustavo was forced to his knees. A guard grabbed him by the hair, and the two holding Yvonne pointed at him, barking orders. They wanted her to see what was about to happen. They wanted her to know it was her fault for resisting them. The group around the bonfire cheered and laughed, their racket rising in volume and fervor.

The guard holding Gustavo's hair pressed a shiv against his brow, like a cellist setting a bow to their instrument, while the second guard held him down. Then, without warning, the guard slit the blade across Gustavo's forehead, slicing a deep gash from one temple to the next. Searing pain erupted from the cut, and Gustavo wailed.

The guard seized his hair with both hands, pressed a knee on Gustavo's shoulder, and started to pull. Bit by bit, Gustavo's scalp peeled away from his skull. A smiling red mouth yawned on his forehead, drooling blood over his face. The agony was so otherworldly that Gustavo couldn't even scream. Instead, his bloodied face twisted into a frozen grimace, every muscle in his body petrified with pain. Yvonne stared at him, white as a sheet, looking like she might pass out.

The cannibals howled and danced around the fire, exalting the violence and the chaos. One of them blew into a bone horn, and it was as if the night itself had come alive with a frenzied, blood-drunken screech. The paralysis in Gustavo's throat loosed, and he joined the cacophony with his own screams.

Yvonne snapped out of the shock. She wiggled herself free from her guards and threw herself on the ground next to the remains of the tribe's previous victim. She picked something from the victim's belt and tossed the item into the bonfire. She shouted for Gustavo to take cover but was interrupted when one of the guards drove a shiv into her stomach.

The guard tried to pull out the blade, but Yvonne yanked him close, refusing to let go. She hurled the guard between herself and the bonfire, using him as a human shield for what was about to happen.

A bright flash turned everything white, and an ear-splitting boom swallowed all sound. The bonfire blasted wide as if possessed by some raging demon, and a gust of scorching air swept through the camp. The fire devoured the tribespeople closest to it, while splinters the size of kitchen knives shot through the air, skewering those further back.

A dead weight collapsed over Gustavo. It was his scalper, a stake lodged in the back of his head.

The explosion caused by the hand grenade was—

CHAPTER TWENTY-ONE

A hand grenade?!" Oscar asked, interrupting Gustavo. "Where'd you get a hand grenade?"

"From the tribe's previous victim," Gustavo replied. "Yvonne spotted them on him."

"And the mountain folk just left the grenades lying there?" Oscar asked. "Well, at least now we know we're dealing with idiots."

"I think they had never seen a grenade before," Gustavo said.

"Please tell me you didn't take any of those things with you," Nathaniel interjected. "Guns, grenades, all that shit—they're not stable here. Who knows how long they've been corroding in the ground?"

Gustavo and Yvonne exchanged a quick glance.

"We escaped after the grenade went off," Gustavo continued, ignoring Nathaniel's question. "We stopped for a moment to tend our wounds, but otherwise we've been on the move this whole time, trying to get out of this Hell within Hell."

Nathaniel scratched his chin. "Any chance you could draw us a map where all of this happened?"

Gustavo shook his head with a resigned look.

"Great," Oscar muttered, burying his head in his lap.

He was seriously starting to question if he could go through with all this. Sure, he'd been in over his head ever since he crawled out of his grave, but this... this was too much. The odds had been steadily stacking against him and now loomed over him like an impenetrable wall. This valley was where his luck would run out. He just knew it.

Daria sat down beside him, nudging his shoulder. She tossed a casual nod: *We got this. No big deal.*

Oscar scoffed and shook his head. He didn't believe her for a second, but the sentiment still warmed him.

Nathaniel held his part of their agreement and summarized the group's journey through the cannibal territories. The consensus was clear: Gustavo and Yvonne wouldn't be safe from the mountain folk until they reached the western desert. Hearing this, they slumped in exhausted defeat.

It was time to say goodbye. After wishing each other good luck, the two groups parted ways. As the trio climbed out of the stony pit, Oscar glanced back at the weary couple. Gustavo was struggling to keep his eyes open, probably due to sheer exhaustion or the pain radiating from the gash on his forehead, now hidden under the blood-soaked turban. Yvonne, slipping in and out of consciousness, looked drained, her adrenaline spent and no longer able to dull the pain of her stab wound.

What prospects did these two have? Oscar wondered. What were the odds they'd make it to the desert? He felt their despair, and suddenly, leaving them behind didn't come so easy.

Yvonne's eyes fluttered open, meeting his gaze. "Just go," she murmured, her voice frail and tired.

Oscar hesitated, torn. But he knew his pity wouldn't help them survive. If anything, it was hurtful, demoralizing. He nodded at her and followed his friends deeper into the hunting grounds.

They roamed through the hillside as dusk deepened and the sky turned leaden. A black carpet of grass, dotted with withered shrubbery and scattered trees, replaced the jagged outcrop.

Softer ground—Oscar had needed this. After the gravelly desert, the root-cluttered forest, and the rocky mountain range, his feet were now more blister than skin, and he was already on his third (and last) pair of shoes. He figured he couldn't have traveled as far as they had if he were still alive. Death had riddled him with a spectrum of deficiencies, but it had also made his body unnaturally resilient. Physical exhaustion never quite reached its peak, and a few hours of rest always seemed to cure the worst of his weariness.

But death hadn't cured the blisters on his feet, the abrasions on his shoulders from hauling the duffel bag, his broken nose, the knotted lump in his belly, the chronic aches, the random twinges of pain, or the feverish chills. Whatever small advantages death offered weren't enough to outweigh its miseries. Still, treading on soft grass did feel nice.

Oscar noticed Nathaniel dragging his left foot, his expression grave with discomfort. "Something wrong?" he asked.

"Just a diversion," Nathaniel replied. "If the mountain folk are watching, it's better to have them underestimate us. Best case scenario: they'll cut down the size of their hunting party."

"I see," Oscar said. "'Just some old man with a limp and a couple of newborns. The rest of you, head home. We'll take it from here.' That kind of situation?"

"Old?" Nathaniel raised an eyebrow. "But yes, something

like that."

"Smart."

Daria pointed at Nathaniel's limp. "Hurt?"

"It's just for show for the cannibals," Oscar said.

"Show?" Daria spun her hand, searching for a synonym she knew. "Fake?"

Oscar clicked his tongue and mimed a finger gun—a callback to Daria's earlier gesture when they'd scaled the mountain. The attempt was so clumsy it made him cringe. Daria smiled, sensing his embarrassment.

Oscar shook his head and turned back to Nathaniel, now limping a few strides behind. "One thing bothered me about Gustavo's story."

"Just one?" Nathaniel quipped.

"Why would Nobu lure travelers to the mountain folk? I mean, he wasn't their prisoner or anything."

"Maybe he was. Gustavo told us Nobu was missing an arm, right?"

"What's that got to do with anything?"

"It's called the pin puppet method," Nathaniel said. "Someone severs a limb of their victim and threatens to inflict pain on the removed piece if the poor bastard doesn't do exactly as they're told. Remember: the dead still have sensation in their amputated parts. The mountain folk might've forced Nobu's hand—no pun intended—to bring them more people to hunt. Extortion, plain and simple."

Pin puppet method, Oscar thought. The idea made his stomach churn, but then skepticism seeped in. "You're so full of shit," he muttered.

Nathaniel shrugged.

"Nobu and Ernie same, maybe," Daria suggested. "Have home here. Cannibal keep safe. Nobu pay with people."

Pay with people. Oscar shuddered. It seemed such a casual, expendable thing for some, the worth of others.

"Maybe," Nathaniel said. "Nobu did express a fondness for solitude." He paused, his tone shifting to something more pointed. "But more importantly, what did we learn about the mountain folk?"

"Gustavo and Yvonne encountered both tribes, didn't they?" Oscar said. "The first tribe they came across used battle cries. Then they heard a war horn after crossing into the second tribe's territory. So, the first tribe's called Battle Criers, and the second one's War Horns."

"Please don't name them," Nathaniel said, rubbing his brow. "But yes, you're right. The first tribe lured prey to their land using Nobu's services. That hanged skeleton Gustavo mentioned? It sounds like they plan their attacks with care. They go to great lengths to get the preparations right. The hunt is a ritual. The good news for us is that this makes them predictable. The other tribe, though, attacked them on sight. No theatrics, no bullshit. Just pragmatic and to-the-point."

"Although they did take their sweet time tormenting them afterward," Oscar pointed out.

"True," Nathaniel said, nodding grimly. "And here's something else: both tribes announce themselves before attacking. That makes a stealthy ambush less likely."

"We can use that to our advantage, can't we?" Oscar asked, feeling a flicker of hope somewhere inside.

"Maybe."

Oscar stopped abruptly. His skin prickled with goosebumps. A realization had just struck him. "Wait. Back at the cemetery, how did Ernie alert Heinrich?"

Nathaniel frowned, thinking it over. Then his eyes widened. "He blew a horn."

"The way Gustavo described the war horn—it kind of sounded like the one Ernie used. And we know Ernie and Heinrich had a deal with one of the tribes. It's not too far-fetched to think they might've had one of their horns, right?"

"It fits," Nathaniel agreed.

"I guess this means they had a deal with the War Horns, right?" Oscar said.

"Or the other tribe stole the horn and gave it to Ernie and Heinrich," Nathaniel said. "Does it matter?"

"I guess not," Oscar shrugged. "You didn't happen to see the horn when you looted Ernie's place? Could've been useful."

"I didn't." Nathaniel exhaled sharply. "Fuck."

Oscar sighed. Connecting the dots had been invigorating, but what practical value did it really have? How did it improve their chances of escaping the tribes? Disappointment settled in. Oscar sighed again.

The hillside leveled into an open field where waist-high grass stood stagnant beneath a shroud of evening mist. The group veered toward a nearby forest and stuck to the tree line where the branches arched over them like outstretched claws, their black leaves forming a slumping marquee.

Oscar noticed something was bothering Daria. She seemed hesitant, as if debating whether she should speak up or swallow whatever was troubling her.

"Daria, what is it?" he asked.

She hesitated some more, then blew air through her nose. "Stop."

Oscar and Nathaniel did as instructed and faced her, waiting.

"You say... Ernie's horn?" she asked.

Both men nodded.

Daria slung her backpack off her shoulder, rifled through it, and pulled out a blow horn crafted from bone. The grotesque instrument was decorated with pearls, braided hair, and strips of skin, and its yellowed surface and scythe-like shape brought to mind the talon of some long-extinct beast.

Oscar froze, wide-eyed. There it was: the cannibal war

horn.

He figured she must have taken the horn after freeing Ernie's child prisoners and ransacking his hideout, right before he and Nathaniel had arrived. Maybe she'd thought it might prove useful. Or maybe it was just another trophy.

"Holy shit," Oscar said breathlessly. Beside him, Nathaniel's eyes glistened with excitement, as if he had just stumbled upon some priceless relic.

"Horn," Daria concluded, holding it out for their inspection.

"Daria, you crazy fucking Slav, I could kiss you!" Nathaniel laughed.

Oscar's smile died instantly. "Please don't."

Nathaniel extended his hand, palm up. "Can I have it?"

Daria's eyes flicked between Nathaniel and the horn. An indecisive hum escaped her throat. Oscar suddenly understood why she hadn't shown them the horn earlier. She didn't trust them, at least not fully. The horn had been her trump card, something to wield as leverage if needed. But now, she was offering it up for the group's benefit.

"It's okay, Daria," Oscar said.

He doubted his input would sway her, but then, having come to a decision, she clicked her tongue and handed the horn to Nathaniel.

The group spent much of their time in the valley sticking close to the edges of forests. It was a strategic medium, providing both decent visibility and a place to hide if they were attacked. They always had a rendezvous point they'd agreed upon beforehand in case they had to scatter. This was a place they picked out whenever they entered new terrain, a place with an easily identifiable landmark, one they could all navigate to on their own.

When they made camp, they scouted the perimeter and secured it with tripwires. They built decoys by piling branches and rocks and covering them with cloths. In the dark, they made a passable imitation of sleeping travelers—hopefully, the mountain folk would strike the decoys first, buying the group precious moments to escape.

They took turns keeping watch. The guard on duty always huddled in the bushes a short distance from camp, holding a rope connected to the others, ready to tug it in case of danger. It was a silent alarm that might just give them an edge if they had to suddenly flee.

Their precautions were thorough, and they considered themselves about as prepared as anyone could be in this situation. Yet there'd been no sign of the mountain folk. No pagan installations. No mad howls. No screeches of horns. No visitors in the night. Just silence, thick and oppressive.

The suspense felt like a swarm of insects under Oscar's skin, a maddening itch that only deepened with every step forward. And in this heightened, wired state, even something as simple as glancing over his shoulder became an act of immense courage—a small motion that now demanded an internal pep talk before he could muster the will to execute it. Because what if he *did* spot someone lurking in the shade of a forest or crouching in the tall grass of an open field? What if meeting their gaze provoked the stalkers to initiate the hunt while simply keeping his head down might avert it?

The valley had grown eyes—not only because Oscar felt watched, but because checking his surroundings felt as intrusive as making eye contact with another person.

And yet... part of Oscar almost appreciated this fear.

He had noticed that whenever he felt safe—or safe enough, at least—his mind drifted from the minutiae, from the here and now, to deeper woes.

One such woe was his worsening stomachache. The pain

had now become constant, raising the question: how far would it progress here in the never-ending? Would it ever cease? Nathaniel suggested it was a symptom of prolonged stress, but Oscar's intuition told him otherwise. The worsening pain concerned him more and more, but when the fear of the mountain folk took over, its weight receded, fading to the background.

Another woe: during a quiet hour at camp, Oscar realized that ever since Heinrich had imprisoned him and Nathaniel, he hadn't thought once about his sister. The revelation struck him with a stab of guilt, but the pain wasn't as sharp as it probably should have been. Losing her, and the thought of her losing him, felt… oddly numb. If this sensation too was progressive, would he eventually stop missing her altogether? By the time she'd lived a full life and entered this world, would he even care anymore?

All these worries the immediate fear erased. It confirmed what Oscar had already begun to suspect: in Hell, danger and its intoxicating rush of adrenaline were things to covet. It offered a reprieve from the maddening eternity, the decline of humanity, the lost loved ones, and the haunting knowledge that they too would one day face the same horrors. Danger nullified the pointlessness of it all. Danger made it feel like there was still something worth fighting for.

One could even go as far as to say that Oscar wanted to be hunted.

CHAPTER TWENTY-TWO

The group had made it halfway through the valley when they came upon an abandoned campsite in a small patch of forest. Amber light filtered through the sparse ceiling of branches and leaves, illuminating a moss-covered outcrop with the remains of an extinguished bonfire. They approached cautiously with Nathaniel leading the way, their blades unsheathed, their postures tense.

Oscar wanted to ask if they shouldn't move as far away from this place as possible, but he was too nervous to open his mouth. He told himself, as he'd done many times before, that Nathaniel knew what he was doing. Maybe studying the site would yield crucial information about the mountain folk. Maybe Nathaniel could determine which direction the campers had gone, so they'd know which route to avoid. Maybe—

I don't fucking know, he thought. *I don't know the first thing about any of this.*

Nathaniel knelt beside the fire's remains and hovered a hand over it. "It's still warm. They must have camped here last night."

"So they're not far." Oscar's throat felt like sandpaper. "We're obviously not on the safe passage. Shouldn't we head south?"

Nathaniel shook his head. "We don't know which tribe left this fire. We might already be south of the safe passage, in which case heading south would only lead us deeper into their territory." He paused. "There's also the chance that we're on the safe passage right now, and this fire belonged to some random group. You could go with that if optimism is your thing."

"I'd rather assume the worst."

"Me too." Nathaniel stood and brushed the ash from his hands. He gestured at the mulled dirt around the fire. "I'd say this was a small group. No more than six people. Doesn't seem like this place has been in regular use, so I don't think there's an outpost close by. They probably just stopped for a rest on their way somewhere."

During this exchange, Daria had been walking around the camp, studying the tracks and traces. She caught Oscar and Nathaniel's attention with a loud gasp. They turned to her. She stood there, trembling, eyes brimming with tears. She was holding something she'd just picked up from the ground: a pair of glasses, one of the lenses cracked.

"Yung," Daria said, her voice tinted with a hopeful shiver.

Nathaniel looked confused. "What about him?"

Daria lifted the glasses to emphasize their significance. "Yung!"

"They're Yung's glasses," Oscar said in disbelief. "I remember him wearing them at the cemetery."

Nathaniel's brow lifted, realization crossing his face. "How about that."

Daria wiped her tears and began pacing around the campsite, her eyes fixed on the ground. She stopped close to the edge of the outcrop and pointed at a path leading deeper into the thicket. "*Tut!* Yung go here."

Oscar was no tracker, but he too saw the numerous footprints, the snapped branches, the trampled foliage. The story was clear: after purchasing Yung from Ernie, the mountain folk had traveled through here, leaving behind a trail to follow.

The problem was that the tracks led north and deeper into the forest. The group's plan was to head east, and one of their cardinal rules was *never* to venture too far into a forested area.

"We go now. Help Yung, yes?" Daria nodded frantically, eyes wide and gleaming.

Oscar looked at Nathaniel for support, but Nathaniel only shook his head and turned away. For that brief moment, Oscar hated him. But he also understood him: Daria was part of their group because of Oscar. It was his responsibility to tell her the bad news.

"It's too dangerous," Oscar said, his throat burning with shame.

"*Shcho?*" she asked, breathless, then translated: "What?"

Oscar pointed at the trail. "Danger." Then he pointed east. "Safe."

"No..." she whispered. "Oscar, please."

"We can't go." Oscar struggled to keep his voice steady. "I'm sorry."

Daria stared at him, stunned. "I... I can't leave Yung."

Oscar placed a hand on her shoulder. "I'm—"

"No!" she shrieked and swung her hatchet at him.

Oscar jumped back, narrowly evading the blade.

"Daria!" Nathaniel barked, his tone sharp with authority.

She froze. Her mouth twisted downward as she stared at him defiantly, tears streaming down her face.

"Listen here." Nathaniel's voice took a patronizing edge.

"We don't know what's out there. These people are hunters. Do you think they'd leave such obvious tracks behind? It's a trap." He jabbed a finger toward the trail. "Fake, understand? Staying safe is our number one concern. Just being here is dangerous enough. We go east, and that's final."

Daria stood stiff, her back ramrod straight, arms rigid at her sides. But the fire in her eyes dimmed, the fury waning to something brittle.

"You know we're right," Nathaniel said, softening his tone. "You probably figured it might be a trap even before I did. I understand the urge to go and make sure, but Oscar said it best: it's too dangerous."

Daria stared down at Yung's glasses, tinkering with the frames with shaky hands. A tear fell on the cracked lens. Her shoulders slumped, and defeat washed over her, snuffing out the embers within.

Dusk fell fast, and the group made camp in a ditch between the forest and a field where chest-high grass shielded them from prying eyes. A heavy silence had hung over them since they'd left the abandoned campsite. Oscar couldn't bring himself to look at Daria directly but instead watched her out of the corner of his eye, analyzing her every action and expression. What words did she leave unsaid in her silence? he wondered. What was her distant stare focused on?

She'd stopped crying soon after they'd left Yung's last known location, but this sad stubbornness was worse. Oscar felt he had failed her, and her quietness seemed to confirm it: *Yes, I* do *think you're a coward, and I never should have trusted you.*

Once they finished setting up camp, Daria volunteered to take first watch.

"Are you sure?" Oscar asked.

"No sleep. Too much here," she said, tapping the side of her head.

Her voice carried a strained calm, one that Oscar took as a form of acceptance. Maybe she was, after all, coming to terms with the reality that Yung was beyond rescue? Of course she had a lot to process—Oscar certainly had back when he realized he would never see his sister again.

"Probably best if you hide in the thicket over yonder," Nathaniel said. "There, yes? Good. Wake me up when you get tired."

He tied a rope around his wrist and passed the loose end to her. Oscar followed suit. Daria coiled the ropes around her palm and gave a curt nod.

"Are you sure you're okay?" Oscar pressed, frustration itching in his throat. Her behavior unnerved him. She'd always been vocal and honest about her emotions, but now she felt much harder to read. He felt disconnected from her. Despite their challenges in communication, this was the first time he actually sensed a barrier between them.

A sad smile rose on her face. She nodded and reached out to pat his cheek. "*Nadobranich*, Oscar."

"*Nadobranich*, Daria."

Oscar felt a hand on his shoulder, shaking him awake from half-sleep. He blinked and looked around to reorient himself. The first light of dawn squinted through the clouds, but here in the secluded ditch, darkness still held on. A lantern flickered faintly beside him, its flame set low. Nathaniel sat next to him, staring at him, his features etched with ghoulish tension.

Nathaniel was about to say something, but Oscar cut in, the words tumbling out on impulse: "She's gone, isn't she?"

Nathaniel frowned. "I'm sorry, Oscar."

The confirmation struck him like a blow to the chest. His

chin began to tremble. He'd known this would happen; Daria couldn't leave Yung behind. But he hadn't wanted to accept it. He'd purposefully misinterpreted the telltale signs, as if his denial might somehow keep her with them.

"She left us a message." Nathaniel handed Oscar a piece of paper.

Wiping his tears, Oscar read the letter: *I help Yung. Don't follow. Meet after mountains.*

Anger surged through him. He crumbled the paper and threw it to the ground. "She knows it's a fucking trap!"

"She knows it *might* be a trap," Nathaniel corrected. "Besides, if there's anyone who can outsmart them, it's her."

"Don't do that," Oscar snapped. "Don't pretend like she's going to be alright. You don't believe that."

"But I do. She survived Ernie and Heinrich. That's no small feat. I've kept a close eye on her. She's got that fire inside her, Oscar—the fire for survival. Shit, she's probably better off without us."

"Yeah, well, *we're* not better off without her." Oscar rubbed his eyes, feeling a piercing headache closing in. "I'm not better off without her. I need her."

"In that case, we better do as she says and meet her east of the mountains."

"Nathaniel..." Oscar sighed. This kind of forced optimism, especially from someone as pragmatic as Nathaniel, set his teeth on edge.

"Why do you insist that she's *not* going to be alright?" Nathaniel countered. "What else can we do but take her word for it? She's obviously made up her mind, so going after her would be useless. We can't force her to come with us. She's not our slave."

Oscar pressed his lips together. He still wasn't buying Nathaniel's optimism, but that didn't really matter because, in the end, the man was right. Again. There was nothing else to do but head east.

"Then I guess we better hurry up," Oscar said, resigned, tasting venom in his voice.

They trudged through the valley all day in defeated, morose silence. Oscar felt abandoned, hopeless, and, he hated to admit it, jealous. Daria had chosen Yung over him. He knew it was juvenile and selfish to feel that way, but he couldn't help it. His heart was broken and now leaked something poisonous deep inside him.

At dusk, his spiraling thoughts were momentarily interrupted when he and Nathaniel stumbled upon something unusual. As they crossed through a small forest, they spotted an entrance to what appeared to be an underground tunnel. It nestled in a ditch walled with bedrock, shaded by arching trees. Cobblestones framed the entrance, and dead vines and thick strings of moss shrouded its dark, gaping mouth. They hid in the shrubbery a little ways from the tunnel, studying their discovery.

"What is that?" Oscar whispered. "The mountain folk did this?"

"I don't know," Nathaniel replied. "Looks abandoned. And old." He paused. "Let's have a look."

"Wait. Shouldn't we just—"

Oscar choked on his words as Nathaniel hurled a rock into the tunnel. The stone clattered in the dark, casting echoes that disappeared one by one into the unknown. They listened and waited, but nothing inside the tunnel stirred or responded.

"We're good." Nathaniel got up and headed for the entrance.

Oscar followed reluctantly, every step tightening the knot of dread in his chest.

Nathaniel stopped in front of the entrance and lit his

lantern. The flame flickered nervously, teased by a faint draft blowing from the depths. "There's another entrance somewhere," he said. "Maybe several of them."

They pushed the curtain of vines aside and entered. Darkness that had likely loomed here for centuries shrank from the lantern light. The ceiling propped just three feet above Oscar's head, and roots of trees pushed through its cracked structures and stretched along the surface like a mutated mycelium. The stench of old decay was strong here, and Oscar had to fight back a coughing fit.

"I don't think the mountain folk did this," Nathaniel said. "I think this has been in the valley a lot longer than they have."

He led the way with Oscar trailing a few steps behind. The man's silhouette slouched forth, the hazy glow of his lantern radiating around him. Then, Nathaniel came to an abrupt stop, and Oscar nearly bumped into him.

"What's this?" Nathaniel's whispers traveled down the tunnel and broke into echoes, searching for a reply. Oscar's skin prickled with goosebumps.

Nathaniel raised the lantern, its light revealing rows of coffin-sized cavities lining the stone walls, stacked like bunk beds. Some were sealed with hardened mud or flat discs of stone, but most yawned open and empty. Between the cavities, the stone walls were etched with worn and weathered illustrations: clouds shaped like humanoid faces, bizarre spirals resembling snail shells, stars forming constellations.

One engraving stood out to Oscar—a man lying on his back, a bulky creature perched on his chest. The stone had crumbled where the creature's face had once been. Oscar couldn't explain why, but this particular image sent a sharp shiver down his spine.

"It's a catacomb," Nathaniel whispered.

Oscar's stare drifted from one sealed grave to the next, the dread expanding in his chest like a balloon. "Don't tell me there are still people inside."

Nathaniel didn't reply. Instead, he continued following the tunnel as if something there had cast a spell on him.

They came to a crossing where the tunnel branched into three passages. Seeing the intersection, Oscar was struck by a sensation he knew all too well: claustrophobia. Crammed spaces and people who had been buried alive didn't bode well together. His windpipe contracted to the size of a pinhead, and his skin tightened like a snare drum. Was the tunnel shrinking? Were his lungs? Were those faint clatters behind him an indication that the tunnel was about to collapse?

Nathaniel seemed unfazed by the setting. He chose one of the three corridors at random and followed it further. Up ahead, the light revealed a staircase descending deeper into Hell's hidden corridors.

"Shouldn't we head back?" Oscar had to force the words out—they felt too big in his throat.

Nathaniel stopped, shining the lantern back on him. The sight of Oscar's pale, haggard face seemed to surprise him. "Clearly. Sorry, I got distracted."

They turned back, and the weight on Oscar chest eased with each step.

The open air of the dimming forest greeted them as they exited the catacombs. Oscar inhaled deeply, and the fog in his mind began to clear. Then he slipped on something.

Nathaniel grabbed him by the shoulders before he could hit the ground. "Careful," he said.

"Thanks," Oscar muttered, embarrassed. He looked down at what he'd slipped on and was immediately struck with visceral horror.

A severed tongue lay on the cobblestone, twitching and flapping like a fish on a pier. Dead flowers and red-dyed rocks circled the slab of meat.

The mountain folk had left them a present.

CHAPTER TWENTY-THREE

Oscar and Nathaniel abandoned the catacombs in a haste and moved through the forest as the black clouds above spread like mold, foreshadowing the coming night. They zigzagged through the sprawling trees, cut through the unkempt thickets, and sneaked along the dry creeks. Oscar moved with the grace of a clay sculpture, fear seeped deep into his core. He didn't have to move fast, though; Nathaniel held on to his faux limp, keeping the pace frustratingly slow and restrained.

Now more than ever, Oscar wished Daria was here with them. Nathaniel's skill set brought experience and a kind of pragmatic cunning to their group, but somehow Oscar could imagine Daria being the perfect fit for dealing with the hunters. He pictured her racing swiftly through the forest, vicious and sly, as if it were her natural habitat. She would have a wild, alert glare in her eyes, scouting the perimeter for intruders, her hatchet ready and her mind fixed on one goal:

survival.

They spotted a tree line up ahead. A fog-shrouded swamp pooled beyond the sparse trees, its watery mush dark and lifeless like outer space. On the other side of the swamp, the forest thickened and climbed up a hill. And beyond the hill, maybe a couple hours' hike away, waited the mountain range. The eastern rim of the valley. They were close to making it out, but not close *enough* to make it in one push.

"Here's good," Nathaniel said, winded.

"Good for what?"

"For a break. We have to save our strength in case they attack. My guess is they're watching us. Probably have been for some time."

"Oh Jesus," Oscar whispered.

"Based on the installation they left for us," Nathaniel said, "I'd say we're dealing with the tribe that uses battle cries. Remember Gustavo's story?"

"Right, right," Oscar nodded frantically. "It's a ritual for them."

"Exactly. We haven't heard their cries yet. I think they're just toying with us. They want us scared. They want us fumbling in the dark. We have to keep it together."

"I'm way past keeping it together," Oscar laughed nervously.

"You're doing fine," Nathaniel said. "Once we get out of here, we're going to work on that confidence, kid."

Oscar smiled. He had needed that.

They didn't bother setting up camp this time. They huddled around Nathaniel's lantern, their backs turned to each other, weapons ready. Oscar scanned the woods for movement while Nathaniel watched the swamp beyond the tree line. If either of them saw or heard anything in the dark, they would alert the other, circle the swamp, and head for the hills, no questions asked.

They spent half an hour in silence, hearing nothing, seeing nothing.

Finally, Oscar asked, "Is it safe to talk?"

"They know where we are either way, so..." Nathaniel shrugged. "I don't see any harm in that."

"That tunnel... why would the dead build catacombs?" Oscar asked.

"I don't think it's the dead who built them."

Oscar mulled this over. Then it hit him. "So it's the same as the cemetery. Some people get transported to the catacombs after they die?"

"Right. Or maybe it *used* to be where people got transported to," Nathaniel said. "People aren't buried in catacombs anymore, so the place doesn't produce corpses. It's an ancient ruin."

"I guess it was kind of narrow-minded to assume the cemetery was the only burial ground in Hell," Oscar shrugged.

"I suppose it was," Nathaniel agreed.

"Speaking of burial rites," Oscar said, "when exactly does the shift from the living world to Hell happen? I mean, it can't be the moment you die. When I got out of my grave, I was wearing a suit, but I'm pretty sure I didn't die wearing one. But it can't be after the funeral, either. By then, you've been through an autopsy. You've been dissected, gutted, and pumped full of chemicals."

"Let's be clear: it's not your original body that transfers here," Nathaniel noted. "Otherwise, all the graves in the living world would be empty. What transfers must be your consciousness, your essence, your soul—whatever you want to call it. The way I've figured it, a person lies in a sort of dormant state between the moment they die and the moment they're buried. During this dormancy, clothes, items, and whatnot adapt to one's essence and transfer to Hell with them. But I guess you've already figured that out, right? That things adapt to us?"

Things adapt to us, Oscar echoed in his mind. He was quiet for a moment. A thought was taking shape. He said, "You know, I think I read somewhere that the human body is infested with microbes from the surrounding environment—so much so that they can even outnumber the body's original cells. Have you heard about this?"

When Oscar didn't get a reply, he glanced over his shoulder and saw Nathaniel looking at him, an eyebrow raised in surprise. "No, I haven't," he said. "Is that right?"

"Yeah. These microbes also affect your behavior. They can influence brain function, mood, mental health... So in that sense, you might be even more of your environment than you are, like, yourself." Oscar paused, pondering his own words. "Maybe that's what makes people act the way they do here: apathetic, depressed, violent, batshit crazy, all that. It's Hell's microbiota. It attaches to us and begins to affect our behavior. I think everything else we've discussed about behaviorism and stuff still applies, but I'm just saying there might also be, like, a biologically valid explanation for it."

"Hell's microbiota. Death bacteria." Nathaniel sounded almost reverent. "Fascinating. You know, it might—"

He was interrupted by a rustling sound in the dark. Both men froze.

Deeper in the forest, about thirty feet from them, a torch flared to life, illuminating a woman's face. She stared at them, smiling a joyless smile: her cheeks had been slit from the corners of her mouth halfway to her ears, the cut skin hanging limp like the wings of a dead bat. Her teeth had been filed unevenly sharp, now gritted together, grinning like a shark. Her shaved eyebrows accentuated the sickly white of her skin and the pearly blackness of her eyes. All this was framed by a dirty mess of tumbleweed-like hair, making her look more like some demonic entity than human, her face hovering there in the dark.

"Jesus fucking Christ!" Oscar shrieked and jumped to his feet.

He saw Nathaniel do the same, cursing, his limp miraculously recovered. Both men broke into a sprint and headed toward the swamp.

A shrill, primal scream erupted from somewhere in the forest.

It's on. A cold pulse throbbed inside Oscar's skull. *The hunt is on.*

Another scream answered the first. Then a third one joined in. Then a fourth. And then more and more. The screams united in a haunting chorus, forming a dissonant chord. The pitch rose higher and higher, reaching an almost inhuman register.

Nathaniel took the lead, lighting their way with his lantern. They leapt over roots and pits, charged past trees and boulders. Bony branches reached out, scraping their faces and snagging their hair. In the lantern-lit, high-speed blur, the forest looked as if it were coated with molten skin, as if it were alive, as if it didn't want them to escape.

They reached the swamp. A heavy mist hovered above the sludge, obscuring the view to the other side. The cannibals held up their battle cries, now mixed with mad howls that added to the disorienting cacophony. The duo pressed on along the shore; the swamp to their left, the forest to their right. Knee-high grass clung to their ankles, and black mud splashed beneath their feet, turning their escape into a slow, awkward nightmare.

Despite the obstacles, Oscar realized the worst trap was his own malfunctioning body. Random twinges of pain came and went without warning, and it wasn't out of the question that he or Nathaniel might suddenly double over from an ill-timed spasm. Then again, the same problem applied to their pursuers.

By the time they were halfway across the swamp, Oscar was gasping in panicky staccatos. The muscles in his throat had clamped up, and his heart convulsed in sharp throbs. He felt some reassurance from Nathaniel's fox-like composure, though: the man radiated vigilance, determination, and an almost eerie dissociation from fear.

The cries scattered. Some came from behind them, some from the forest, and more from the opposite shore of the swamp. It was impossible to discern how many voices made up the choir. It could have been five or twenty-five. All Oscar knew for sure was that he and Nathaniel were outnumbered.

Up ahead, the shoreline curved inward, encircling the swamp. The opposing shores would meet, and they would come in contact with the mountain folk closing in from the other side. So, instead of following the shore any further, they veered into the woods.

More roots lay scattered along their path, slick with moss. Oscar tripped over something and slammed to the ground. Nathaniel pulled him up so quickly that Oscar barely registered what had happened.

A new shriek erupted close to their right, forcing them to steer away from it. This led them closer to the mountain folk on their left, but there was nothing else they could do. Trying to hide or rely on diversion tactics was pointless until they gained more distance from the cannibals or at least determined how large the hunting party was.

The pursuit led them up a hill, and the bald hilltop peeked through the thicket. Oscar saw firelight up ahead, flickering through the black foliage. His guts twisted. The mountain folk had guided them like cattle, driving them to the hilltop. And yet they pressed on. There was nowhere else to go.

They reached the crest of the hilltop, and in the middle of the grassy clearing, three headless, naked bodies hung from a gnarled tree. Oscar and Nathaniel came to a halt, petrified by the grotesque sight. The bodies were strung by their feet, their hands bound behind their backs. The old tree creaked in protest as the bodies floundered, swirled, and swung like trapeze artists. Torches encircled this macabre display, and the blood-soaked grass glistened in the firelight, the crimson spatters tracing their chaotic dance. Red pebbles and wilted flowers had been plugged into the various stab wounds dotting their bodies. Blood sputtered from their open necks, the stream weak and sporadic like a clogged faucet.

Based on their build, Oscar recognized two of them as Gustavo and Yvonne. The third looked like the body of a slim teenage boy. It took Oscar a moment, but then it hit him: it was Yung. Whatever little life remained in Oscar drained away instantly.

As if on cue, the cries of the mountain folk fell silent.

"Let's keep moving." Nathaniel nudged Oscar's shoulder, snapping him out of the shock.

They hurried toward the opposite side of the clearing where the forest stretched on. As they were passing the headless bodies, a torch flared to life in the dark tree line up ahead. They shifted course, but another torch blazed in that direction as well. They changed direction again—a third torch ignited. One after another, more fires ignited in the black shrubbery. Soon, a dozen torches formed a circle around the field, and the message was clear: the mountain folk had them surrounded.

A high-pitched cry screeched from behind. Oscar and Nathaniel spun around and saw five Battle Criers emerge from the thicket—three men and two women, each as ragged and demonic as the next. Human-based ornaments and trinkets covered their bodies; some were sewn on their sparse clothing, some on their skin. Their cheeks were slit open, revealing unevenly filed teeth that reminded Oscar of the Cheshire Cat, and they carried hatchets, knives, and spears forged from bone.

One of the men, already slathered in blood, held a meat cleaver and carried a floral-patterned tote bag over his shoulder—the very same one, Oscar realized, that had belonged to Gustavo and Yvonne. This man must have been the one who'd decapitated them.

The five hunters spread out and approached slowly, shoulders hunched and weapons ready. Their every movement was calculated and sly, their demeanor quiet and ruthless.

"Nathaniel, do something. Please," Oscar stammered.

Nathaniel dropped to his knees and rummaged through his satchel. Oscar's eyes darted back and forth between the advancing Battle Criers and Nathaniel, who was now using his knife to cut something inside the satchel.

"You want the treasure?!" Nathaniel shouted at the hunters as he sprang up from the grass. "You can fucking have it!"

He hurled a pouch at the butcher—the one carrying the tote bag—who instinctively caught it against his chest. The pouch burst open, drenching him in lantern fuel. The two hunters beside him stepped closer, apparently intrigued by the prospect of treasure.

Nathaniel acted fast. He grabbed one of the torches set around the hanged bodies and threw it at the butcher. The torch struck its mark, and the night burst into brilliant orange as the fire wrapped its roaring wings around him. The two hunters nearest to him stumbled back in shock while the butcher wailed and thrashed, the flames controlling him like a puppeteer, forcing him to join their erratic dance.

"Run!" Nathaniel bellowed.

They bolted across the field. Two hunters emerged from the thicket up ahead, screeching madly, charging at them with their spears extended.

Oscar glanced back and saw three more hunters come out

of hiding to aid the butcher now engulfed in flames. Just as they reached him, a ball of fire erupted from the butcher, consuming them all. The clearing turned blindingly bright, and the deafening blast of the explosion warped into a distorted crumble, as if Oscar's eardrums had been turned to paper.

Something swooshed past Oscar's face like a bullet, continuing its trajectory toward the two spear-wielding hunters. The high-velocity projectile tore through one of them, leaving a nickel-sized hole in his throat. He let out a series of choking gasps as blood began spilling from the wound in a thick, syrupy arc. He collapsed to the ground, panic and terror peeking through his permanent smile.

The second hunter, half-blinded by the explosion, stared at his fallen comrade in confusion. Nathaniel lunged at him, driving his knife into the hunter's side as they hit the ground, the hunter's mouth agape in a silent scream of pain.

"Jesus Christ!" Oscar screamed. He couldn't hear himself through a high-pitched whine that pricked his ears like a needle.

Nathaniel pulled out the knife and motioned for him to keep running. Oscar did as told.

His ears cleared, and the muffled tinnitus was replaced by a cacophony of chaos and agony. The mountain folk wailed and screamed on the other side of the clearing as the fire illuminated the aftermath of the explosion. Their shredded remains lay scattered, and Oscar saw severed limbs in the grass, twitching spasmodically. Gustavo's headless body slumped on the ground, his rope apparently cut by shrapnel, while Yvonne and Yung still hung from the tree, unmoving. Mountain folk unaffected by the explosion—five of them by Oscar's count—scrambled frantically to help their fallen.

"Are you hurt?" Nathaniel asked.

"No, I'm good," Oscar heard himself say. "I'm good."

A couple hunters shrieked a battle cry, their gleaming

eyes locked on the two men. More hunters joined the cry, but Oscar and Nathaniel had gained enough distance for a decent head start. They stumbled to the edge of the clearing and vanished into the dark forest.

CHAPTER TWENTY-FOUR

The cries of the cannibals filled the night with a gospel of raging vengeance. But the further Oscar and Nathaniel ran through the woods, the more distant the screams became. And soon there were only echoes; then, echoes of echoes.

The terrain rose, the trees thinned out, and bedrock replaced the forest floor. Nathaniel kept the lantern's flame low, just enough to illuminate their path. They stopped in the shade of some boulders to catch their breath.

"So those were the mountain folk," Nathaniel said, his voice hyper and tense. He leaned against a rock, his trembling fist still clenched around the bloodied knife, his free hand tugging at the shoelace under his shirt. "I thought they had us. My God, what a night."

Oscar collapsed to the hard ground and slumped his head between hooked knees. He felt a panic attack approaching and began rubbing his chest. It wasn't working. He had never been this terrified. Ever since he had crawled out of his grave, fear had been as constant as breathing, but this level of horror was almost incomprehensible. He felt as if something in his mind had sprained. Both he and the world around him felt altered—he could barely recognize either. It didn't help knowing that there would be only more terror in the never-ending to come.

But what he feared the most was what would happen to Daria. She was alone in the valley with these blood-starved maniacs, chasing a ghost. The Battle Criers had finished Yung before she had found him, condemning him beyond saving. But Daria wouldn't know that. She was running straight toward the same—or worse—fate as Yung. The thought was so horrible and frustrating that Oscar began sobbing helpless, exhausted tears.

"That third one hanging from the tree… it was Yung, wasn't it?" Nathaniel asked quietly, apparently guessing from Oscar's demeanor where his thoughts were.

"Yes." Oscar wiped his eyes, though more tears kept flowing. "And now Daria's on a wild goose chase. She's putting herself at risk for nothing."

Nathaniel was silent a good while, then said, "I'm sorry, Oscar."

Oscar wished Nathaniel would've had a solution to helping Daria, but it was no surprise that all he could offer were his condolences. Oscar understood the situation without Nathaniel having to spell it out: backtracking to where Daria had left them and picking up her trail would have been whatever a dead man's equivalent for suicide was. Besides, as terrible as it was to admit it, Oscar no longer harbored an iota of hope that she would make it out of this place. The mountain folk were the masters of this valley, and the only reason Oscar and Nathaniel had managed to escape was because of dumb luck in its purest, rarest, most improbable form. It would be foolish to think she would stumble upon the same fortune.

Nathaniel sat down beside Oscar. Oscar lifted his head from between his knees and saw the man staring at his bloodied hands. His eyes brimmed with tears, too.

Oscar placed a hand on Nathaniel's shoulder. Nathaniel flinched at first, then accepted his support. He broke down in quiet, suppressed cries. Oscar let his own tears fall freely, too. The two friends took their time in this moment.

The battle cries had ceased, and the valley slumbered in silence. Oscar and Nathaniel's nighttime wanderings had led them to the base of a mountain—smaller and less steep than the one they'd climbed back west. Trenches wound through the uneven ground, and ten-foot-tall boulders jutted from the bedrock as if it was the spiked shell of some colossal beast.

They came upon a half-dry mountain river. Ashen trees arched over the riverbed like vultures spreading their wings. Soggy moss crept along the bank, and water trickled in weak rivulets from somewhere up the mountain. They followed the river upstream and soon reached a trail flanked by high stone berms.

"This is our ticket to the mountain pass," Nathaniel said. "We're close. Real close."

Oscar said nothing. All he could think about was how every step forward took him further from Daria.

But suddenly, he stopped, ears straining. "Nathaniel," he said. "You hear that?"

Somewhere nearby, groups of people were speaking in a language he couldn't recognize. The overlapping conversations blended into a low chatter, the kind one might hear in a market square.

Nathaniel's shoulders tensed. He killed the lantern and pulled Oscar into the shade of a stone berm—the noise came somewhere from the other side. They waited and listened, but the chatter remained the same. Oscar pointed at the top of the berm and raised an eyebrow. Nathaniel nodded, and they crawled up the mound.

The top of the berm leveled into a cliff overlooking a canyon, enclosed by steep mountain walls on three sides, shaped like an amphitheater. A dense forest barricaded its open side, secluding the area from the rest of the valley. In the shadows of the mountains hid a small village, illuminated by its many bonfires and torches.

Oscar and Nathaniel crawled to the edge of the cliff, studying the scene below. A muddy plaza lay at the center of the village, surrounded by shacks and huts with firelight weaving through the corridors and small yards between them. At the edge of the plaza stood a stone mound crowned with a building that looked like a chapel. Its black roof slanted at a steep angle over walls built from bones, and human skulls and wicker decorations adorned the peak of the roof. The bone chapel loomed over the village like some hunchbacked boogeyman, observing its domain in silence. A bonfire throbbed in the plaza like a smoldering heart, casting a flickering smile of shadows on the bone chapel's facade.

About twenty villagers moved in the open. *Battle Criers,* Oscar noted. Though they didn't wear human-based accessories like the hunters, their cheeks were slit halfway to their ears, they wore little to no clothing, and exuded the same primal, ghoulish demeanor. The villagers busied themselves with mundane-looking tasks: chopping wood, carrying water, sharpening weapons, crafting ornaments, repairing dwellings, and so forth.

Two watchtowers stood at the village's edge, overlooking the forest that separated the canyon village from the valley. Oscar noticed patches of the forest had been cleared and illuminated with bonfires—probably to aid the watchmen in the towers scanning the woods for intruders.

Nathaniel nudged Oscar's shoulder, steering his attention back to the edge of the village. There, by the tree line, a tunnel dove into the ground. It seemed all but identical to the one they had seen in the valley.

"Catacombs," Nathaniel whispered. "They're using the catacombs to move through the valley undetected."

As if on cue, a hunter burst from the tunnel, shouting something to the villagers, his voice panicked and breathless. He sprinted to the plaza, gesturing wildly for the villagers to gather, then hurried back to the tunnel entrance. The villagers abandoned their tasks and crowded around the entrance, their chatter rising in a worried crescendo.

Soon, more hunters emerged from the tunnel—some carried by their comrades, others limping on their own. They bore a gruesome array of injuries: deep gashes, charred patches of skin, missing limbs. The villagers gasped and cried out at the sight. Some collapsed to their knees and covered their mouths in shock.

Next, four hunters brought out two shoddily crafted stretchers from the tunnel. The first stretcher held a jumbled heap of severed limbs and burnt flesh. The second carried the mangled remains of a man—only half a torso, a head, and one arm were still intact, all charred black with horrible burns. A ragged moan escaped his mouth in one long continuous note, like the howl of a mournful wind in a seaside cave. The villagers' cries swelled into hysteric wails.

"Are those—" Oscar started, but he couldn't finish. He felt like he might retch if he uttered another word.

"The hunters from the hilltop," Nathaniel said, sounding dazed.

The hunters trudged forward in a sluggish, defeated line. The villagers rushed to meet them, offering water, relieving them of their weapons, and helping to carry the injured across the plaza.

Out of the corner of his eye, Oscar noticed movement beyond the village. His gaze shifted to the mountain wall on the opposite side of the canyon. A figure hunkered there, observing the mountain folk, partially hidden in shadows, partially illuminated by the village fires.

Oscar's breathing stalled. He recognized the figure.

"Daria!" he cried.

Nathaniel slapped a hand over Oscar's mouth. "Not a sound."

Oscar pulled Nathaniel's hand away. "It's Daria," he whispered urgently. "Look—on the rocks. Do you see her?"

Daria hadn't spotted them, and from her position and angle, likely wouldn't.

"Well, holy shit," Nathaniel said, winded.

Oscar tried to stand, but Nathaniel grabbed his arm and yanked him back down. "Easy now. They'll see us before she will. Let's be smart about this."

The parade of injured hunters trudged toward the bone chapel. Its black doors creaked open from the inside, inviting them in, and the hunters shuffled through. The villagers stayed outside, many crowding the entrance to comfort each other, while a few returned to their tasks, looking grim and defeated.

"We need to tell her about Yung," Oscar said, his voice tight with urgency. "How can we reach her?"

Nathaniel surveyed the distance between them and Daria. "Let's... let's just get off the cliff first."

They retreated and climbed down the berm back to the mountain road.

"The tracks probably led her here," Oscar said, tingling excitement racing through his body. "She's still looking for Yung. We need to hurry before she does something reckless."

Nathaniel kept his eyes on the ground, saying nothing.

"We could cut through the forest to the other side," Oscar continued, but his confidence was waning. Nathaniel's silence unnerved him. Dread crept into his chest. "Nathaniel? Say something."

But Nathaniel stayed quiet, and this was answer enough.

An acrid sensation flared inside Oscar. "You're not seriously thinking about leaving her... *again?*" he spat, feeling his lips pull back.

"After everything we've been through," Nathaniel said, his voice low and heavy with regret, "after being *this* close to getting out, it's just too risky. We don't know what kind of patrols they have in that forest."

"No. You can't be serious."

"She chose her path, Oscar. I won't throw ours away for the choices she made. The way out is right there."

"I... I can't believe this. She's right over there, about to walk into danger for nothing." Oscar's voice trembled with fury and frustration. He felt Nathaniel was deliberately missing the point. His stammers took a defensive edge. "I know we can do this. We'll use the dark as our cover. Do it smart, do it your way."

"The smart thing to do would be to get out of this valley right now." Nathaniel sounded pained. Taking this stance wasn't easy for him. But Oscar didn't care. The man was simply wrong. "We could be done with this nightmare before dawn," he continued.

This can't be happening, Oscar thought. Nathaniel wasn't debating the issue—he had already made up his mind. Oscar felt as though he had lost his grip on something and was now falling. The sensation pulled at the pit of his stomach.

"Don't do this," he pled, voice cracking. "Nathaniel, you can't do this. Please. *Please.*"

Nathaniel took a deep breath, his irritation breaking through. "She chose this. She fucked up. It's done."

"She fucked up? You really want to talk about fucking up?" Tears streamed down Oscar's cheeks in hot, itching trails.

"Fine, let's talk about fucking up. How about this entire journey? You promised to keep me safe, but all I've ever felt is the opposite with you."

"And you blame *me* for that?" Nathaniel's eyes filled with disappointment. "You really don't get this place, do you? You think grave looters and the mountain folk are the only threats in Hell? There's danger everywhere. This is it, Oscar. You don't have a scratch on you except for that broken nose. You think that's something anyone could pull off? All things considered, I've done a pretty fucking stellar job at keeping you safe."

Oscar fell silent, his skin simmering with resentment.

"This proves how short-sighted, impatient, and impulsive you are," Nathaniel said, shaking his head. His voice turned low and serious. "You're a smart kid, Oscar, but you're also a fool."

"Yeah? Well, I guess I was a fool to follow you. You don't really care about me. If you did, you'd help me go warn Daria. But you just want to get to Dean Theodore, and you won't even tell me why."

Nathaniel's face twisted with hurt. "All the things I've done for you… you don't think that's caring? Let me say it again because you don't seem to get it through your skull: the way out of the valley is *right there*." He gestured toward the mountain road for emphasis. "Why would I be having this conversation with you if I didn't care? I could just leave."

"Well, maybe you should." Oscar's voice hardened, and he straightened his posture. "I'm not leaving her, and it's clear you're too selfish to help me."

"Selfish?" Nathaniel let out a hollow, humorless laugh. "Finding Dean Theodore and delivering my discovery to him is the only way to achieve relief in this place, understand? We can change things. That's hope. I gave you *hope*. And you call me selfish?"

At the mention of Dean Theodore, Oscar felt that familiar

pull he had experienced the first time Nathaniel had spoken of him. It had swayed Oscar then, but it worked no longer. Daria mattered more.

"I don't need hope. I need her," he said, the words solidifying his resolve.

"Oscar—"

But Oscar had made up his mind. "Go find Dean Theodore yourself. We're done."

With that, Oscar turned his back on Nathaniel and walked away. He headed back toward the river, mapping a path in his mind from the mountain base to the forest that concealed the village. He could avoid the fires, make his way across the forest to reach Daria...

A shiver crept up his spine. Someone had snuck up on him. Before he could react, an arm looped tightly around his throat.

"Get off me!" Oscar gasped, eyes bulging.

"I can't let you go and get yourself ripped apart," Nathaniel murmured through clenched teeth, applying more pressure to Oscar's neck.

Oscar fumbled for his machete but dropped it. He sank his elbow into Nathaniel's side, but the hit lacked force. He clawed at Nathaniel's arm with the few fingernails he had left, only to feel the man's grip tighten. He grabbed a handful of Nathaniel's hair and pulled. None of his efforts worked. His hold remained unyielding.

Oscar's windpipe welded shut. He didn't need to breathe, but instinct kicked in, forcing him to fight the suffocating sensation. A void began to form before his eyes, expanding until his vision was swallowed by darkness.

The metallic clatter of a chain snapped him back to reality. With his free hand, Nathaniel had retrieved a pair of handcuffs from his satchel. Oscar might have been a fool, but he knew one thing: he would never be handcuffed again.

With the strength of this newfound resolve, he broke out of the void and twisted his arm to an awkward angle, managing to slip his hand under Nathaniel's shirt. He immediately found what he was looking for and yanked it with all the strength he could muster.

Nathaniel cried out, all vigor escaping his body. His grip loosened, and Oscar wriggled himself free. The handcuffs clattered to the ground. Nathaniel dropped to his knees, and half an arm's length of his small intestine slipped from beneath his shirt, pink and slick, dangling below his waist like the tongue of a dead animal. His mouth opened in a stunned *o*, his eyes wide and vacant. He collapsed onto his side, unconscious before his head hit the ground.

Oscar gasped for air and backed away, rubbing his throat, two-thirds of a bloodied shoelace tangled around his fingers.

CHAPTER TWENTY-FIVE

Making his way toward the forest, Oscar crept down the mountain base. The night held firm and visibility was low, rendering the descent over the rocky hillside a challenge. But Oscar wasn't overly worried. His eyes had adjusted to the dark, more or less, and the night offered him perfect cover against the mountain folk. He could do this—or at least that's what he told himself.

He'd seen from the cliff's vantage point that the forest was dotted with bonfire-lit clearings, presumably to protect the village against stealthy infiltrations. But Oscar's plan wasn't to approach the village. His plan was simply to cross the forest. He would use the bonfires as landmarks to navigate through the woods, making sure to stay out of their light and avoid the two guards manning the watchtowers. Oscar knew the plan wasn't perfect, but neither were the village's security measures.

And once he reached Daria, he would tell her about Yung and convince her to rejoin the group. They would return to

Nathaniel and patch him up, Oscar would reconcile with him, and they would all escape together. Simple.

Time, however, was a great concern. Oscar had to reach Daria before she left her hiding spot and ventured into the village. After his confrontation with Nathaniel, Oscar had studied the village one last time and seen Daria still in the same place, probably memorizing the patrol routes or scanning the village for signs of Yung's whereabouts. She could head off at any moment, and all Oscar could do was hope she wouldn't.

Despite the time pressure, Oscar felt confident in his plan—not that he could afford to doubt it. The window for doubt had closed the moment he had ripped open Nathaniel's shoelace sutures and eviscerated him.

It doesn't matter, Oscar told himself, trying to ignore the guilt. The damage was done. From here on out, everything depended on instinct, reaction, and pushing forward at full speed. All he could do now was embrace the adrenaline, embrace the not-looking-back, and *act*.

His determination nearly dwindled altogether when he reached the forest. As he slid down a rock and jumped into the thicket, his feet sank knee-deep into watery sludge. This wasn't a forest after all. It was a swamp.

The black surface of the water stretched before him like a mirrored floor. Crooked trees emerged from the stillness like misshapen pillars, their gray, moss-draped branches reaching down to the water to trace their own reflections. The bonfires stood on mounds of rock and dirt, casting flickering slices of yellow on the obsidian water. Mist hovered over the scene like a slow nightmare, disorienting and full of unknowns. Partial skeletons and human-made ornaments hung from the trees—maybe set as warnings, maybe carrying some spiritual significance.

Doubt sank in deep, offering all kinds of enticing reasons to give up. But Oscar refused to listen. He remained committed to his plan. He squeezed the handle of his machete and gritted his teeth. *Don't think. Embrace the not-looking-back.*

He waded through the watery slough toward the first bonfire, its flames roaring about a hundred and fifty feet away in the distance. The bottom of the swamp was a slimy mush that shifted beneath his feet, giving the sensation of treading on something uniform, malleable, and alive. Each movement sent ripples through the water, the sound like a drooling whisper in the silent dark.

Oscar stuck close to the trees, keeping himself hidden from the watchtowers looming above. Their rickety observation decks looked like oversized bird nests and the watchmen perching on them like owls, scanning the swamps for small animals to kill. But despite their vantage, they had yet to spot him. That was all that mattered. His plan was working.

Progress through the swamp was awkward and grueling. There was suction in the sludge, making every step a small battle for balance, but thankfully the bottom was thick enough to prevent him from sinking in entirely or getting stuck. Still, he'd already lost a shoe shortly after entering the swamp. After what felt like ages, he passed the first bonfire and set his sights on the next one, its glow blooming in the mist like a phantom flower.

He hunkered under a mess of branches adorned with human-based talismans and circled a cluster of trees. Then he noticed a wooden boardwalk with a rope railing cutting through the swamp a short distance away. Portions of the wobbly structure had sunken beneath the surface, but much of it still rose above the waterline and looked solid enough to mount. The boardwalk led from the first bonfire to the next but also branched off in other directions, weaving between the trees like the segmented trail of a centipede.

Oscar figured that on any other night, guards would be patrolling the swamp using the boardwalks. But this wasn't any other night, was it? The village had suffered severe losses after the encounter at the hilltop. They were mourning, licking their wounds, and running short on guards.

Fucking A, you bastards, Oscar thought, a grin creeping across his face.

He forded through the swamp until he reached the boardwalk. He vaulted the rope railing. The branch-woven walk creaked, wobbled, and sank beneath his weight, leaving his feet submerged in the water. No matter—it was still better than trudging through the swamp and would make the rest of his trek to Daria much easier.

He removed his remaining shoe, sank it into the swamp, and moved cautiously down the boardwalk toward the second bonfire. He kept a constant eye on the watchtowers and used the trees as cover whenever possible.

Up ahead, the boardwalk split in two: one path led directly to the second bonfire; the other veered behind a dense thicket of moss-covered trees.

Then Oscar spotted the flicker of a torch through the trees, moving toward the intersection. He froze. Blood pounded in his head.

The torchlight bobbed closer. Once whoever was carrying it reached the junction, they'd see Oscar. He scanned his surroundings in a panic. There was a cluster of trees nearby that offered partial cover, but he wouldn't make it there in time. Everything else was just swamp—still, dark, and dead quiet.

Oscar glanced down at the submerged boardwalk beneath him.

Oh, God.

He slipped back into the water, lay flat on his back, and slid beneath the boardwalk. Just as he did, he caught a fleeting glimpse of two torch-wielding hunters arriving at the intersection. But then they were out of his sight, as he was of theirs.

All he could do now was wait.

The boardwalk was elevated just enough to keep Oscar's face above the surface, although its slimy underside pressed against him, cold and unyielding. The swamp felt less like water and more like some thick, chunky soup. Underwater weeds clung to his back, neck, and ears like the tentacles of some otherworldly creature.

The boardwalk creaked and wobbled. The hunters were approaching. His heart hammered so violently he feared they might feel its beats through the wooden structure. The waddling above grew heavier, now accompanied by the sloshing sound of footsteps. Oscar moved his hand to his face, pinched his broken nose, and drew in deep, calculated breaths.

Through the narrow slits between the woven branches, he could only see the dark sky and the ashen treetops. Then, suddenly, the sole of a foot blocked his view, and the weight of the two hunters pressed him under the water.

The swamp floor embraced him with reeds and moss, their slimy tendrils wrapping around his body. A jagged stone buried in the sludge dug into the small of his back, its sharp edge sending a nasty jolt up his spine. A scream rocketed up his throat, but he fought it back. He stayed still, lungs burning, one hand clamped over his nose, the other clutching his machete like a lifeline.

After a moment with no change in his situation, a new kind of panic began to seep in. The hunters should have passed him by now. They'd been simply walking through—hadn't they? So why had they stopped right above him?

The answer revealed itself half an arm's length away: something began pouring into the water in a steady stream, making it slosh and bubble in the underwater hum. One of the hunters had stopped to take a piss.

Oscar's chest felt like a pressure chamber on the verge of imploding. His pulse accelerated, each throb a signal broadcasting panic through his body. The instinct to inhale clawed at his throat, demanding relief. Claustrophobia closed in like a malicious embrace. Oscar's eyes were shut, but now a different darkness invaded his sight. He was back in the airless confines of his coffin, immobile, suffocating. His body stiffened, and his jaws began to part involuntarily, letting water in.

But then the stream of piss ceased, the weight above him shifted, and his body rose back to the surface. He forced himself to stay quiet as the boardwalk wobbled above him. Only when the swaying stopped did he dare to breathe.

He drew a lungful of air, relief cutting through the terror.

Oscar slogged through the knee-deep swamp, moving in a clumsy half-crawl, half-swim. He reached another section of the branch-woven walk, closer now to the third and final bonfire. He hoisted himself out of the water, his eyes darting wildly, scanning the twisted trees and the jittering shadows cast by the fire—no sign of the mountain folk or their torches.

Instead, he realized this stretch of the walk led straight to the shore. He hurried along its length until his bare feet met solid, dry ground. Standing there, soaking wet and shivering, he fought the urge to drop to his knees and kiss the forest floor.

Then, just beyond the shore, something caught his eye. In the thicket lining the edge of the swamp, illuminated by the glow of the nearby bonfire, a pale face emerged from the shadows, watching him intently.

Oscar's breath hitched. "Daria."

She blinked, and recognition settled in. Her eyes softened and filled with tears, and a smile of pure relief broke across her face.

A high-pitched cry interrupted their reunion.

Shock coursed through Oscar like an electric current,

locking his muscles in place. The cry came from somewhere close. Too close.

Two hunter-guards emerged from behind a cluster of trees, one with an extended spear, the other with a drawn longbow. Both weapons were aimed squarely at Oscar.

The guards—a man and a woman—wore the typical Battle Crier hunter's attire: their death-paled skin was adorned with human-based ornaments, making them look like high-ranking warlords of some occult army, and unevenly filed teeth gleamed from behind their dissected cheeks, ground together like rusted cogs. Their round, browless eyes, gleaming black in the dim light, were fixed on Oscar with manic intensity.

They barked orders in their rattling, consonant-heavy language. Oscar acted according to instinct: he tossed the machete to the ground and shot his hands up in surrender. Terror blanketed him like wax, and his body succumbed to a submissive numbness.

The guards advanced and settled in front of him. Behind them, Daria rose silently from the thicket, hatchet in hand, her face cast in shadow. Oscar forced himself not to look at her, not to give away her position.

She crept closer, raising the hatchet. But before she could strike, a third guard burst from the bushes behind her. The guard swung a wooden club, striking the back of her head with a vicious smack. Daria crumpled forward, landing facedown in the dirt between the two guards.

Cold realization washed over Oscar. He had made a terrible mistake.

CHAPTER TWENTY-SIX

The three guards herded Oscar and Daria through the swamp along the branch-woven boardwalk. Oscar's hands were bound with a rope, and one of the guards kept a spear pressed against the small of his back. The other two guards dragged Daria by her arms, her head lolling as she drifted in and out of consciousness. Blood slicked her hair and ran in a heavy rivulet down her back, gluing her T-shirt to her skin.

An animal howl echoed from above, and the guards waved to the watchmen in the towers. The watchmen waved back, signaling the village below.

The group clambered over a barricade of boulders and entered the secluded village's muddy plaza. A large bonfire crackled at the center, its flames spitting sparks into the night and casting flickering shadows over the surrounding shacks and cabins.

Some of the villagers dropped what they were doing

to gawk at the captured intruders. Soon, a crowd of fifteen—most crippled by ancient injuries—trailed them across the plaza, their slit mouths stretched wide as they sneered insults, hurled chunks of mud, and spat on the prisoners.

Oscar lowered his head, trembling with fear and humiliation, tears mixing with the grime and spit dripping down his face. Daria, lost in her daze, remained unresponsive to the hostile crowd's jeers and assaults.

They passed the bonfire, and the chapel loomed ahead. Slits of light and curls of smoke seeped through its bone walls, shrouding the structure with an orange fog—like a cage for some infernal beast, the air around it heavy with its smoldering breaths. As the convoy approached the chapel, Oscar realized with deep dread that they were being led inside. It was here, at this grotesque altar, that he and Daria would be maimed, dissected, and consumed. Their bones would be hung on a tree somewhere, and they would have to endure this agony forever and ever.

The weight of this realization shattered the last of Oscar's composure. He broke into hysterics, thrashing against his restraints. "No! No!" he screamed, voice cracking with terror.

The guard subdued him with a sharp jab of the spear into the back of his thigh. The blade didn't sink deep and was out before Oscar even realized what'd happened, but the pain was immediate and electrifying, sending a violent spasm through the muscle. He crumpled into the mud, wailing. The villagers laughed and swarmed him like vultures. They tore at his hair and clothes, and one even tried to jam a finger into his eye socket. But before any real harm could be done, the guard barked a command and shooed them away. Oscar lay curled up in the muck, his cries reduced to ragged sobs.

The guard hauled him upright, and the convoy ascended the mound leading to the chapel.

The black doors groaned open, and a figure emerged from

inside. An old woman, draped in a hooded crimson robe, stood at the threshold. She leaned on a cane adorned with bone rosaries and dead flowers, her presence exuding an air of somber authority.

The guards greeted her with deep bows and presented the spoils of their hunt. Her gaze swept over Oscar and Daria with disdain so palpable it almost made Oscar want to apologize for his ragged appearance. She spoke, her voice low and morose, each word carrying the weight of command. The guards listened in silence, their heads still bowed.

Then, without so much as a nod, the old woman turned and retreated into the chapel, leaving the door open behind her.

The inside of the chapel was illuminated by a hundred sparkling candles, and the air was thick with the scent of incense. Smoke coiled from bundles of smoldering herbs, creating an atmosphere that hung heavy, humid, and suffocating. Ornaments, dreamcatchers, and stick figures dangled from the rafters like trapped birds, casting a cobweb of shadows that swayed over the dilapidated wood-and-bone surfaces of the chapel hall.

At the center of the open space, twenty or so hunters sat around a long table. Raw meat was piled high on trays set along its length, interspersed with bone chandeliers, sorry-looking flower arrangements, and human skulls repurposed as chalices, brimming with a dark, viscous liquid. The hunters dined in solemn silence, the quiet punctuated only by the clatter of cutlery.

At the head of the table, a skeleton slouched on a wooden throne. Its skull lolled to the side, jawbone slack as if caught mid-yawn. It wore a rusted crown, and tarnished jewelry adorned its bones. A tattered cape draped from its shoulders, framing a ribcage stuffed with withered flowers, their petals brittle and gray.

The hunters around the table barely acknowledged Oscar, Daria, or the three guards entering the chapel. Even when Oscar doubled over and vomited at the sight of the macabre feast, the hunters offered only a few irritated glances before resuming their meal.

The old woman—the village shaman, Oscar presumed—clicked her tongue in disapproval and snapped an order to the guards. They shoved Oscar, now huffing and gasping, and the dazed Daria toward the edge of the hall where four wooden poles stood supporting the ceiling.

Here Oscar noticed another prisoner: a man with a bulky frame leaned against one of the poles, tightly bound with ropes. His face was battered, blood smeared the side of his shirt and ran down his leg, and his right arm ended in a stump just below the bicep. The stump looked old, its surface a shiny lattice of keloid scars.

Oscar blinked in confusion. If he didn't know any better, this had to be Nobu—the man from Gustavo and Yvonne's story, the man who'd sold them out to the mountain folk.

The guards bound Oscar to the pole beside Nobu. Daria was tied to the adjacent pole, her body slumping against the ropes, her head lolling forward.

Nobu watched the newcomers through a mask of bruises, his expression tired but calculating. Oscar met his gaze but quickly looked away. *Why's he here?* he wondered. Nobu was supposed to be an ally to the Battle Criers, yet here he was, beaten and bound. Then it clicked. *He fucked up, didn't he?* He let Gustavo and Yvonne escape and now was paying the price for it.

One of the guards looped a noose around Oscar's neck and yanked it tight, slamming the back of his head against the pole. His vision dimmed for a second, then returned, blurrier this time.

The guards gave the shaman a final nod and exited the chapel. She turned to the long table and began chanting in low, guttural murmurs. Her voice filled the space, each syllable reverberating with ritualistic weight. She swayed around the table, the bone rosaries of her cane rattling softly with every step. She stopped next to the throne a few times, leaned in close to the skeleton seated there, and pressed her ear to its slack-jawed mouth. She nodded slowly, eyes closed, then returned to her chants and rituals.

"Hey. Boy," Nobu slurred through a mouthful of bruises. "Do you speak English?"

Oscar pried his eyes away from the shaman and glanced at Nobu. The ropes prevented him from fully turning his head, so he could only catch him from the corner of his eye. Nobu waited, but Oscar remained quiet. He had nothing to say to this traitor. Besides, it was probably better to keep him in the dark about what Oscar already knew.

The corner of Nobu's battered mouth twitched, attempting a smirk. "Yes, you understand me."

Damn it.

"Did you do this?" Nobu nodded toward the feast table. His voice dropped to a whisper, careful not to draw the mountain folk's attention. "If you did, it is an impressive mess. They only eat their own when someone is beyond recovery. This way, the fallen stay with them forever. This way, the hunt never ends."

Oscar furrowed his brow, absorbing the information. He reassessed the hunters around the table, and what had initially seemed like oppressive tension now read as solemn reverence. There was no gluttony in their feast, only a grim devotion. They honored their "dead" by consuming them.

It struck Oscar that some of the hunters must have recognized him from the hilltop. Yet, whatever hatred they harbored, they kept it contained—this was a holy ritual, and disrupting it would be considered sacrilege.

"How do you know all this?" Oscar asked, keeping his voice low.

"Don't worry about that," Nobu muttered. "What you should worry about is this: once they are done with their fallen, it will be your turn."

Hearing his worst fear spoken aloud made it all the more real. Despair clamped down on Oscar's chest, and the lump in his belly gave a nauseating twitch. For a moment, he could have sworn the lump had *squirmed.*

"We should work together. Plan an escape." Nobu's voice quivered with poorly restrained enthusiasm, his words bubbling out in a rapid whisper. If he kept this up, the mountain folk would hear him. "There is—*nandakke?*—a grave tunnel at the back of the village."

"A catacomb?" Oscar whispered.

"Yes, catacomb!" Nobu said, a bit too loud. "It digs into the mountain and comes out the other side."

Oscar's mind raced. He'd seen the catacomb at the front of the village, the one by the tree line, but he had no knowledge about another one at the back. Was Nobu telling the truth? The man was a traitor and couldn't be trusted, but what reason would he have to lie about the catacomb?

"What do you say?" Nobu asked.

Oscar opened his mouth to reply but stopped, realizing the chapel had fallen silent. The mountain folk, their faces painted with crimson smears, glared at Nobu with seething disdain. He was desecrating their ceremony.

The shaman spat an order, blunt as ever. Nobu's face went slack with dread—whatever the shaman had said, he understood it.

A large, brutish hunter arose from his seat, sending the chair skidding across the floor. He nodded at the shaman and approached Nobu with a determined stride, unsheathing a bowie knife from his belt. The other hunters roared in approval and raised their blood-filled chalices in a macabre toast.

Terror gripped Nobu. He thrashed against the pole, shrieking, hyperventilating, unable to get a word out.

The brute seized him by the throat and cocked back his knife-wielding arm. Oscar averted his eyes just as the blade plunged into Nobu's mouth. He couldn't escape the sounds, though: the sharp crack of teeth popping loose, the wet slosh of blood hitting the floor.

The mountain folk erupted in cheers, their fists, cutlery, and chalices pounding the table like a war drum. The sound swelled, drowning out Nobu's weak whimpers.

The shaman gave the brute another command, gesturing toward Oscar and Daria. Oscar's insides turned to goo, and all the moisture drained from his mouth. He didn't need to understand their language to grasp her meaning: *Now do the same to these two.*

His eyes flicked to Daria; she remained slumped, still lost in a concussed daze. *Good. Maybe she won't feel it,* he thought.

The brute marched to Oscar, seized a fistful of hair, and yanked his head back. The sheer force of it convinced Oscar that this man could tear his head off if he wanted to. The brute's icy blue eyes locked on his, gleaming with cruel intent. Slowly, deliberately, he brought the bowie knife toward Oscar's face, putting on a show for his brethren. The mountain folk around the table cheered and laughed.

Oscar's pulse throbbed violently in his throat. He was certain now that the lump in his belly was moving around, as if writhing in protest.

The tip of the knife pried through his puckered lips and slid past his gritted teeth. The metallic taste of Nobu's lukewarm blood spread across his tongue. Oscar squeezed his eyes shut. He didn't know what else to do.

The knife stopped still. The brute petrified, and Oscar felt the man's cold shiver pass through the blade.

The chapel fell silent, the jeers and laughter snuffed out in an instant. A strange, ugly screech had just carried in from somewhere outside. The sound was short and jagged and stopped as suddenly as it had begun.

The brute's grip on Oscar's hair loosened slightly as the hunters exchanged tense glances. For a moment, everyone in the chapel held their breath, all eyes turned toward the door.

Then the screech returned, louder and more confident this time, its pitch bending into a low blast of menace and doom.

Chaos erupted. The shaman shrieked orders in rapid succession as the mountain folk scattered from the table. Chairs scraped against the floor, cutlery clattered, and chalices toppled, spilling blood across the table and floor. The shaman's sharp commands cut through the clamor like a whip as the hunters rushed to an arms rack near the entrance, grabbing spears, bows, axes, and clubs. The brute yanked the knife from Oscar's mouth and sprinted to join them.

The war horn fell silent, replaced by the rising screams of villagers outside. One of the hunters opened the chapel doors, and Oscar glimpsed two cabins engulfed in flames. The bright roaring pyre consumed the cabins hungrily and dyed the night with citrine and blood like a doomsday sunset. Guards and villagers gathered around the blaze, some carrying buckets of water, others scanning its surroundings for the saboteurs, their postures tense and ready.

The cannibals poured out of the chapel, their piercing cries forming a dissonant chorus. Only the shaman and a single hunter remained inside. The hunter, holding a bone blade, stood alert and wired, eyes flicking between the entrance, the shaman, and the throned skeleton. The heavy chapel doors slammed shut behind the last of the exiting warriors.

Oscar, blood rushing in his head, twisted against the

ropes, trying to break free. He felt both dread and hope surge through him. The war horn, the fires—it all had to be Nathaniel's doing.

"Oscar?" Daria's faint voice broke through his focus.

His heart leapt and flooded with relief; he'd feared the blow to her head had been the kind people didn't recover from, but that didn't seem to be the case. She blinked, eyes scanning the room, her breathing shallow and panicked.

"Daria," Oscar said. "We're getting out of here. Don't worry. I—"

Oscar jolted in his restraints as a portion of the chapel's rickety back wall came crashing in and a man burst through the hole, shoulder first, tumbling to the floor.

"Nathaniel!" Oscar cried.

Nathaniel clenched a rusted sickle, and his open vest, shirt, and trousers were soaked in blood. Matted strands of hair clung to his pale, sweaty face, and his eyes burned with unhinged madness. He looked like a rabid animal.

Nathaniel scrambled to his feet and charged at the hunter like a blood-crazed demon. The hunter jumped in surprise, but that was all the protest Nathaniel got out of him. The sickle flashed across his face, carving a deep gash from brow to jaw, splitting his features in two. The hunter spun, and a wide arc of blood whipped through the air. He collapsed to the floor, curling into a shuddering, screaming ball.

Oscar and Daria bellowed with a mix of shock, fear, and triumph.

The shaman shrieked as Nathaniel lunged at her. She drew a dagger from her sleeve, slashing wildly, but Nathaniel dodged and caught her wrist. He drove a fist into her face, sending her reeling to her knees. The dagger clattered to the floor as her head lolled in a daze. Moving with skillful efficiency, Nathaniel produced a rag from his jacket pocket and gagged her. Next, he took out a pair of cuffs and secured her hands behind her back.

With the shaman subdued, Nathaniel picked up her dagger and strode toward Oscar. His gaze darted between Oscar and the writhing shaman, but his movements were purposeful, his grip on the weapons firm. Seeing this new, unsettling side of the friend he'd betrayed, Oscar felt an involuntary shudder ripple through him—what if Nathaniel hadn't come to save him, but to avenge the betrayal?

Nathaniel grabbed him by the throat. "Look what you made me do," he snarled, voice cracking, tears streaming down his face.

"Wh— Me?!" Oscar cried. "I didn't ask for this! Why'd you come if you didn't want to?"

"Because I can't lose you, damn it!" Nathaniel screamed.

"Nathaniel, I—"

"Don't," Nathaniel hissed through gritted teeth. He slid the dagger between Oscar's wrists and sliced through the bindings. Then he shoved the sickle into Oscar's hand and turned to haul the squirming shaman off the floor, the dagger now pressed against her throat. "Hurry up," he spat over his shoulder.

Oscar wasted no time. He slipped the noose from around his neck, sliced through the ropes binding his ankles, and stumbled to Daria.

"You're safe," he stammered, brushing her blood-streaked hair from her face with trembling hands. "We're gonna get out of here. We're going to make it."

"Oscar, Oscar, Oscar," she wailed, her lips trembling, trying to smile.

"I'm here, sis. I'm here," he choked out. "Are you okay?"

She nodded frantically. He cut her loose with the sickle, and she collapsed into his arms, hugging him tight and kissing his cheek. Then, she scrambled toward her backpack which the guards had tossed into the corner, her belongings scattered on the floor.

"No time," Nathaniel snapped, his eyes narrowing at Daria. "We have to leave."

"Yes, yes," Daria murmured. She picked up her hatchet, kissed the blade, and wrapped the wad of Ernie's hair around her fingers. Everything else she left behind.

"We need to circle back to the mountain pass," Nathaniel said. "How? No fucking clue."

"There's another catacomb at the back of the village," Oscar said. He looked at Nobu, who was now slumping from the pole, unconscious, a steady stream of blood still dripping from his mouth. "It digs into the mountain. It'll get us to the other side, out of the valley."

"I saw something like that, too. Looked like a cave entrance." Nathaniel raised an eyebrow. "You're sure it'll get us out?"

If Oscar knew one thing about Nobu, it was that he was a liar. So, no, he wasn't sure. But he also knew the catacomb was their best shot, and explaining all this to Nathaniel would only hinder their escape. "I'm sure," he nodded.

Nathaniel stayed quiet, holding the squirming shaman steady.

The cannibal cries outside swelled. Oscar's chest tightened. "Nathaniel?"

"I'm thinking," Nathaniel muttered. Then, a sharp exhale: "Fuck it. Out the back. Let's go."

Oscar watched Nathaniel drag the shaman toward the hole in the back wall. "She's coming with us?"

"The whole village is looking for an intruder. We're not sneaking our way out of this one. We need the leverage."

As they were heading out, a guttural cry stopped them. Nobu had lifted his head, blood dribbling from his mouth as he struggled to speak. The words came out unintelligible, but his pleading eyes said enough: *Don't leave me.*

Nathaniel's gaze landed on the one-armed man apparently for the first time, brow furrowing in recognition. "Is that…?"

"Yes," Oscar said. Avoiding eye contact with Nobu, he gestured for Nathaniel to keep going, and the group slipped out the back.

CHAPTER TWENTY-SEVEN

The hole in the wall opened to an elevated rock mound that overlooked the chapel's dimly lit backyard. The group froze as they spotted two figures huddled at the foot of the mound. One was a young guard, lying on his back, his throat slit, blood pooling in the mud. The other, an old villager, knelt over him, pressing his hands against the wound, his back turned to the group.

Oscar figured this was Nathaniel's handiwork, and the old villager must have discovered the guard afterward. Lucky for them, his first instinct had been to help the guard instead of alerting the others.

Before any of them could react, the shaman let out a muffled cry through her gag. The old villager whipped around, his eyes wide with surprise.

"Daria," shot Nathaniel.

Daria sprang into action. She jumped down the mound, hatchet raised. The villager uttered a dry gasp, then the blade came crashing down on his brow, splitting his head open. Blood sprayed across Daria's face in a vicious burst, leaving a red mist lingering in the air. The villager collapsed over the slain guard, spasmed once, then went still.

Daria yanked the hatchet free and cleared her sinuses with a farmer's blow—some of the blood must have sprayed up her nose. The red mist around her settled, but she remained huddled over the villager, frozen in a daze.

"Let's keep moving." Nathaniel dragged the shaman down the sloping rock mound. She slumped forth without resistance—witnessing Daria's attack had driven all fight out of her.

Oscar followed, shooting frantic glances around the yard. Beyond the surrounding huts, the glow of torches rose over the rooftops, lighting the streets as search parties scoured the village. The number of lights wasn't overwhelming—most of the villagers were likely still preoccupied with Nathaniel's fires—but all it would take was one lookout to spot them, and the entire village would be on their trail.

"I saw the catacomb entrance at the end of that alley," Nathaniel said, nodding toward a passage on the other side of the yard. "You two take point. I'll cover the rear."

"How'd you even know we were in the chapel?" Oscar asked, the thought just occurring to him.

"I saw them drag you across the plaza." Nathaniel's tone darkened, venom seeping into his words. "This was after I stitched my stomach back together."

A sharp twinge of guilt shot through Oscar. *I deserved that. But so did he.*

Oscar turned to Daria. "Come on. We've got to move."

She blinked, refocused on the task at hand, and nodded. Together, they led the way through the yard, creeping toward the alley with Nathaniel and the shaman close behind.

They were halfway across the yard when five villagers

emerged from behind the chapel, their demeanor brimming with tension. Both parties noticed each other simultaneously. The villagers wasted no time. They raised a cacophony of battle cries, their voices ringing out like alarms across the village.

Nathaniel pulled the shaman closer, holding her as a human shield, the dagger pressed firmly against her throat. His eyes gleamed with defiance, while his prisoner squirmed and wept through the knotted gag. Seeing their revered shaman like this, the villagers cried out in dismay.

One villager broke from the group, attempting to circle the escapees, but Nathaniel tightened his grip and yanked the shaman's head back as the blade pressed deeper into her neck.

"Get the fuck back! Don't come any closer!" Nathaniel roared, shaking her. His gaze flicked over his shoulder. "Why are we stopping?! Move!"

Oscar jolted into motion and continued leading the way, his legs trembling with every step. Daria stayed at his side, hatchet in hand, her blood-splattered face set in a wild, unhinged snarl.

The pursuing mob grew larger as more mountain folk joined the original five—three more, two more, then another five. They advanced with deliberate, vigilant movements, as if trying to catch fish with their bare hands.

The group entered the alleyway. Bleached skulls and dried human remains adorned the shacks like carnival decorations. Oscar forced himself to ignore the grisly trophies and focus instead on the fire-lit catacomb entrance at the alley's end.

"Pick up the pace," Nathaniel snapped. "And keep an eye on those doors."

Oscar glanced back: behind them, the mob was now cramming into the alley. But something didn't add up. Back in the yard, there had been at least fifteen villagers. Now he counted only eight.

Nathaniel noticed it too. "They're circling us!" he screamed.

Right then, a man burst from one of the shacks lining the alleyway, spear raised, his mouth stretched wide in a frenzied grin, eyes locking on Oscar.

Oscar halted, feeling like a deer caught in headlights. The sickle slipped from his hand, landing in the muddy ground. The man drew back his spear, ready to skewer him.

Before he could strike, Daria darted in from the side. Her hatchet flashed in the torchlights and sank deep into the nape of the man's neck. She twisted the blade free, tearing flesh, cracking bone. The man slumped to his knees with a heavy thud, blood gushing from the wound like water from a broken pipe.

Daria turned to Oscar and slapped him across the face. This shook him out of his paralysis. He looked away, cheeks burning with shame.

The mob erupted in furious cries, a collective of rage and bloodlust. In response, Nathaniel pressed the dagger deeper into the shaman's throat. The blade bit into her skin, drawing blood. She wailed in panicked, muffled hysteria, her struggles intensifying.

"We have to hurry!" Nathaniel roared.

"Make a run for it?" Oscar stammered.

"Yes! Go!"

Oscar and Daria took off, sprinting toward the catacomb. They skidded to a halt in front of the entrance, turning back to wait for Nathaniel.

Nathaniel dragged the shaman forward, but she resisted with all her strength. Screeching like a cornered animal, she clawed at the air, her body jerking wildly as she tried to break free and reach her people. Her terror and despair seemed to have overridden any sense of self-preservation.

Nathaniel was done giving warnings. He buried the dagger into the shaman's neck and dragged the blade across her throat like a can-opener.

The mob froze, their cries faltering as they watched blood jet from the gash like a hissing viper. Nathaniel shoved the shaman's limp body toward the crowd and bolted down the alley.

The mountain folk surged forward to catch their spiritual leader. They laid her on the ground, pressing hands against her gushing throat and clutching her limp fingers, murmuring words of comfort as she gasped and gagged and choked on her blood, eyes hazy and unfocused.

Nathaniel was two shacks away from Oscar and Daria when something flew past his head, leaving a cut on his cheek. An arrow sank into the mud at his feet.

"*Na dakhu!*" Daria cried.

"On the roof! Eight o'clock!" Oscar shouted.

A hunter sprinted across the rooftops, bow in hand, already notching another arrow. Without breaking stride, Nathaniel spun and hurled the dagger at him. The hunter dodged at the last second but, as a result, tripped over his own feet. He trampled down the sloped roof and plummeted facedown into the dirt with a neck-snapping thud.

Nathaniel had barely regained his footing when another villager barreled out from a side street, tackling him hard. They crashed against the wall of a nearby shack, its structures groaning from the impact.

The villager sank his jagged teeth into Nathaniel's shoulder, ripping through fabric, skin, and muscle. Nathaniel screamed, his voice raw, his face contorted in agony, tears streaming down his cheeks.

"No!" Oscar cried helplessly.

"*O Bozhe,*" Daria gasped, covering her mouth.

Nathaniel drew his knife and plunged the blade deep into the villager's side. The man's mouth stretched open in a scream of agony, and Nathaniel wrenched himself free with a desperate shove.

Most of the villagers who had stopped to aid the shaman were now back on the hunt. They ran down the alley, their eyes burning with red-hot fury, while more mountain folk joined the chaotic flock from the side streets.

"Come on, come on, come on!" Oscar yelled, voice cracking, as Daria bounced anxiously beside him.

Nathaniel reached them, and the group dashed into the catacombs. Vacant graves lined the tunnel in uneven stacks, their rows warped and jagged from the slow shifting of the mountain. Torches hung from the walls like cocooned moths, flickering in the faint draft that must have funneled from somewhere further ahead.

Nathaniel took the lead, and Oscar and Daria followed close behind. Behind them, the mountain folk surged into the catacombs in a disorganized wave, their cries echoing through the narrow space, amplifying into ear-splitting feedback. Luckily, the confined corridor offered the escapees a critical advantage: the mountain folk's momentum broke as they clogged the entrance, forcing them into single file.

"We can outrun them!" Oscar cried, his voice alight with sudden hope.

Daria's eyes sparkled with the same realization. "Yes, yes, yes!" she gasped, tears and snot streaking her blood-smeared face, carving pale lines through the crimson mask.

"Then keep running and stop talking," Nathaniel snapped over his shoulder. But Oscar also caught a glimmer of hope beneath his gruff exterior. This invigorated him even more. He felt almost giddy.

Up ahead, the corridor branched: to the right, the tunnel stretched forward, its path lit by a steady row of torches; to the left, a darkened spiral staircase wound upward into the unknown. The torches on the right flickered calmly, untouched by the draft, while a thin howl of air traveled down the staircase on the left.

"The stairs," Nathaniel ordered, snatching a torch from the wall in mid-run.

They charged up the spiraling staircase. Loose stones scattered the steps, and deep cracks and hollows snaked across the arched ceiling overhead—a promise that one day these corridors would all come crashing down.

The staircase wound forth. Behind them, the mountain folk reached the bottom of the stairs, and the flickers of their torches danced on the curving walls, their advancing shadows merging into a uniform, writhing cluster. The clatter of their weapons echoed in sync, a mechanical rhythm of war and destruction.

Suddenly, the staircase came to an abrupt end. The tunnel ahead was blocked by a massive cave-in. The ceiling had collapsed, forming a dense wall of rubble.

Oscar's lungs squeezed dry. "No, no, no," he cried, clawing at the debris.

"In here," Nathaniel said, gesturing at a narrow crack in the rubble—an escape route Oscar hadn't noticed. "We can squeeze through."

He grabbed Oscar's shoulder and pushed him toward the gap. Panicking, Oscar crammed himself in, twisting his body to fit. As he turned, he saw Daria kneeling on the stairwell, her back to them, fiddling with something.

"Daria?" he called, voice cracking with urgency.

She stood up, revealing a shiv wedged into the rubble, its blade pointing upward. "*Pastkoyu,*" she smirked.

"Yes, a trap. I get it," Oscar said. "Now, please—come on!"

He wriggled further into the collapsed passage. Nathaniel followed, passing his torch to Oscar. Oscar shone the light ahead. Beyond the cave-in, another grave-lined corridor stretched into the shadows. He tossed the torch through, then grabbed onto the surrounding rubble and hauled himself out.

But as he did, the rubble shifted. A deep rumble erupted

right behind him, echoing through the catacombs like a guttural groan. He turned just in time to see a boulder slide from the pile and ram into Nathaniel, pinning him against the wall.

Nathaniel let out a strangled cry, then quickly gathered himself and tried to wiggle free. But he couldn't.

His eyes widened, and his breathing quickened in panic. "I'm… I'm stuck." His face drained of color. "Jesus Christ, I… I can't move."

Behind Nathaniel, Daria burst into a dismayed scream—she too had come to the same realization. Nathaniel was blocking her way out.

"No…" Oscar cried, grasping at the boulder. He pushed, pulled, and shook it with all his strength. "We can get you free." Even as the words left his mouth, he knew it wasn't true. Neither Nathaniel nor the boulder would budge.

From the staircase, the mountain folk's battle cries drew closer, their voices sharpening with every step.

Nathaniel let out a high-pitched, near-hysterical laugh. His eyes shone with disbelief. "I think… I think this is it."

"No," Oscar whispered, the weight of the situation sinking in, becoming too much to bear.

Behind Nathaniel, Daria's voice rose in terror. "Oscar! Help!"

Oscar's legs buckled, and he sank to his knees, trembling. Nathaniel and Daria weren't going to make it. He was about to lose them both. He knew this now.

The mountain folk's cries stopped, leaving a chilling stillness in their wake. They had made visual contact with Nathaniel and Daria, and the hunters knew their prey was trapped.

"*Ni! Ni!*" Daria screamed. "Go away!"

"Oscar, listen to me," Nathaniel said. He swallowed hard, his throat dry. "You get past this mountain, and you're safe. The cannibals won't leave their valley."

"No, Nathaniel. Please," Oscar stammered. "I can't go on my own."

Nathaniel ignored his pleas. "On the other side of the mountains, there's a canyon. It's close. Find it and follow it east."

A pained shriek tore through the cave-in—someone had stepped on Daria's trap. She roared in desperate triumph, ready to go out with a fight. Her hatchet whooshed through the air a few times, striking nothing. Then, a sickening crunch as the blade found its mark. More screaming, more pain.

Nathaniel's breathing quickened, each word spilling out faster than the last. "Follow the canyon east. There's a hillside. You'll find Dean Theodore there. Tell him I sent you. If he doubts you, say 'parasite.' He'll know. He'll do right by you."

"I just… I can't…" Oscar sobbed.

Daria's cries of triumph changed to those of anguish. Then came a muffled thud, heavy and decisive like the last beat of a heart. Silence followed.

Oscar couldn't see her through the cave-in, but whatever had befallen her, it had been final. For her, there was no more fight to fight. She had lost. Understanding this, something inside Oscar died. It was too much. All of it—too much.

Ghoulish panting echoed down the corridor on Oscar's side of the cave-in. Something stirred inside him. The mountain folk must have known another route to reach this side. They were trying to flank him.

"They're here," he whispered, barely recognizing the words as his own.

Maybe it's best to give up now, he thought. At least then, he wouldn't have to leave his friends behind. But then that stubborn survival instinct kicked in with a counterargument: *Stop now and your friends' sacrifice will mean nothing.*

"You have to go. Right now." Nathaniel's voice snapped

him back to reality. He thrust his knife-wielding arm toward Oscar. "Take this and *go*."

"Nathaniel, I—" Oscar stammered.

"Go, you son of a bitch! *Go!*"

At that, a rush of resolve shot through Oscar like a spike of lightning. He grabbed Nathaniel's knife, picked up the torch, sprang to his feet, and bolted down the corridor.

Up ahead, a noise that reminded Oscar of TV static swelled and rose in volume. It almost drowned out the cries of the mountain folk and Nathaniel's screams of agony—almost.

Soon enough, the torch revealed a yawning pit of darkness where the floor had collapsed, cutting off his escape. Somewhere far below, water rushed and roared, its relentless torrent carving through Hell's subterranean aqueducts.

The light of his torch caught the edge just in time. He skidded to a halt at the brink of the pit, sending loose rubble into the abyss.

"No," he whispered, his voice swallowed by the chasm.

Heart pounding, he turned and saw them. The mountain folk, half a dozen or so, crowded the corridor, their blades and spears extended, their mauled mouths hanging agape in an eternal smile, dripping spit.

Beads of cold sweat broke through Oscar's skin. He raised the knife with a trembling hand. The blade offered no thrill, no security, no strength. He might as well have been holding his palm open—that's how much confidence the knife gave him. *Why even bother?* he thought. If Daria and Nathaniel couldn't beat them, how could he?

The mountain folk gave him no more time to assess the situation. They lunged at him as one, their battle cries screeching like twisting metal, clashing against the staticky roar of the currents below.

Oscar staggered back instinctively, but there was no ground left beneath him. His foot slipped, and he toppled into the pit.

The cries above shifted from frenzied triumph to bitter frustration, but suddenly the mountain folk felt like the least of his worries. The darkness swallowed him whole, and the roar of the river rose until there was nothing else.

As he slammed into the water, his body was seized by a sudden, paralyzing coldness. The currents swept him with violent force as if he'd been shot from a catapult. The sheer velocity twisted his insides and wrung the air from his lungs. He tumbled, limp and lifeless like a rag doll, as the relentless river pulled him deeper and deeper into its unforgiving embrace.

Something slammed into his head—*hard*. The impact rang hollow and muffled in the underwater world. Hot pain flared briefly, then extinguished, fading into numbness. His strength waned. He surrendered to the whims of the currents as consciousness slipped from his grasp.

CHAPTER TWENTY-EIGHT

Something was making its way up Oscar's throat, and with this sensation, the first shreds of awareness returned to him. He rolled on his side just as a lungful of water surged up his throat and spilled out of his mouth. Air rushed in, and with each ragged breath, more and more of his consciousness emerged from the dark.

He blinked, taking in his surroundings. He lay sprawled on a riverbank, his soaking wet clothes clinging to his skin like a heavy exoskeleton. The river meandered in a steady, knee-deep stream over jagged bedrock at the base of a looming mountain. Upstream, a cave hunched in the shadows, the rumbles of heavier currents drifting from somewhere deep within.

Above him, light cascaded through a sagging ceiling of clouds, casting the mountain in hues of rusted bronze. The river's ripples sparkled like a stream of fireflies, and trees bent low over the water, washing their wilted leaves in the stream.

Oscar dragged himself farther from the river. With each movement, pain flared along his side, sharp and cold like a knife. He pressed a hand against his torso, wincing. *I think I broke a rib.*

He began probing his body for other injuries. Everywhere he touched, stiff bruises responded with throbbing ache. When his hand reached the back of his head, he paused, feeling a deep dent. His fingers came away dry. No blood. The wound had already stopped bleeding.

His eyes followed the river upstream to the cave. *How long was I in there?* The thought sent a shiver down his spine.

Although the river had battered him good, nothing seemed beyond repair. What bothered him the most was a jarring migraine blooming behind his eyes, making his vision swim. Oscar sat up slowly and pressed his head between his knees, focusing on steadying his breath.

Something caught his eye—a glimmer in the water. He reached in and pulled it out. It was a knife. Nathaniel's knife.

The sight snapped his mind into focus, and the events that'd led him here came rushing back. Nathaniel and Daria were gone. Oscar's posture crumpled under the weight of the realization. A sob rose from his chest and soon spiraled into a full-blown meltdown. The grief felt like a physical force, like a membrane stretching over his skin, growing more oppressive and suffocating by the second.

And from this grief, a poisonous thought seeped through: *You did this.* This was his fault. If he hadn't gone after Daria, maybe the guards wouldn't have found her. Was she even heading to the village when he intercepted her? Perhaps she'd already decided Yung wasn't there and had been on her way to the mountain pass to escape the valley. If that was true, Oscar should have listened to Nathaniel and followed him. Maybe then they'd have all reunited by now. They'd all be together, and Nathaniel and Daria would be safe.

A dizzying vortex of what-ifs and maybes, of guilt and heartbreak, formed in his mind. But no matter how many hypotheticals he came up with, no matter how severely he beat himself up, Nathaniel and Daria were still gone, most likely already consumed beyond rescue.

But there was one thing they'd left in their wake: the journey they'd been on. It was still in motion. The expedition party had dwindled from three to one, but the goal and the means to reach it remained the same. Oscar owed it to them to see the journey through. Besides, what else did he have left but Dean Theodore? He recited Nathaniel's words in his mind: *Dean Theodore will do right by you.*

He tinkered with Nathaniel's knife, hands trembling, and his gaze fell to his fingers. Five of his fingernails were missing—had been for a while now—but only now did he realize they no longer hurt. The frail skin once shielded by the nails had now hardened, adapted. He squeezed the knife's handle, and his hands stopped shaking.

Oscar rose to his feet and began limping downstream, each step weighted by exhaustion. The mountain base bedrock gradually gave way to gently sloping hills, revealing a barren wasteland that unfolded like an apocalyptic omen: gravelly plains, clusters of jagged stone formations, and patches of withered scrubland stretching endlessly under the black-streaked amber clouds.

A handful of solitary hovels scattered throughout the desolation, hunkering against the harsh terrain, their decayed frames barely standing. To the south, the half-buried skeleton of a town lay clinging to the hazy distance. Whether it was inhabited or abandoned was impossible to tell. Here and there, nomads scoured the wasteland like shadows without origin. The nearest seemed miles away, and Oscar doubted they'd welcome his company any more than he'd welcome theirs.

Follow the canyon east. There's a hillside. You'll find Dean

Theodore there.

His eyes drifted north, settling on a deep fissure that split the wasteland in two and veered eastward, away from the mountains. Was this the canyon Nathaniel had spoken of? It had to be. Judging the distance, Oscar figured it would take him about an hour to reach it, maybe a little longer with his limp.

He set off toward the canyon, callused fingers wrapped around the knife as if it were some precious heirloom.

By the time Oscar reached the canyon, dusk had settled. The fissure stretched twenty feet across, and beyond it lay nothing but more wasteland—the same as on Oscar's side. He crept toward the canyon's edge and peered down. Unsurprised, he found no bottom, only a chasm that dove into the dark.

He backed away from the ledge and resumed his trek, following the canyon deeper into the eastern wastelands. The terrain was uneven, and the dusk had smothered the landscape with shadows, so he couldn't see how far the canyon stretched. Oscar now knew what he had already suspected: he wouldn't reach his destination before nightfall.

He swallowed dryly and fought back a shiver. He'd never spent the night alone in Hell. He had no equipment, no fire, no makeshift alarms. All he had were his soggy clothes and a knife that felt like a plastic toy against the lurking horrors. Feeling helpless in Hell wasn't anything new, but this was the first time he'd felt lonely here.

How lucky had he been to have someone like Nathaniel and Daria by his side? Without them, Oscar felt like an abandoned child in a foreign country. He knew he wouldn't last long by himself. He was no lone wolf. He needed his friends. He belonged in a pack.

Frustration sizzled on his skin like a maddening rash.

Why had he been the one who got to escape the valley? Why him? Of the three, he felt the least deserving of escape. He simply wasn't worthy of carrying the torch. In his mind, guilt and self-loathing had become cold, indisputable facts.

By nightfall, Oscar had found shelter beneath a boulder-strewn outcrop. A narrow gap under a rock provided just enough space for him to crawl in. Feeling humiliated, he settled on the hard dirt and cradled the knife, swallowing his cries to remain undetected.

The darkness was so complete that, after a while, he had to blink just to confirm his eyes were still open. Every now and then, a distant scream pierced the silence, sending his heart into a wild sprint. When a howl rose into a higher register, it twisted in his ears into a battle cry. And just like that, he was back in the catacombs, fleeing deeper into the claustrophobic unknown as the agonized cries of his friends faded behind him. In these visions, Nathaniel and Daria screamed Oscar's name, though he was pretty sure that hadn't really happened.

When the night finally grew quiet and his pulse steadied, Oscar's mind drifted back into the old cycles of ifs and maybes, into the vortices of self-blame and guilt. The sensory deprivation of the dark allowed him to delve deeper into himself, and from that darkness, more fragments of his past life began to surface.

The memories extended from his late teens to the age of twenty-one, his final year alive. His death and the events leading to it remained a blank—hadn't Nathaniel said no one remembered their own death?—but everything else unfolded in his mind like a story.

He succumbed into these memories, glad for the momentary reprieve from Hell.

Despite all the drinking, angst, and Mom's relentless discouragement, Oscar managed to stumble through high school without dropping out.

"Who would have thought?" Mom had said after the graduation ceremony (which she hadn't attended).

The next couple years of Oscar's life drifted by in an aimless haze of drinking and occasional drug use. He felt like he was treading still in a vast ocean, directionless and adrift, not knowing what else to do but stay afloat. Nothing motivated him, but then again, nothing *un*motivated him, either. Life didn't move him one way or the other. The world of responsibilities and long-term plans felt distant and unrelatable, like the mysterious rites of some ancient culture.

On Oscar's twentieth birthday, Mom kicked him out of the house. From a practical standpoint, it had little impact because he rarely went home anyway. But on a symbolic level, it hurt. A lot.

He called his sister to tell her what had happened. They both knew reasoning with Mom would be pointless—she'd rather die than change her mind. Instead, they agreed he could crash on his sister's couch in her cramped one-room apartment until he figured something out. Her only condition was that Oscar would have to stop drinking.

Oscar agreed without protest. There was no great drama there. He was tired of being either drunk, high, or hungover all the time, and an ultimatum from someone who cared was exactly what he needed. At twenty, he was still young and relatively healthy, and a little support went a long way. Agreeing to drop a habit he'd never really enjoyed didn't feel like much of a sacrifice. With nothing but a bag full of clothes and enough money for a bus ticket to his name, he moved to his sister's place.

After what felt like a month-long hangover, Oscar's mind began to clear. Each thought rushed in like a fresh breeze, and for the first time, maybe ever, he felt like he could breathe.

While his sister was away—usually at campus working on her master's or teaching undergrads—Oscar spent his days combing through her bookshelf, packed with titles from various fields of social sciences. With his mind clearing, he discovered an appetite for knowledge that only grew with every book he devoured.

He never told his sister about this new passion. He wasn't sure why. Maybe he didn't want her to think he was trying to follow in her over-achieving footsteps. He knew she wouldn't see it that way, but years of Mom's ridicule had cemented self-deprecating thought patterns into his brain that refused to bend to reason. And so, for this reason or something else entirely, he kept it a secret.

His sister never gave the impression that his extended stay was a burden. She'd learned from Mom's mistakes. Despite Oscar's low self-esteem and tendency to assume the worst about himself, he genuinely believed she enjoyed having him around. And, of course, he loved being with her. They'd watch movies and binge TV series together. They'd talk about novels and music, and look up weird stuff online. Oscar contributed to the household by regularly cleaning the apartment. Despite being stellar in pretty much everything, tidiness was the one thing his sister couldn't seem to get right.

In their moments together, he felt he'd achieved his childhood dream: the two of them getting by without their mother. But he knew it wouldn't last. She'd recently started dating someone, and it probably wouldn't be long before the relationship consumed all her spare time.

Still, being accepted and appreciated worked wonders. Oscar began to get a grip on his life. His uncle, a recovering alcoholic who was big on second chances, offered him a job at his firm, where he was assigned with low-pressure office tasks.

Life goals and plans still felt foreign and distant, but no

longer in an estranging way. They intrigued him now.

This must have been near the end because from this point forward, the memories grew blurry and disjointed. He might have moved out of his sister's place and rented his own apartment, but he couldn't be sure. He never contacted Mom after she kicked him out, and he remembered asking his uncle not to tell her he was working for him. His uncle didn't protest—he and Mom weren't on speaking terms, anyway.

One could argue things had worked out for Oscar in the end. Some might even say he'd lived happily ever after—brief though his ever after had been. But, looking back, the leading feeling was that he'd left the living world unfinished, incomplete. He didn't know if he would've ever tried to reconcile with Mom, but he would've at least liked to have the chance to do so. He never got to see what great things his prodigy of a sister would accomplish, either. The last he knew, she was still working on her master's and teaching undergrads.

Just when life had begun to make sense, it had ended. The memories tasted all the more bittersweet because of it. But then, would he have missed life *less* if it had all been a tragedy? Did it even matter now? So much had happened in Hell that his former life felt alien—literally another lifeform. He could no longer conceive of a universe where Hell and endless existence weren't part of the natural order of things.

One more memory surfaced. During his recuperation period at his sister's apartment, Oscar had picked up a book on psychopathology. It was a broad overview of the field, likely from one of her freshman courses. One page had been earmarked, leading him to a passage on the psychoanalytic theory of something called *death drive*.

The theory suggested that humans harbored an aggressive, toxic, self-destructive compulsion that worked against their instinct for safety and survival. It pulled people toward reckless acts, repeated mistakes, and decisions made against their better judgment. This drive, according to the theory, stemmed from the idea that the ultimate goal of all life was to return to an inanimate state. Death.

The theory, Oscar had gathered, was outdated and highly speculative, but it had resonated with him nonetheless. At the time, though, he hadn't understood why.

Now, in Hell, reflecting on that discovery, Oscar realized his sister had probably earmarked the passage thinking of him. She had always been aware of his daredevil recklessness, his penchant for self-destruction. She knew he took foolish risks and was often drawn to situations where he'd end up hurt. Her scolding lectures had been frequent, and, to his guilt, Oscar had taken a twisted comfort in her concern.

But having died and discovered Hell, Oscar knew something the psychoanalysts behind the theory didn't: the "inanimate state of being" was a myth, a fairytale. The dead couldn't die. Existence was an unbreakable constant.

And yet, if there was one place where the fantasy of true oblivion persisted, it was Hell. Here non-existence was the ultimate dream. Oscar had seen it. He had felt it. Every fiber of his being yearned for it. But of course, no one could end the never-ending. To act on that urge was futile—a stunted whim, a vestigial instinct from the world of the living. The death drive was a lie, whispered from the collective subconscious of a species that never truly understood what came after.

The thought conjured an image Oscar had seen many times before: a cornered animal, claws tearing at a brick wall, desperate for an escape that didn't exist.

Futile or not, Oscar had also felt that self-destructive pull countless times in Hell, hadn't he? He had even recognized this sensation, this death drive, just not by its true name. Until now, he'd called it something else: *the thrill.*

The thrill had puzzled him from the start. At first, he'd suspected it was a latent violence within him, but that never seemed to quite fit. Hadn't he proven time and again that he wasn't a violent person? Apart from attacking Heinrich's defenseless body—an incident he now viewed as a misguided experiment on his capacity for violence—he had forfeited every chance to act aggressively. Even when circumstances demanded it, even when self-defense would have been justified, he simply couldn't do it.

No, the thrill didn't stem from violence itself but from the danger it carried. Hurting others wasn't what had lured him; it was the potential for danger, for destruction. His death drive had thrived on that potential.

Oscar realized his death drive operated in two contradictory ways. First, it made him yearn for oblivion, for freedom from this endless existence. Second, it made him feel *alive.* For someone already dead, it was hard to say no to such a sensation. The danger, the surge of adrenaline, the fear of losing something—it all fed that primitive impulse within him, the part of him that refused to accept the reality of immortality.

Now that he understood the source of this urge, Oscar wondered: could he fight it? And more importantly, would he want to? Would he deny himself the only sensation that made him feel alive, even if chasing that feeling came at the risk of severe, irreversible injury? It seemed irrational—it *was* irrational—but anyone who had entered Hell knew these were the kinds of questions its multi-faceted absurdity forced upon you.

Oscar turned these thoughts toward his current mission. Was his quest to find Dean Theodore just another self-destructive compulsion? Or would reaching him absolve Oscar from that cycle? Nathaniel had said Dean Theodore would do right by him. Whatever that meant.

The way Oscar saw it, there was only one way to find out.

CHAPTER TWENTY-NINE

Oscar left his hiding place at dawn and resumed his trek along the canyon. He moved stubbornly without pause, each step driven by teeth-gritted resolve. Every ache and throb in his battered body was drowned out by feverish focus. He pressed on until the canyon walls leveled out into a small gravel field, encircled by rugged hills. His heartbeat quickened, and something between hope and fear surged through his veins. *This is it. It has to be.*

He descended into the valley, the loose gravel biting into his bare feet like sharp teeth. His eyes swept across the uneven terrain. The resinous glare of the overcast sky washed the landscape in a ghostly light, while deep shadows lingered in the cracks and crevices of the hills. It felt like the hills were watching him. The thrill tingled on his fingertips and made the hairs on his arms stand up.

Oscar cleared his parched throat, took a deep breath, and screamed: "Dean Theodore!"

The name cracked against the hills like a whip and bounced back and forth from one wall to another. He stood rigid, back straight, fists glued to his sides, and listened as the echoes faded into nothing. He waited, but there was no response.

Oscar called out again, but this time his voice broke, producing only a strained, high-pitched wheeze. He collapsed to the ground, his body folding in on itself. He rocked back and forth, face twisted into a desperate frown. He hadn't realized before just how tired, how utterly exhausted, he was of all of this.

What if no one was here? Or what if Nathaniel had tricked him? *No,* Oscar stopped himself. *Haven't you been through this already? He wouldn't do that to you.*

Something glimmered in the corner of his eye. He looked up and saw firelight illuminating a cave entrance in the hills. Someone was standing there. Their hunched figure was silhouetted against the reddish glow emanating from deeper within the cave. The figure raised an arm, gesturing for Oscar to join them, then retreated into the cave. The firelight vanished, and the shadows returned to conceal the entrance.

Oscar rose and unsheathed his knife, fear gnawing at his nerves. He could still back away, disappear into the wastelands, and… what? Spit on everything he, Nathaniel, and Daria had fought for? No. There was only one way to go about this.

He set off toward the hill and ascended the slope with slow, deliberate steps. He reached the cave entrance, perched on a sandy balcony halfway up the slope. The entrance led into a tunnel, its floor and walls clustered with dead mold poppies, like a mouth infested with spider eggs. The cataract-colored heads hung from their stems, their lifeless posture mirroring Oscar's own weary state. At the back of the tunnel, stripes of firelight projected faintly on the walls, partially obscured by the cave's uneven contours.

A voice echoed from within: "Step inside, lad. You needn't fear." The voice was low, raspy, and rich with calming frequencies.

Oscar felt tempted to lay his unease to rest and believe the voice, but even he wasn't *that* naive. He tightened his grip on the knife.

"Who are you?" he called out, wincing at the tremor in his voice.

"Theodore," came the reply. "I'm the Dean."

Oscar felt like crying out of relief, but he caught himself. He took a few wary steps forward and noticed each one felt lighter than the last. Slowly, he followed the poppy-coated corridor until he reached a doorway veiled by a curtain of vines. Firelight peeked through the gaps. He tucked the knife behind his back and pushed through.

The tunnel opened into a dome-shaped chamber, its walls and ceiling swelling with clusters of those strange flowers. Their pearly heads bathed in the warm glow of a campfire that crackled in the middle of the chamber. The flames painted the flowers with a rose gold hue that shifted with the flickering light.

In all this warmth, millions of spores floated in the air, refracting the firelight into a dazzling prism of sparkle, like a star-spattered cosmos captured in a snow globe, swirling with arcane dust.

The sheer beauty of the space struck Oscar with melancholic ache. The contrast between this celestial haven and the horrors outside was almost too much to bear. The weight of everything it had taken to get here hit him like a wave, and tears welled in his eyes.

He also felt a sense of familiarity about this place. It was like stepping into a long-abandoned childhood home and finding it still warm. As the nostalgic sensation flowed through him, he realized his headache had faded. Even the lump in his stomach had ceased its broadcast of pain signals.

A man in his fifties sat on a shawl by the fire, one elbow resting on a hooked knee, his mouth curved into a faint smile—Oscar's flabbergasted reaction must have amused him. The man's aura seemed perfectly aligned with the warmth of the chamber.

As soon as Oscar's eyes settled on the man, he became transfixed. A deep scar cut from his brow to cheek, giving his wise features a charismatic edge. He wore a dark sweater over a collared shirt and a pair of corduroy pants, tattered and frayed by time. At his feet lay an open book, shoddily bound, its cover facing up. Despite the wear and tear Hell had inflicted upon him, he carried himself with an air of academic elegance.

So this is Dean Theodore.

"Pray tell," Theodore said, his voice stern but calm, "what do you intend to do with that knife?"

"It's for protection," Oscar said. He tried to mimic his sternness, but the words came out small and apologetic. Under Theodore's calculating gaze, he felt exposed, as if the man knew things about him that even he wasn't aware of.

"I see," Theodore nodded slowly, the tone in his voice saying, *I suppose it's alright*. He closed his eyes, and a shadow passed over his expression. "I take it Nathaniel didn't make it."

"No," Oscar whispered, fighting the burning in his throat. But then a troubling thought struck him. "Wait. How did you know I was traveling with Nathaniel?"

"We will discuss this forthwith," Theodore said dismissively. He gestured toward the fire. "Come, sit if it pleases you. We'll palaver."

Oscar detected a blend of gruff Scottish and polished American academia in his intonation. Theodore seemed to belong to an era before Oscar's time—something about the man's cadence made it clear.

Slow and reluctant, Oscar sat on a tree trunk by the fire, across from Theodore. He fidgeted with the knife, realizing it had become little more than a stress toy in his hands. Who was he fooling? He wasn't going to use it on anyone.

"You must be parched, lad," Theodore said, producing a canteen from behind his back.

Oscar eyed the canteen warily. "You first."

"Aye, of course." Theodore took a long swig, swished the mouthful of water around, then gurgled loudly before swallowing. He passed the canteen to Oscar, raising an eyebrow: *Satisfied?*

Oscar sniffed the cork and gave the canteen a shake. He wasn't entirely sure what he was looking for. Either way, the water appeared clean. The canteen sloshed reassuringly. He tipped it back and drank voraciously. The cool liquid rushed down his throat, and an invigorating freshness swept through him.

"Keep it," Theodore said. "There's plenty more."

Oscar nodded his thanks and drained the rest of the canteen in one go.

"I don't believe I caught your name."

"Oscar." He wiped his mouth. "I'm Oscar."

Theodore tipped his head in greeting. Then: "What happened to Nathaniel, Oscar?"

Oscar's expression darkened. "Ever heard of the mountain folk?"

Theodore's posture sank—yes, he had heard of them. He drew a measured breath. "How much did poor Nathaniel tell you about our arrangement?"

Oscar hesitated, wondering if the proper course of action would be to withhold information until he got a better sense of the man. He quickly decided against it. He had no leverage here, no cards up his sleeve. He was tired of playing games that couldn't be won. Wasn't that what Hell was? A never-ending game that only led to loss after loss.

Oscar recounted what little Nathaniel had shared: "He told me you've studied Hell extensively and gathered results only a few have managed to uncover. Nathaniel found something significant—a discovery—and his goal was to deliver it to you. He said this would change things."

"Nathaniel has sung far too many praises of me," Theodore scoffed, swatting the compliment away. "We have a school of like-minded scholars here. Our research is a collective effort."

"There's other people here?" Oscar's eyes darted around the cave. Until now, he'd been so captivated by the spore-sparkling space that he hadn't noticed the alcoves carved into the poppy-coated walls. Darkened indents and cracks hinted at tunnels branching off into deeper caverns.

Theodore apparently caught the realization in Oscar's expression. "Aye, it's a whole cave system," he said, his tone reassuring. "Fear not. I've requested privacy. We won't be bothered."

Oscar gave a tight nod, saying nothing. He shifted in his seat, making a mental note to keep an eye on the shadows.

"How did the two of you come to work together?" Theodore asked.

"Nathaniel found me in the cemetery," Oscar said. "He needed someone to help him on this journey. Later, he told me that he also wanted to spare someone from experiencing what he'd endured in Hell."

Oscar's voice wavered, and he trailed off. Despite the horrors they'd faced, Nathaniel had done everything in his power to shield him from the worst. Hell was an unconquerable beast in that and many other regards. And yet, despite his own downfall, Nathaniel had managed to deliver Oscar here. That in itself felt like a monumental achievement—a testament to the man's resilience and devotion.

"I see," Theodore said. "And this discovery—did Nathaniel

perchance reveal it to you?"

"Not exactly. Right before the mountain folk got him, he told me to find you and bring you this message: *parasite*. He said you'd know what it means." Oscar hesitated, then added, "He said you'd do right by me."

The Dean rested his chin on his folded hands. "Uh-huh."

Oscar's heart shrank. He'd expected the word *parasite* to be a spell that would unfold some magical revelation where it all would finally make sense. But Theodore's lukewarm response only suggested the opposite: disappointing, anticlimactic indifference.

He glanced down at the knife in his hands. The leather grip had started to peel from all the nervous fidgeting. "You didn't answer my first question," he said, eyes still fixed on the blade. "How did you know I was traveling with Nathaniel?"

Theodore's penetrating stare focused on Oscar.

"Because you are the discovery."

Oscar's mind went blank. He opened his mouth, but no words came out.

Theodore continued, "I assigned Nathaniel to find your grave in the cemetery and bring you here."

"Wh—me?" Oscar stammered. "You've mixed me up with someone else."

Theodore didn't blink. "Have you been experiencing headaches? What about double vision? Nausea?" His questions felt more like confirmations, as if he was filling a form for Oscar, checking the boxes before he got a chance to reply.

"Yeah, but... those are just death symptoms," Oscar protested. "They could apply to anyone."

Theodore leaned forward. "Then let's be more specific: do these flowers stir nostalgia? Have you felt persistent pain around your chest or abdomen? Have you noticed an abnormal growth forming there—a lump, perhaps?"

Something inside Oscar sank, and a deep, exhausted forfeit seized him. There was no point denying it. They both knew Theodore was right.

"There's no mistake, no mix-up," Theodore concluded. "You're the one we've waited for."

Throughout this interaction, there'd been no malice, no shadow of ill will, in Theodore's tone or demeanor. In a way, Oscar wished there were. Maybe this kind of revelation would've been easier to digest if it'd been delivered with some diabolical bravado. But no. Dean Theodore exuded warmth and sincerity, and Oscar resented him all the more for it.

"What is this?" he asked. "What does that mean—'the one you've waited for?'"

Theodore's brow furrowed as he calculated his response. He drew a steadying breath and began: "As you know, our school is dedicated to studying Hell and the nature of afterlife. Nathaniel was correct—our research has indeed led to significant discoveries. In fact, our focus has expanded to advanced lifeforms beyond our realms—cosmic entities capable of perceiving higher dimensions and comprehending the infinite nature of existence. We call them the Wanderers, and we follow in their footsteps."

It got very quiet in the chamber. Even the hum of the cave system seemed to dim. Oscar stared at Theodore, trying to decide whether he should laugh or simply get up and walk out.

"Listen," Oscar said after a long pause, taking the diplomatic route, "maybe you've been alone in this cave for too long, and—"

Theodore scoffed and shook his head, cutting him off. "Instructor Agnes," he called, his voice carrying into one of the darkened recesses. "Would you be so kind as to prove to our guest that I am not psychotic?"

Oscar's grip on the knife tightened, and he shifted into an alert position, every muscle wound tight.

A young woman emerged from the shadows. She appeared

to be around Oscar's age, but something stern and grave in her aura suggested to Oscar she'd been in Hell far, far longer. Her curly dark brown hair was tied back in a bundle, emphasizing the fox-like sharpness in her pale eyes. An old, grotesque scar ran across her throat, deep and jagged, like a line drawn into wet sand. A longbow rested on her back alongside a quiver bristling with arrows.

Her demeanor exuded a strong sense of level-headedness. Her hands rested neatly on her lap, one over the other, and her gaze shifted between him and Theodore with measured assertiveness. An embarrassed self-consciousness flowed through Oscar in a queasy wave. He was way out of his depth with these people.

"Do you see her?" Theodore asked.

"Yes," Oscar said, his body still tense, ready to flee.

"Then we can agree," Theodore continued, "that she—and by extension, any of my colleagues—are not figments of my imagination?"

"Unless you're imagining all of us," the woman countered, "including our guest here."

Theodore chuckled. "Very good."

"Is there anything else, Provost?" she asked, respectful but direct.

"One more thing, dear Agnes," he said, raising a finger. He turned to Oscar. "Ah, before we proceed... you do know what 'metamorphosis' means?"

"Yes," Oscar replied, slightly offended.

"Excellent," Theodore said with a smile. "Now, Instructor Agnes, please enlighten young Oscar here on the metamorphic stages of a Borbos descendant, if you would."

A Borbos descendant? The words hung in Oscar's mind, stirring unease.

Agnes fixed her calm gaze on Oscar. "In the living realm, mold poppies release spores that seek to inhabit human hosts.

If conditions are optimal, these spores evolve into a parasite within the host. The next stage for the parasite is to form a cocoon to protect itself and to ensure its metamorphosis progresses uninterrupted."

She paused briefly, letting the words sink in, then continued, "Unfortunately, the human often dies before the cocoon is fully formed, before it's strong enough to withstand the death of the host. When that happens, the parasite's metamorphosis halts. It dies an animal death—a death devoid of self-awareness, a death devoid of afterlife. The theory is that if the parasite manages to spin a fully-formed cocoon before the host's demise, the parasite might survive the transition from the living realm to Hell. Here it could continue its evolution, culminating in a lifeform capable of perceiving higher dimensions—a lifeform superior to humans."

"We've encountered half-formed cocoons," Theodore interjected, his tone scholarly but also tinged with excitement. "But no Borbos descendant in recorded history has ever survived the death of its human host. Until now, that is."

"Until now?" Oscar echoed. He glanced between the two, waiting for clarification. The weight of their silence was answer enough. "You're saying I'm a host?" A hollow laugh escaped him.

"Indeed we are," Theodore said, his expression grave. "We have strong reason to believe that the descendant within you has survived the transition."

Oscar's insides churned with a sickening twist. The hardened lump pressed to his side suddenly felt heavier, more prominent, more *alive.*

"This is insane." He stood up, paced back and forth, slicking back his hair, fighting back nausea. *Why am I crying?* he thought. "You're both insane."

"Is it any more insane than discovering an existence beyond death?" Agnes countered with a confident tilt of her head. The gesture reminded Oscar of Daria, and his heart broke all over again.

"Yes," Oscar said, his voice a strangled mix of laughter and sobs. "Yes, it is."

"Believing life and death are the only forms of existence—*that's* insane," she shot back, her pale eyes sharp.

Theodore cut in, "Even science in the living realm acknowledges the possibility of higher-dimensional lifeforms. By entering this plane of existence, by studying it, we've proven it correct."

Oscar hesitated. The logic gnawed at him, unwelcome but undeniable.

"I can see it in you, lad," Theodore pressed. "You've already accepted it."

"How would I have even gotten infected by the parasite?" Oscar countered, defensive. "You're saying mold poppies caused this? Before Hell, I didn't even know they existed."

"It's a... complicated procedure," Theodore said blandly. "Agnes provided you with the simplified version so as to not overwhelm you."

"Overwhelm me?" Oscar laughed. He paused. A new thought came to him with dawning horror. "Say you're right. What happens when the parasite... hatches?" The last word burned like bile at the back of his throat.

Theodore and Agnes exchanged a weighted glance.

Oscar closed his eyes, hot tears streaking down his cheeks. "And don't you dare lie to me."

"We will extract the parasite," Theodore said. "You will undergo surgery—"

Surgery. That was all Oscar needed to hear. Whether or not he believed in the parasite was irrelevant now; Theodore and his cave-dweller scholars believed, and they intended to cut him open for it.

Oscar stepped back, raising his knife toward Theodore.

Defiance burned in his eyes, but his hands shook so violently that he had to grip the knife with both hands to steady it.

"Easy now, Oscar," Theodore said, rising slowly, his hands held up in surrender. "We can talk this through."

"You're not extracting anything, okay?" Oscar barked, his voice raw. "I'm leaving right fucking now!"

"Lower your blade," Agnes commanded with cold resolve. She had drawn her longbow, an arrow already notched and aimed at him.

"Agnes, don't," Theodore warned, his tone sharpening. "You might hurt the descendant."

"You're more important," she replied, her bowstring taut, her eyes locked on Oscar.

"Nothing's more important than—" Theodore froze in mid-sentence as Oscar yanked up his shirt, revealing the lump on his side. He pressed the tip of the knife against it, a daring, defiant gleam in his eyes.

"Listen to your dean, Agnes," Oscar said, his voice low. Beneath the pressure of the blade, the lump shifted.

Agnes hesitated, her eyes flickering between Theodore and Oscar. After a tense beat, she cursed under her breath and lowered her bow.

"Oscar. Think this through, lad," Theodore said. "You won't make it out there."

"I'll take my chances," Oscar spat.

"You don't understand. The parasite isn't merely confined to your abdomen. It's spread. Headaches, double vision—this means it's already reached your brain."

Oscar paused. His retreat faltered. The knife trembled in his hand, its tip pressing against the lump on his side, piercing skin and drawing a thin line of blood.

"If you leave it unattended," Theodore continued, "the parasite will hatch on its own. Is that your want? To be out there, alone, without help, when that happens?"

"At least with us, you'll be tended to," Agnes added. Her voice was measured, almost clinical. "We'll sedate you. Minimize your pain."

Pain. The word lodged squarely in the center of Oscar's mind. Behind one corner, it dulled; behind another, it sharpened. But it was always there—a persistent, shape-shifting intruder that refused to leave. He was so tired of it. Tired of everything.

"You have a key inside you," Theodore said, his eyes bright with fanatic devotion. "A key that can unlock the door beyond death."

Agnes took a step toward Oscar, and now there was warmth in her voice: "Your contribution could potentially alleviate so much suffering."

Potentially, Oscar thought. That was the operative word. *Potentially* didn't amount to much when you were being asked to sacrifice yourself. His glassy stare drifted to the campfire's erratic dance.

Wasn't self-destruction what he'd been chasing all along? Coming here, ignoring every warning sign—wasn't that proof of his resolve? Maybe all this time Dean Theodore's conviction was the order Oscar had yearned for to subdue the chaos within. Theodore's near-religious fervor must have rubbed off on him because for the first time, it felt like it all made sense.

"Nathaniel was right," Theodore said. "The discovery will change everything. I can see you shared something meaningful with him—it's written in your grief, lad. So, if not for anyone else, do it for him."

Oscar blinked, his eyes lifting slowly from the fire. "Did he know?" he asked, his voice hollow. "Did Nathaniel know what you'd do to me once he brought me here?"

Theodore hesitated. "I don't know," he finally admitted.

"Bullshit!" Oscar shouted, jamming the knife deeper against his side.

"It's the truth!" Theodore's voice sharpened, the measured calm in his voice faltering. "I assigned Nathaniel from the outside. 'An independent contractor' I believe were his words. I know he'd studied our work, but how extensively he did this—I've no idea. You've spent more time with him than I ever did, Oscar. If someone knows the answer, it's you."

Oscar's eyes darted without a point to focus on as he searched for an answer—any answer. The leaden exhaustion weighed on him, and gravity strengthened its pull. At last, he exhaled shakily and sank to the ground. The knife slipped from his grasp and clattered to the stone floor.

There was sweetness in giving up.

He looked up at Theodore, his figure framed by the shimmering spores and the rose-gold poppies that pulsed gently to the ever-throbbing heartbeat of the fire. The Dean's expression held no triumph, no arrogance—only quiet, understanding acceptance.

"Will you please help me?" Oscar asked, his voice barely above a whisper.

CHAPTER THIRTY

The sedatives were taking hold. Oscar's limbs grew heavy and unresponsive, and his tongue felt swollen, filling his mouth. The rough grain of the wooden operating table pressed against his bare back. He felt himself melting into it. The wood fibers intertwined with his tissue, its ancient essence blending with his own, and he found himself marveling at its silent wisdom.

These probably aren't just sedatives, he realized. But the thought didn't trouble him. He welcomed this oneness, feeling content with blissful surrender. A lopsided grin spread across his face, and a stream of spit slid down his cheek.

Instructor Agnes leaned over the table and gently wiped the drool from his mouth. He tried to thank her but only managed to mumble drunken gibberish. She offered a soft yet troubled smile and a pat on his shoulder before turning back to prepare the surgical instruments laid out on a side table: scalpels, scissors, clamps, bone cutters, retractors.

The delicate clink and clatter of the tools echoed softly in the cavernous space, like chimes in an empty temple.

Oscar's eyes roved sluggishly, registering his surroundings. He had a hazy recollection of Agnes leading him here. They had traveled through the labyrinthine tunnels of the complex cave system, eventually emerging into this anatomical theater, constructed inside a vast high-ceilinged cavern. Steep scaffolding surrounded the central stage where the operating table had waited under the glow of torches.

At the time, the seats of the scaffolds had been empty; now, Oscar became aware of the hushed chatter of the fifty or so spectators that had gathered around him, their voices buzzing softly in his ears. The lights had been arranged so that the crowd remained shrouded in shadow, but he still felt fascination exuding from their ranks, directed squarely at him.

Lying there, naked and drugged, surrounded by faceless onlookers, self-awareness swept over him. He felt ashamed, humiliated. *No negative thoughts now,* he reminded himself. *Let's not make this a bad trip.*

He forced his attention to the operating table's immediate surroundings. Agnes was still there, her back turned, cleaning the surgical instruments. Beside her sat a heavy glass jar filled with a viscous, translucent liquid. Spores floated lazily within, stirring nostalgic sensations of things Oscar couldn't remember. He figured the jar was meant for the parasite once it was extracted. The thought drifted through his mind with eerie calm. No fear. Just a drug-induced acceptance of what was to come.

The murmurs in the anatomical theater faded as Dean Theodore entered the stage from a side door. He wore a white apron over his collared shirt, sleeves rolled up. The attire reminded Oscar more of a butcher than a surgeon. Theodore gave Agnes a brief nod before moving to Oscar's side and gently squeezing his hand with fatherly affection.

Oscar managed an appreciative smile in response, while Agnes began wrapping restraints around his wrists and ankles. The padded fabric was soft and snug, and the restraints embraced him with a protective warmth.

Theodore surveyed the crowd around them. The dark figures rose from their seats, looming over the railings like a ghostly jury, their collective focus fixed on the scene below.

"Good evening, dear colleagues and student body," Theodore announced, his voice carrying a firm yet gentle authority. "As many of you have heard, we are indeed in possession of a live descendant of the Wanderer Borbos Mollus."

A charged silence fell over the theater. Oscar could feel the electricity in the air, like a cloud of tiny pinches that plucked at the fine hairs on his skin.

"Young Oscar here, host to the pupal parasite," Theodore continued, "has discussed his situation at length with Instructor Agnes and myself. He has given his full consent to the parasite extraction process."

The crowd murmured in awe. One person began clapping, and soon the entire cavern erupted in applause. The sound washed over Oscar, amplified by the drugs coursing through his veins, magnifying their admiration into something euphoric. His chest swelled with gratitude, and tears stung his eyes in a good way. Theodore turned to him, smiled proudly, and patted him on the shoulder.

With a raised hand, Theodore silenced the crowd into a reverent hush. "Now," he declared, "as this operation with a live parasite is the first of its kind in recorded history, I shall perform the surgery under the guidance of The Trickster."

The Trickster? The word rang hollow in Oscar's mind. He tried to voice it, but his tongue lay limp and lifeless like a dead slug.

"Instructor Agnes," Theodore said, his voice growing grave. "The mask, if you would."

Agnes stepped out of Oscar's field of view. She soon returned, cradling a mask in her hands—a mask made of skin. It had been peeled cleanly from someone's head—face, scalp, hair, and all. The grotesque thing sagged in her hands like a wet rag, its boneless features paralyzed in a leering grin.

She handled the mask delicately, as though it were an injured bird. Her fingers brushed a long strand of black hair away from its face before she presented it to Theodore.

A few horrified gasps rippled through the crowd.

Oscar's breath caught in his throat. His eyes fixed on the slumping mass of skin, and cold dread began to seep through the sedated fog. He recognized the face from somewhere.

Theodore received the mask with grim reverence. He studied it a beat, then let out a heavy sigh. "I know many of you find this appalling," he said. "And I share your sentiment. Let it be understood: this phase of the ceremony is not conducted lightly, nor with disrespect. But the mask is a window to the visions. This is the way, and the way we follow."

A dispersed, arhythmic murmur rose from the crowd: "In the footsteps of the Wanderers."

Theodore slipped the mask over his face.

The sight of the masked figure struck a primal nerve in Oscar, triggering forgotten dreams. Two previous encounters returned to him: one occurred in an abandoned shack in the western desert, the second one in a mountainside cave. Both times, the encounters had been preceded by a full-body paralysis—a trap between dream and death—and a visit by the cackling creature.

Oscar's mind swirled with questions and hasty conclusions. Was this Trickster Theodore had mentioned the creature from his dreams? And had Dean Theodore somehow visited him through visions conjured by The Trickster? Merely forming such questions forced Oscar to confront just how far he'd drifted from the realities of the living world and descended into a realm governed by nightmare logic.

As if summoned by his thoughts, an oversized bald head rose from behind the foot of the operating table. Dead fish eyes followed, glassy and unblinking, locking onto him.

The euphoria drained from Oscar's veins and was replaced by all-encompassing horror. The drug-fog cleared and Oscar's mind sharpened, but still he couldn't react or retaliate. His body remained unresponsive, paralyzed by the drugs.

"Ke ke ke," The Trickster cackled, the sound originating from somewhere deep within its throat.

Its very presence seemed to warp the environment, and something malignant took over the cavern's ecosystem: the surfaces glistened with a sickly, poisonous sheen, and the shadows thickened as if they'd gained mass. The air turned dense with an oppressive weight, and even the golden glow of the spores in the glass jar dulled, graying to ash.

No one else in the cavern seemed to react to the creature nor its effects on the atmosphere, the nightmare unfolding around them.

Why am I the only one who can see it? Oscar thought. *Or rather, why does The Trickster show itself only to me?*

Theodore asked Agnes for a scalpel.

As she handed him the instrument, The Trickster hoisted its hulking figure onto the table, perching at Oscar's feet like some grotesque primate. Its scaly hands rested on hooked knees, partially obscuring a smile that stretched wide across a shadowed face. Those gelatinous black eyes gleamed like obsidian pearls, brimming with malicious curiosity as they drank in Oscar's plight.

"Get that fucking thing away from me," Oscar tried to say, but all that emerged was a slurry of sobbing gibberish.

Agnes settled a hand on Oscar's head and stroked his hair gently. She leaned in close, her voice a soothing hush in his ear: "You're fine. Don't look at all that. Look at me."

She cupped his face and gently turned his head. But instead of Agnes, Oscar saw Daria.

Daria's hazel eyes locked on his, and the two shared a silent connection, the kind preserved only for close friends. A smug yet warm grin tugged at her lips. This calmed him. All the panic drained away, and the fog returned, enclosing him in a warm embrace. Daria was whole again—no signs of injury, no deathly pallor. She radiated vitality. Life.

"It's okay, Oscar." Her hand continued to stroke his damp hair. "It's okay."

With her mere presence, she erased every trace of fear. Oscar knew this was a hallucination, but Daria stood *right there*, sharper and more vivid than anything else in the cavern. She felt more tangible, more real than the scalpel cutting into him. How could he not give in, embrace this fleeting moment, and lose himself in its comforting illusion?

Everything beyond the bubble he shared with Daria felt distant, muted, as though filtered through a body of water. The crowd leaned over the railings, ravenous for every glimpse of the parasite's birth. Their voices rose in a great, rapturous chant: "In the footsteps of the Wanderers." The Trickster joined their ritualistic fervor with its guttural, staccato cackles.

From the corner of his eye, Oscar caught the glass jar reflecting Theodore's surgical work. Matted strands of the mask's black hair swayed close to the incision. Blood flowed in thick ribbons down his naked torso, pooling on the table and dripping on the floor. Yet, Oscar felt no pain.

Theodore spread the wound with a pair of retractors, then reached in with steady hands and began pulling out… something. A pulsating, writhing lump emerged, slick with blood and quivering with grotesque vigor.

The Trickster ceased its laughter. Strangely, its silence seemed to occupy more space than its cackling, and Oscar found the creature all the more disturbing for it. It fixed its glassy black eyes on the bloody lump, tilting its head from side to side as though studying a specimen. The Trickster's wide, shadowed grin remained, but something in its stillness made it seem… content.

The audience's chant faltered and broke into murmurs of awe, then picked up again with renewed zeal: "In the footsteps of the Wanderers! In the footsteps of the Wanderers!"

Oscar tried to shut it all out, anchoring himself to Daria. She was all he had left.

The lump was out of his stomach now, but Theodore kept pulling. Long, sinewy tendrils followed, slick and taut, stretched like bass strings between the gaping incision and the squirming lump in Theodore's hand.

Oscar felt a violent *tug* deep inside his skull, another sharp pull at the nape of his neck, and several smaller, stabbing jerks all across his body. His face prickled and sizzled. His left eyelid fluttered uncontrollably, like the wing of a moth. His body began to convulse.

"Stay, Oscar," Daria urged, her voice now edged with fear. She leaned closer, cradling his head in her hands. "Stay with me."

But how could he? He was barely here anymore.

Everything screeched—the cavern, the parasite, the very fabric of his existence. His body spasmed, caught in a seizure, teeth grinding so hard his jaw threatened to crack. His mouth filled with the sweet taste of peaches; his nostrils permeated by the acrid stench of burning hair.

With his last shreds of comprehension, he focused on Daria. She was the last peek of sunset in the horizon, her presence the final rush of euphoria before everything unraveled.

Then, with a sudden yank, he was pulled into a new kind of darkness.

EPILOGUE

The black desert sand shifted under Oscar's callused feet, tracing the arhythmic stagger of his poorly coordinated movements. For the time being, he had the strength to remain upright. Once he didn't, he would crawl until his muscles locked and refused to carry him further. Only then would he rest.

This grueling routine wasn't born of will or foresight—Oscar no longer comprehended such notions. Saving his strength or finding shelter simply didn't cross his mind because he had no mind for thoughts to cross. He operated purely on whims, impulses, and reflexes, his cognitive abilities barely above that of a simple sponge.

Nowadays, half of his face sagged in paralysis and old scars decorated his young skin, the most prominent of which, to this day, remained the fist-sized crater of keloid on his side. His clothes had disintegrated away a long time ago, but he'd since found a tattered shawl to drape around himself. It wasn't modesty or self-awareness that compelled him to do so (he had neither), but because it comforted him, and comfort was a thing he had learned to appreciate.

Oscar marched forth, his feet carving erratic paths in the sand. Last night, he'd seen lights in the distance and felt compelled to follow them. Before that, he'd followed some other distraction, already forgotten by the time this new irritant had stolen his focus.

Now, under the amber illumination of noon clouds, the lights had vanished from Oscar's line of sight. Yet he stayed on course, compelled by inertia, until a ramshackle town materialized ahead. Towns meant people, and people meant trouble—Oscar had learned and forgotten this lesson time and again. But the town was an interruption in the monotonous, unstimulating wasteland and thus beckoned to be explored.

He entered the town through one of its quieter neighborhoods. The huts slumped along the streets were a crude assemblage of rock, mud, and wood, all united by a deep-set wretchedness. At least in this part of town, the dead were few and scattered. One hunkered on a patio, crafting arrows. Another shuffled along the street, muttering to herself, rubbing her temples. A third lay curled on the sidewalk, hugging his knees, shivering. They ignored Oscar, and he ignored them.

But what did get his attention was a barrel filled to the brim with water. It stood in front of a small wooden shack, the faint glimmer of its surface wooing him. Without hesitation, Oscar stumbled forward and plunged his head into the water. His dirt-smeared face dyed the water black as he slurped greedily, the refreshing liquid rushing down his parched throat in unregulated gasps.

One of the few things he had learned was that water eased the drought within him and quieted the weary protests of his strained body. Water was a good thing, a pleasurable thing. Water was a Stimulus. Most other sensations weren't so much displeasing as they were simply meaningless static in the emptiness that had become his existence.

As he drank, something snapped against the back of his head. He ignored it and continued to gulp down the barrel's contents. Another snap—this one harder, more forceful. He lifted his head, water streaming down his face, and saw an old woman looming over him. One of her eyes was milky white with cataract, the other sharp with fury. She was screaming and waving a wooden stick like a deranged conductor.

Oscar met her glare with vacant eyes. She swung the stick again, cracking it against Oscar's fingers gripping the edge of the barrel. He pulled his hand away and stumbled backward, cradling it, his mouth hanging open in confusion. He labeled the woman an Agitant.

The woman spat at him and retreated into her shack, muttering curses and shaking her head.

Oscar studied his trembling hand and noticed that one finger wouldn't hook or stop shaking. The finger, too, had become an Agitant. There was no pain, though. Oscar hadn't felt pain for a long time.

Sounds from the livelier parts of town drifted toward him, and his interest in the broken finger faded.

He followed the sounds down the street which led him into a bustling bazaar. Desert dust billowed over the streets from the constant scurrying of townsfolk. Merchants peddled their wares: water, oil, weapons, clothing, trinkets, holistic remedies, and services ranging from survival training to occult rituals. Some townsfolk lounged on porches or leaned out of open windows, watching the dead shuffle by. Along the sides of the streets, the severely impaired—physically, mentally, or both—begged for alms, help, salvation.

Oscar drifted through the busy streets. His slack-jawed demeanor, erratic movements, and the open shawl revealing his nakedness acted as natural repellents, forcing the crowds to steer clear of him.

At a market square corner, a man sat slumped on the dusty ground, a frayed jacket bundled beneath him as a cushion. He stared vacantly into the distance, blending in with the beggars lining the streets. Yet his presence stirred something unusual in Oscar—something akin to curiosity.

Oscar rarely hesitated when something piqued his interest, but this man was different. He was both a Stimulus and an Agitant—an anomaly Oscar had never encountered.

Wary but compelled, Oscar sat down on the other side of the street to observe the man. His matted hair hung in oily streaks, framing a face marred by various old and crusted deformities: a missing eye, a caved-in cheekbone, a torn cheek exposing rows of blackened teeth. His torso was a patchwork of scarred pits and gaping holes, some so deep that bone gleamed beneath the ragged tissue. His left arm had been amputated at the elbow, while his right hand retained only three fingers. He also had only one leg, the cauterized stump resting on his bundled jacket.

But it was the man's midsection that truly grabbed Oscar's attention. An old, barely visible scar ran across it, a shoelace crisscrossing through the skin like a crude seam.

Suddenly, the man turned tense and alert. Oscar lifted his gaze from the scar and met the man's single eye. Their gazes locked. Something stirred within Oscar—something that went beyond his usual primal responses. For the first time in a long time, he felt something.

The sensation was both soothing and exhilarating, resurrecting stagnant synapses that now tingled with electricity. Oscar didn't know his body could do such things. The working side of his face lifted into a smile. He didn't understand what any of it meant, and his acknowledgment of the smile was akin to a sleeping dog wagging its tail. But no matter how confusing or ultimately insignificant the sensation was, it still felt good. A smile was a smile.

The man, however, didn't return the gesture. He stared back with a dull expression, then broke their connection with a blink, shifting his gaze elsewhere. He planted a crutch beside him and hoisted himself upright, deliberate and careful. Dust billowed as he shook out the jacket and slung it over his shoulder, draping it over his missing arm.

Oscar remained seated and watched the familiar stranger limp down the street. Soon, his figure disappeared into the crowd. Only a ghost of a memory remained.

ACKNOWLEDGMENTS

I'm not sure whether I should be proud or embarrassed to admit it took me ten years to write this novel. Either way, that's a long time to spend in a place like Hell (though what's ten years in eternity?). Fortunately, I've been visited by some wonderful people along the way. I would now like to thank them:

To Richard Blandford and Russel McLean, your developmental feedback provided many revelations and elevated this story to heights I couldn't have reached alone.

To Sami and Toni, thank you for reading some of the early drafts, sharing fresh perspectives, and offering words of encouragement when I needed them most.

And, finally, to my wife, Essi, who has read more versions of this story than anyone ever should and, for reasons beyond my comprehension, has gifted me with her unwavering support: thank you for keeping me grounded in this world while my mind wandered in the next.

Author photograph © Kristian Tilander

MATIAS YLIKANGAS is a Finnish author focusing on speculative fiction. In addition to writing, he works as a graphic designer and holds a Master's degree in Arts. He also releases music under a solo project, **Madu**.

Born and raised in Finland, he writes in English, bringing a distinctive and unconventional voice to his storytelling. *Hell Pulp* is his debut novel.

matiasylikangas.com **maduism.bsky.social** **maduism**

Curious about what's next in my creative work? Scan the QR code or visit **matiasylikangas.com** to subscribe to my monthly newsletter, **Zinemadu**, for exclusive updates, behind-the-scenes insights, and new tales delivered straight to your inbox.

Printed in Dunstable, United Kingdom

70147475R00180